*To all of the lovers of M/M romance,*
*especially those of you who read and reviewed*
BORROWING BLUE.
*And to the other authors whose advice has made all the difference,*
*I thank you from the bottom of my heart.*

# TAMING TEDDY

A MADE MARIAN NOVEL

LUCY LENNOX

Jennifer,
Brrr!
lucylennox ♡

Cover Designer: Angstyg - www.AngstyG.com

Editor: Hollie Westring - www.HollieTheEditor.com

# ABOUT TAMING TEDDY

**Teddy:** If there's one thing I don't do, it's commitment. You don't become an award-winning photographer by staying in one place. I'm always on the road, looking for the next shot, the next award, the next hot body. Which is how I end up on Dr. James Marian's front porch in the middle-of-nowhere Alaska. He's known as the Wildlife Whisperer, and I want to photograph him in action. He's reluctant at first, but I can be persuasive.

Soon enough I have him in bed saying yes over and over and over again, but my ability to shoot and scoot is frozen by a Denali snowstorm.

**Jamie:** I always thought of myself as the marrying type. Until I got left at the altar. Now I have a new motto: never commit and never fall in love. So when a cocky nature photographer decides I'm the key to his next masterpiece, it seems like the perfect arrangement: the hotshot's only in town for a brief assignment and then he'll be gone. No commitment, no strings, and no chance of getting my heart broken again.

There's just one problem: I think I'm falling in love. Now I'm afraid that maybe I'm the marrying type after all. And he definitely is not.

# 1

# TEDDY

How do you trap a wildlife veterinarian? I was one of *National Geographic*'s most well-known wildlife photographers, and Dr. James Marian was the most elusive animal I'd ever tried to capture.

I'd sent Dr. Marian at least six emails requesting permission to photograph him, and he hadn't responded to a single one. I wasn't the kind of guy to give up easily, so I just needed to get creative.

The man was known as a wildlife whisperer, someone who attracted animals and made them feel like he was one of them. Wild animals flocked to Jamie Marian as though he was fucking Noah with the ark or Cinderella trying on her damned dress. I'd come across a photo of him cradling a grizzly bear cub and I couldn't get past the visceral connection between the man and animal that was apparent even in an amateur photograph.

Plus, the man was a motherfucking masterpiece of masculine beauty. Not that his looks had anything to do with... whatever, never mind. I just knew for damned sure I needed to capture that man and his animals with my camera.

The good doctor was currently living in Denali National Park near Fairbanks, Alaska. Since I lived in Manhattan, it wasn't as though I could pop in for a quick visit to convince him in person. The emails had started off polite and professional, but my patience was wearing thin.

The last email fell more into the begging category. I told him Alaska was one of my favorite places to shoot and that despite my impending assignment in Australia, I was free to talk anytime on the international calling plan I had.

Finally, I got a response. At least now we could have a discussion instead of my continued soliloquy.

~

*From: James Marian*
*To: Theodore Kodiak*
*Subject: No thank you*

*In my field of work, I prefer to avoid media exposure. Sorry for the inconvenience. You are welcome to come to Denali and snap pics of the wildlife without me, anytime. Just contact the main ranger station.*

*Enjoy your time in Melbourne. Don't overreact to the rumor about the snakes. It's not as bad as people think.*

*Regards,*
*Jamie Marian*

~

*From: Theodore Kodiak*
*To: James Marian*
*Subject: What rumor?!*

*Shit, I hate snakes. WTF? What rumor? And what do you mean "it's not as bad as people think"?*

*Theodore Kodiak*

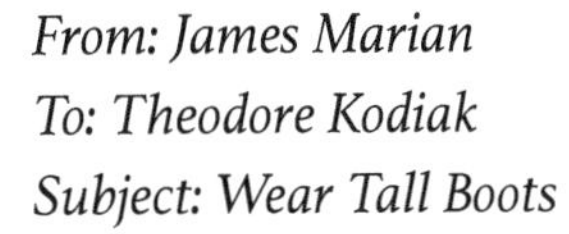
*From: James Marian*
*To: Theodore Kodiak*
*Subject: Wear Tall Boots*

*Australia boasts the largest population of poisonous snakes but there are very few actual fatalities due to easy access to antivenom. Just make sure you're not out in the wild when you get bitten.*

*You're at significantly higher risk of death or injury on an airplane than around snakes anyway. Have a safe flight.*

*Jamie Marian*

*From: Theodore Kodiak*
*To: James Marian*
*Subject: Boarding Death Trap Now*
*Gee, thanks. You're certainly the calming voice of reason. As a wildlife photographer on location in the wild, I probably won't be in the wild when I get bitten by a wild snake.*

*Theodore Kodiak*

I couldn't tell whether Jamie was joking or an asshole or perhaps both. Clearly he didn't understand the lure of an artistic vision.

Regardless of his dry personality, I needed to get through to him somehow. Email wasn't working.

I had an idea and sent another email after I reached Melbourne.

~

*From: Theodore Kodiak*
*To: James Marian*
*Subject: Wounded Peregrine Falcon*

*While on location near a breeding nest, our crew came across a wounded peregrine. I was hoping you would have some advice on what to do. Sorry to bother you.*

*Please give me a call at your earliest convenience. Don't worry about the time difference. This poor little guy is in rough shape.*

*THEODORE Kodiak*

~

MY PHONE RANG while I was taking a sip of water and sitting at a picnic table with my sandwich. It was a gorgeous spring day in Australia, and I was relaxing in a small park two hours outside Melbourne. Kids played on swings and dog walkers enjoyed the warm weather.

"Theodore Kodiak," I answered.

"Hi, Theodore," a brisk male voice replied. "This is Jamie Marian in Alaska."

*Well, hot damn.* My evil plan worked.

"I understand you have an injured falcon? Can you tell me about it?"

"Hi, Jamie. Yes, thanks for calling me so quickly. This poor guy—" I took the phone away from my ear and crinkled my sandwich wrapper over the microphone while I mumbled intelligibly near it.

"What?" Jamie asked. "I can't hear you. What's that sound?"

"Oh no! I'll have to call you back. We think he stopped brea—"

Before disconnecting the phone I heard him yelling, "Wait, wait!"

Immediately a text from him flashed on my screen:

**Jamie:** *Your phone cut off. I'm emailing you the contact info for a nearby wildlife vet. Glad you were there to help the poor bird.*

I chuckled. Now I had Jamie Marian's phone number, and it was his turn to sit and wait.

After my weeklong shoot outside Melbourne, I received the third pissed-off email from Jamie Marian asking if we'd taken the bird for professional help. The first email asked if I'd gotten in touch with the wildlife vet he'd suggested. The second inquired how the bird was doing, and the third accused me of being rude and implied it was probably my own "bumbling around the park" that had caused the injury in the first place.

A part of me wanted to let him in on the ruse that there was no injured bird, but I didn't think that would go over well. Especially since I was still trying to get him to agree to work with me. I finally texted him back.

**Teddy:** *Sorry for the delayed response about the falcon. I have been on airplanes for almost two days and asleep for two more. My days and nights are messed up and I can hardly think straight. Thank you for the vet recommendation. You'll be happy to know that the bird made a full recovery and has been adopted as a mascot by a local orphanage. They named her Princess Petunia Peregrinswaggle, I believe.*

I CRINGED, wondering if I'd gone too far with the ruse. After several minutes, I received a response.

**Jamie:** *There was no bird, was there?*

**Teddy:** *There was totally a bird. Here's proof:*

I flipped frantically through the photos on my phone until I found a shot of a peregrine I'd taken the year before. I texted it to Dr. Marian.

**Jamie:** *That isn't a falcon, it's a tiercel. Also, that's the top of the Yellowstone Roosevelt Arch in the background. Montana, not Australia.*

I looked closer at the picture. Fuck, he was right. That's what I got for trying to be too elaborate in my lie.

**Teddy:** *Ok, you're right. There may not have been a bird.*

**Jamie:** *Are you fucking kidding me? Who lies about an injured animal? Why would you do that? You're an insensitive asshole. Good riddance. May you rot in hell.*

**Teddy:** *Sorry for the small deception. I wanted to get your number and now I have it. I'll give you a call soon to discuss the photo shoot.*

**Jamie:** *You're a cocky motherfucker if you think I'm answering your call.*

The next day I tried, but, sure enough, he didn't answer. That was fine. I had other tricks up my sleeve. In the meantime, I decided to use humor to soften his demeanor through texts. Over the next few days I texted Jamie periodically.

**Teddy:** *Why are mountains so funny?*

**Jamie:** *Fuck you.*

**Teddy:** *Because they are hill areas.*

**Jamie:** *<rolls eyes>*

**Teddy:** *Why do we like volcanoes?*

**Jamie:** *Because they are a good place to dispose of photographers' bodies?*

**Teddy:** *Because they are so lavable.*

**Jamie:** *That is the worst pun Everest.*

**Teddy:** *Why do mountains make good singers?*

**Jamie:** *Your joke telling may have already reached its peak.*

**Teddy:** *They have a lot of range.*

**Jamie:** *Now you're on a plateau. Not that I can find fault with that.*

**Teddy:** *High praise indeed.*

A few days later, I made a quick trip to New Orleans to go over some images with the folks at the wildlife reserve. After the meeting, I asked them if they had an empty office where I could make a phone call from a landline. Once alone, I closed the door and sat down at the desk.

I made the first call to my own cell phone to see what the caller ID would show. "Reserve Institute." Even better than I hoped for. Next I dialed Jamie. It was nearing lunchtime in New Orleans so he should just be waking up in Denali.

"This is Jamie," he answered in a warm, deep voice.

"Well, hello there, Dr. Marian," I said with a smile. I knew he'd be pissed and tried to disarm him before he could go nuclear on me. "I'm sorry about the falcon. You're right, it was an asshole move to make you worry like that."

A beat of silence and then I heard him mutter, "Dammit."

He took a breath before speaking. "What do you want? How many times do I need to say no, Mr. Kodiak?" He hit the "k" sound with a smack.

"Don't get your binoculars in a twist. I'm just calling to talk. Why don't I fly up there on Thursday and we can meet Friday morning? Does that work?"

He hung up on me with an audible huff and I barked out a laugh. Something about the guy energized me. Ever since I'd seen the picture of him with the bear cub, I'd been obsessed. I knew I needed to see more of Dr. James Marian.

It wasn't that I was attracted to him. I didn't even know him, and I was usually only attracted to people I thought would be an easy fuck. Wait, that sounded awful. It wasn't that I didn't respect the people I slept with, but my job took me all over the world, sometimes at a moment's notice. I didn't have time for a relationship, so I looked for quick connections that satisfied my lust in the moment. Plus, I had to assume the guy was straight.

As for companionship and long-term commitment, I had my friends from Pratt. When I went to art school, I was a kid in a candy store. More beautiful, artistic men and women than I knew what to do with. In addition to plenty of dates, I also found some wonderful friends. Jenna, Cat, and Brody were like family to me. Between my college friends and my best friend Mac, I had almost everything I needed.

There was one other thing I needed, however, and that was a top photography award on my résumé. I had won some decent awards, but there was a big elusive award called the Gramling Prize I was desperate to win. Call it a personal goal. To be the best in my field. To finally prove to myself and my father I wasn't that skinny little kid from Dryden who dicked around at art school instead of becoming a big corporate success.

In order to win the Gramling, I had to submit something original, captivating. Something other photographers couldn't capture the way I could. It could be anything, but something kept telling me the magic shot awaited me in Alaska. And to get that shot, I needed Jamie Marian.

## 2

# JAMIE

I was standing on the edge of the wide river about four miles from the truck. I'd hiked in to assess a beaver family I was keeping my eye on. I sat down quietly on a piece of log by the dam and caught my breath. The week's cold snap had broken to give us a warmer afternoon, so my fleece was tied around my waist. I slowly set down my backpack and stretched my shoulders.

One of the reasons I loved my job was the peace and quiet. The sounds of the birds flying through drying leaves and the water burbling over rocks were so much nicer than the sounds of horns honking and music blaring. I felt at home in the park. Denali was my most recent posting, but I could be happy in almost any of them. Give me plants and water and animals, and I would be happy every time.

I sat quietly for a while, waiting. Out of the corner of my eye I saw them. Two kits peeked out at me from behind a crisscross of broken twigs. I pretended to ignore them.

One of these two cuties was the offspring of the monogamous pair who managed this dam. The other was a rescue from Mount Rainier that I had introduced as a baby into this family in hopes they would raise it with their own kit. So far, everything was going well.

Beavers mated for life. They had traditional families like on the show *Leave it to...* well, *Beaver*. This pair had a modest-size lodge and the kits hid behind lodge walls while they figured out what to do with the big scary animal sitting near them (me).

I wore forest colors to blend in—a drab park service green T-shirt with dark khaki cargo pants. Despite popular belief, I wasn't really a park ranger. Everyone assumed I was one because I dressed like one and worked in the park. My official job was independent wildlife consultant. I had a bachelor's degree in environmental science and a doctorate in veterinary medicine with specialty training in wildlife management.

One of the kits poked a nose out of the sticks and started tentatively moving a paw. I could almost sense the moment he recognized me because his posture changed and he came scampering out of the enclosure, his buddy not far behind.

They ran clumsily over branches and rocks before arriving at my boots. One of them sat up on his hind legs and put his tiny front paws on my pants cuff. The other clawed up onto the log and snaked his way onto my lap. I kept my hands to myself and said softly, "Well, hello, tiny friends. Fancy meeting you here."

They chattered at me as if they were telling me about all the adventures they had in the week I'd been away from them. They moved around like little brown flashes of fur and when they ran through the water, shiny drops glistened on their coats. Clearly, the kits still carried the exuberant joy of youth and the ease of not having to worry about food and shelter.

I noticed movement inside the lodge and assumed it was one of the parents. The two adult beavers knew me even though they used caution around me when the kits were nearby. I wasn't surprised he or she was staying hidden. While the babies tittered around me, I told them about my crazy week in Napa with my family and even told them about the arrogant photographer who kept bugging me.

I enjoyed the conversation with Pete and Repeat. Maybe it was because they listened without giving opinions. Telling them I'd be back the following week to check on their work, I stood up and slid my backpack on. Before getting back to the trail I noticed one of the adults come out of the lodge and wobble down a giant tree trunk connecting to the opposite riverbank.

Back in the truck, I drank deeply from my water bottle. I made some notes in my field journal and headed back the twenty miles to my cabin for dinner. My place was very remote down a gravel road. I loved it. The little cabin sat on more than twenty acres of Denali wilderness.

My truck tires turned onto the gravel road with a familiar crunch and a moment later I heard muffled barking. It sounded like Sister was really riled up about something. I pulled up to the front steps and noticed a white Chevy Tahoe I didn't recognize with rental car stickers on it. I saw Sister's big black-and-white paws up on the front windowsill and her slobber made wet tracks on the window.

I retrieved my bear spray from the seat beside me and opened the truck door. Walking around the strange vehicle in a wide circle, I approached the driver's side. As I peered in, the door opened and out stepped my fucking libido.

The man was stereotypically tall, dark, and handsome in a rugged way, but he was also muscled like an athlete and manly as all fuck. As he stood to his full height, I subconsciously stepped back to take him all in. He was several inches over six feet, so he towered over me. His dark hair was shorter on the sides but wavy on top, and he sported at least a day-and-a-half's dark growth on his cheeks. The man had striking blue eyes that bore into me so intensely I should have been afraid, but for some reason I wasn't.

My grip loosened a little on the can of bear spray as I asked, "May I help you?"

"Are you Jamie Marian?" he said as a slow, lazy grin appeared on his lips. *Damn.* I recognized that voice.

"You have *got* to be kidding me." I gawped. "*You're* Theodore Kodiak?"

"My friends call me Teddy," he replied, holding out his hand for a shake. I ignored it.

"How do you know where I live? And showing up with no warning? That's a bit creepy, don't you think? Give me one good reason not to call the cops."

He chuckled and pulled his hand back. "What, out here? Surely it would take an hour for anyone to get here from anywhere. Plus, I'm not here to hurt you. I just want to talk. The people at the ranger station told me where to find you. I'll be as gentle as a kitten, sweetheart. I promise," he said with a wink. He reached into the backseat of the Tahoe to pull out a large well-worn backpack. "Ask me in for a drink?"

Sister had started hurling herself at the door by this point so I threw Teddy an angry glare before going over to unlock the front door and let her out. She came bounding out in a rush of vicious glee and threw herself wantonly at her new love interest. Teddy held out the back of his hand for her to sniff then squatted down to pet the hundred-pound slut.

"Who's this?" he asked.

"That's Sister. And she's very violent. Watch yourself."

I walked into the cabin and slammed the door behind me, twisting the lock. Kicking off my boots, I walked across the wood floor in my socks toward the bathroom.

The interior of my cabin was made up of one big, open room that had a tidy kitchen and a wood table with four chairs on the left and a living area with a comfy couch, an old recliner, and a flat-screen television on the right. Straight ahead was a door to a bedroom with a full bathroom tucked out of view behind the kitchen. There was a ladder up the side of one wall to a sleeping loft over my bedroom in case I ever had guests stay over. When people visited, they usually stayed over rather than driving the long distance back to any kind of civilization.

I heard Teddy knocking on the door. Ignoring him, I headed into the bathroom and turned on the shower.

As I showered I thought about the photographer outside. When he originally emailed me, I looked him up online. His work was stunning. Obviously I was a sucker for good wildlife photography, but these images had something extra that made them stand out. I didn't know much about photography to know what that special something was, but I wasn't the only one who saw it. His work was featured all over the world in magazines, books, and galleries. There were even some displayed in museums. I couldn't believe how popular his photographs were.

I finished showering and put on sweatpants, a long-sleeved T-shirt, and thick socks. I returned to the living area to the sound of more knocking.

"Jamie, open up. I need to use the bathroom."

"Use the woods. Or better yet, head to your hotel. There are bears out there," I responded calmly through the door.

I heard him blurt, "Fuck."

I padded over to the kitchen for a glass of water and returned to my bedroom to sit down at my laptop. I caught up on some email and ordered some new long underwear online.

A few minutes later I looked up at the sound of rain on the window and realized the sky had gone dark. I looked back down at the computer screen for a few minutes before hearing a rap at the bedroom window in front of me. Teddy stood outside my window, soaking wet, holding up a wet Sister.

*Goddammit. I forgot Sister.*

I gestured for him to walk around and I met him at the door. I opened it and felt Sister rush past before giving off a huge sprinkler shake inside the door. My eyes narrowed to warn Teddy against similar behavior.

"Can I come in, Jamie? It's really cold and dark and wet out here. Can I just dry off a little? Please?"

The man was fucking adorable. His hair stood up in wet spikes, and drops glistened on his eyelashes in the light from my cabin. I felt a little sorry for him and decided to calm down.

"Why the hell didn't you just get into your car?"

He looked at me, indignant. "And leave Sister alone out there, wet and afraid? You're a cruel man. I saved your baby. The least you can do is loan me a towel."

I sighed and let him in, walking off to fetch some dry towels. As I dried the dog, I apologized to her. "I'm so sorry, girl. I didn't mean to forget about you out there. Poor Sister."

Teddy rubbed a towel over his hair and tried unsuccessfully to dry off his shirt and jeans. The jeans were plastered to him, hiding nothing. Not the long, muscular legs or the long line of... Anyway, nothing sucked worse than wearing soaking wet jeans. Served him right.

"Why is her name Sister?"

"When she was a puppy her black-and-white markings looked just like a nun's habit. Now that she's much fluffier, it's harder to see. The rescue place named her Cookie, but my friends wouldn't stop calling her Sister. It stuck."

I got up and headed to the kitchen. "Do you want a cup of coffee? I'm going to make some."

"Coffee would be great, thanks. Can I use your restroom?"

I gestured toward my bedroom door. "Sure, before you get to the bedroom door, look left and you'll see a door behind the kitchen."

As soon as he had grabbed his backpack and started walking in that direction, I remembered the care package my brothers had sent me to celebrate my new singlehood. There was a huge box of condoms, lube, outrageous dildos and tacky jockstraps sitting out in the open on the bathroom shelf. I felt blood rush to my face and I started to call out for him to wait. Too late, he was already through the door. Shit.

*Okay, Jamie. The man is clearly old enough to know that men have sex and stupid-ass brothers who send prank shit and who are now going to die. Calm your ass down.*

I busied myself starting the coffee and then checked on Sister. She was happily licking the rest of the water off her before settling onto her bed in the corner. I heard the shower turn on in the bathroom.

*Well, make yourself at home, asshole.*

When he joined me in the main room I saw he had changed into gray sweatpants and a black hoodie sweatshirt that said *Pratt* in bold yellow letters. He was barefoot.

He accepted a mug of coffee with sincere thanks before adding cream and sugar from the counter. When he sat down next to me at the kitchen table and started sipping his coffee, I spoke. "Listen, Theodore—"

"You've decided not to call me Teddy? I feel like I'm at work when people call me Theodore."

"You *are* at work."

"Oh, right. Glad to know I got the job then. Continue," he said with a shit-eating grin.

I looked at him with annoyance at his assumption and then my brain caught up with something he said.

"Hold up. Wait. *Holy shit.* Are you telling me your name is Teddy Kodiak?" I blurted, breaking into uncontrollable belly laughs. "As in Kodiak, the type of bear? ... Are you saying your name is *Teddy Bear*?" I felt tears stream out of my eyes and I almost snorted.

He raised a brow and stared me down before one side of his mouth drew up in a grin.

# 3

## TEDDY

As if I'd never heard that before. It was a joke that was almost as old as I was. It annoyed the crap out of me my parents hadn't thought through the consequences of my name before sticking me with it for life. At some point I decided to own it. That might have coincided with me realizing some people loved dating a real-life Teddy Bear.

I started to grin out of sheer pleasure at seeing Jamie lose it. He was all in. Laughing and crying and snorting. It was flipping fantastic.

He was gorgeous. His hair was shiny brown threaded with lighter brown and gold from being outside all summer. The overgrown waves fell over his forehead as he laughed, and the scruff of his five o'clock shadow was right on the verge of changing from prickly to soft. I wanted to run a finger over it.

"That's right. I flew over four thousand miles to make you laugh, sweetheart. Yuk it up. Be careful though, I'd hate for you to piss yourself."

I chuckled and took another few sips of coffee while he got a hold of himself. I almost told him I'd never made the connection about my name, but I didn't think I could pull it off with a straight face.

He took a long look at me. "Seriously though. Why are you trying to get this photo gig? What do you think is so special about my job that you need to photograph it?"

"Jamie, it's not really your job I want to photograph. It's your ability to get up close to the animals. That kind of engagement with wildlife is what people wish they could have. I want to capture it, or maybe find a way to... I don't know... record that one perfect moment when an animal looks at a human with trust instead of fear. Does that make sense? I don't really know how to explain it, but I'll know it when I see it. I'm considering submitting something for a big award this year, but it needs to be special."

He looked at me with furrowed brows. "Teddy, exposure is part of the problem. If you publish photos of me getting close to animals the way I do, it could be dangerous. People might think they can approach wildlife too. They won't realize I have years of education, training, and experience and I still take a risk every time I do it. Can you see the danger in that?"

I stood up and wandered toward his fridge. "Yes, I can. But there are ways to mitigate that when publishing them." I found some vegetables and cheese in a crisper drawer and snooped around in the cabinets until I came across a jar of spaghetti sauce and lasagne noodles.

*Aha, lasagne. I could go for some lasagne.*

"Like how?" Jamie asked, getting up to feed Sister.

"Well, it depends. I'll try my best to take your concerns into consideration if I submit or publish a photo of you with an animal." I found a pot and started water to boil. Then I chopped veggies to put in the sauce.

"What are you doing?" he asked, looking at me making myself at home in his kitchen.

"I haven't eaten since I left New Orleans."

"So?"

"So, I'm making dinner," I told him. "Do you have a problem with someone making you dinner? I'm making vegetable lasagne because there aren't many options in your fridge. You don't go to the store much, do you?"

"It's a bit out of the way. Wait, you live in New Orleans?"

"No. I live in Manhattan, but I was in New Orleans for work. I came straight here and could eat Sister right about now."

He told me Sister would be way too fatty and then asked me where I was staying.

"Well, it's a funny story actually..." I looked at Jamie expectantly.

"Are you fucking kidding me?" he flashed at me. "You're expecting to stay *here*? With *me*? God, you really are a presumptuous bastard. Forget it, Teddy Bear. You're shit out of luck."

I gave him my best puppy-dog look. "It's not that I was planning on staying here as much as I just sort of hopped a plane to Fairbanks without thinking it through or making plans."

"You didn't make a reservation somewhere? How do you fly to the wilds of Alaska without making arrangements?" he asked with a look of sheer exasperation.

"Honestly, Jamie, I wasn't planning on coming here today. I woke up at the hotel, drove to the airport to catch my flight to LaGuardia, and ended up buying a ticket to Fairbanks instead. When I landed, I got a rental car and headed straight for the Denali ranger station. They pointed me here, and here I am. I'm about as surprised as you are. I didn't even have any cold weather gear. I have my camera stuff and this one change of clothes. I bought a fleece and warm coat in the fucking Denver airport when I changed planes."

Jamie's mouth hung open and he looked at me like I was insane. He wasn't far off. Even I had to admit it was crazy. An unfamiliar feeling of embarrassment washed over me. I hadn't felt this way since I was a sickly, skinny kid in high school.

"Look," I started, "I'm really sorry about this, Jamie. I know my being here is a big imposition. Can you maybe point me in the direction of a place to find a room? Or do you have a number I can call?"

He blew out a breath. "You're for sure out of luck tonight if you don't already have a reservation. The Road Lottery starts tomorrow, and places have been booked for ages. The Road Lottery is like Mardi Gras for Denali as far as accommodations go."

"Shit," I muttered. "Glad I rented an SUV. I can sleep in the back."

"Jesus, Teddy. You can stay in the loft. But you leave tomorrow and fly back to New York. And you don't fuck with me or talk about taking pictures of me. Consider it unmentionable. Understand?" His eyes drilled into mine. I noticed they were a warm brown even when he was peeved.

"Thank you. I promise to be on my best behavior tonight and refrain from discussing your unmentionables." I shot him a knowing look.

Jamie's eyes narrowed at me. "Jackass."

While the food cooked, I asked him what it was like to live and work in a national park. I found flour and searched for other ingredients to make quick drop biscuits. My stomach was driving me at this point, and I found what I needed in a spice cabinet. He watched me work while he told me about the parks he'd selected and explained the reasons why. I asked Jamie what he loved and disliked about each park he'd worked in.

When the lasagne was ready, I replaced it in the oven with the tray of biscuits. By the time I let the casserole cool and set enough to cut it, the biscuits were ready. I had left out the rest of the stick of butter I used in the dough, and it was nice and soft for spreading.

I brought everything to the table, and Jamie didn't quite know what to say. He got up to grab us some beers.

I was ravenous and the lasagne hit the spot. During dinner I told him what it was like to travel all the time. I de-emphasized the photography part and spoke of some of the places I'd been that were particularly interesting.

He had worked in parks all over the US. It seemed as though he was in demand enough to write his own ticket. It was refreshing to talk to someone as passionate about his job as I was. We shared stories about several of the places we had both been.

After dinner Jamie did the dishes. We moved to the living area, and when I sat down on the sofa, he chose the recliner.

"Thanks for dinner. You're a really good cook. I can't believe I had enough food in this place for someone to produce that meal."

I turned to face him, putting my back against the opposite side of the couch. "You're welcome. So… is there a Mr. or Mrs. Marian?" I asked.

"None of your damned business," he replied with a laugh.

"Okay, okay. No need to get aggressive. I'll take that as a no. You're a good-looking guy, so I'm surprised. Let me guess, you're just getting out of a bad relationship?"

He narrowed his eyes at me. "I said none of your business." But his eyes told me the truth. Behind the annoyance I saw weariness.

"With whom?" I pushed. "It's okay to talk about it. I'm a good listener."

"I've known you for ten minutes. I don't care how good of a listener you are; I don't want to talk about it."

I changed my approach. "All right, I'll start. Normally I prefer men, but I was seeing a woman named Lola last year. It wasn't anything serious, but we'd seen each other off and on for several months."

Jamie interrupted with a look of skepticism. "You're bisexual?"

"I'm not a huge fan of labels, but yes. I sleep with both men and women. Anyway, guess who she left me for?" I asked.

Jamie rolled his eyes. "How the hell should I know?" He pulled his feet under him and settled farther back in the chair. "Fine, I'll bite. Who?"

"Lead singer of a Kinks tribute band. You know, the band who sings the song *Lola*?" I snorted before reaching for my beer on the coffee table.

"Liar," he scoffed.

"I swear to god it's true. Made me almost glad it happened because I'm getting a ton of mileage off the story."

"What did she look like?" Jamie asked nonchalantly.

"Who, Lola? She's a tall blonde with really big—"

"Never mind!" Jamie interjected.

"Eyes. Wow, sweetheart. You have a dirty little mind. Now it's your turn to talk. Tell Uncle Teddy all about it."

"Mine isn't a story about missing out on a hot piece of ass. It was a little more involved than some roadie who sleeps with the whole band."

"Who said she slept with all of them? Although, she *is* hot so there's no way to know for sure. I never thought to ask. Huh. Anyway. Start talking, Jamie."

"I was dating a guy named Brian. We dated on and off in undergrad and then met back up three years ago when at the Grand Canyon on a project."

So, this guy was into men. *Jackpot.*

"Is he a wildlife consultant too?" I asked, playing it cool and telling my dick to shut the fuck up.

"No, he is a professor of zoology."

"Ahhh, dating the professor. Go on," I said with a grin. Jamie shot me a look.

"No, he became a professor when I was in vet school. Anyway, we dated long distance, which was hard, and after six months, he popped the question. I said yes, he jilted me, and now you know the whole story." He took a sip of beer and studied the label.

"Sweetheart, you went from the dating part to the jilted part a little fast. Can we rewind?"

"I was left standing at the fucking altar. What do you want from me?"

"Well, how about you tell me when this event took place? I take it from your reaction that it was yesterday."

Jamie glared at me. "It was five months ago. We were engaged for eight months before that while I tried to plan the big-ass wedding he supposedly wanted. What a joke. I never even wanted a fancy wedding. I still don't know what he was thinking or why he wanted to pretend we were going to marry."

"Why did he leave?" I asked.

"Pfft, he never spoke to me again. When I say he left me at the altar, I mean he actually left me standing at the fucking altar. I found out later he was already married. To a woman."

"Oh shit, denial much?"

"Yep. He was a real keeper, that one. The only problem was that he wanted to keep everyone he ever laid eyes on." Jamie got up to grab a blanket from a basket by the fireplace.

"So you were like in a tux and everything? Damn, Jamie. That's harsh," I commiserated.

"Yes, I was standing in a tux in the back of the church. Which is another ridiculous part. I've never wanted to get married in a church wearing a tux. Shit, what was I thinking? I think I sort of forgot who I was, you know? And talk about a confidence killer. I felt like a fool. I *am* a fool."

"Jamie, you weren't a fool to trust someone you had been intimate with for several years. *He* was the fool to have met you and ever let you go in the first place. He, like, got married after dating you in college and then never told you about it when you hooked back up?" I asked.

"I don't know. I assume so."

"Did his wife ever find out about you?"

I was surprised when Jamie tilted his head, looked me over with a cunning look, and said, "Not as far as I know. I'm still plotting my revenge. Wanna help?"

# 4

# JAMIE

Teddy had a surprised look on his face, so I reassured him. "It's not like I'd ever go through with it, but we should brainstorm ideas anyway. C'mon. It'll be fun."

The look on Teddy's face betrayed his hesitation. "What's the matter, hotshot? Too chicken?"

Teddy laughed and got into the spirit of the idea. "Okay, sweetheart. Let's do this. First of all, do we have a name for this lovely lady?"

"Aww, I feel bad for her. She's married to a manwhore. The revenge plot needs to target Brian. His wife is just the innocent bystander who gets injured in the ensuing wreckage. Poor girl. I don't know her name, but let's assume she's a royal bitch. I think we should call her Lola."

He snorted. "Careful, sweetheart, lest you come off as jealous."

"Me, jealous of Lola? *Your* Lola? In your dreams, Teddy Bear. Besides, I've sworn off relationships. As far as I'm concerned, men can go fuck themselves," I replied.

"Simmer down over there. I can see that naming her Lola is going to be a problem. Let's call her Dingbat. Now, do you think Dingbat has any idea about hubby's manwhore status? Where do they live?"

I shrugged. "I don't know what she knows. I got a call from his brother. They live in Seattle."

"So it would be possible for you to arrange an accidental meeting. Isn't Seattle where most Alaskans go for… I don't know… culture? Or something?"

I shot Teddy a look. "You're an idiot. Seattle is over two thousand miles away. By your math, it's halfway to New York from here."

"All right, so we plan something from a distance. Maybe a phone call or an email. Is he on Facebook?"

"I don't know. I'm not on Facebook."

Teddy looked at me like I had three heads. "Not on Facebook? Are you eighty-five years old? What the hell's the matter with you?"

"Well, I used to be on Facebook in college, but then I realized it was stressing me out so I quit. I don't miss it. You know I spend most of my day in the wild, right? So while I have my smartphone with me all day, I only get computer time at night."

"Hmm. That makes it tough. Do you have a phone number for Dingbat?" he asked.

"No, but I still have Brian's number in my phone. I don't know if he's changed it. He ignored my calls after the wedding disaster, but I gave up trying to contact him just two days later when I heard from his brother. He might have let down his guard by now."

Teddy asked for my phone, and I eyed him suspiciously. "What are you going to do?"

"Text him. It'll be fun. You'll see. Gimme." He held out his hand.

"No way. You're crazy," I told him, but a small part of me wanted to see what he would say in the text. "What would you say?"

"You won't know until you give it to me, sweetheart." He smiled.

"Why do you keep calling me that? If you're trying to flirt with me, don't bother. I told you, I'm off the market. For good," I assured him, trying to ignore what the endearment did to my nether regions.

"Jamie, I'm not shopping for a husband, but thanks anyway," Teddy stated.

I looked over at him, offended. "What makes you think I'm

looking for a husband? I was implying you should stop trying to get into my *pants.* Not get into my wedding ring."

"You're not the fucking type. You're the commitment type. No, thanks. I'm more the bang and bolt type. Sorry, gorgeous."

He was really starting to get on my nerves. "What the fuck does that mean? You don't know me. Just because I was engaged doesn't mean I want a husband. Because I don't. Not anymore. And for that matter, I don't want just fucking either. At least not with another jackass who treats sex like coin collecting."

Teddy looked at me with one side of his mouth quirked up. "So, to clarify, you don't want sex with someone serious, and you don't want sex with someone who isn't serious. You don't want a commitment, but you don't want a one-night stand. I see."

"Why are we even talking about this?" I sputtered.

"Just so I understand, why don't you like sex?" His grin widened. *That smug motherfucker.*

"I *do* like sex! I fucking love sex. I just don't want to deal with the shit that comes with the actual fucking man."

He chuckled. "Ahh, now we're getting somewhere. You've decided to become heterosexual. I can see it. Maybe a haircut and a shave. Some khaki pants and a blue button-down. Yep, hetero works for you."

"*Fuck!*" I screamed, accidentally waking Sister from a dead sleep on the sofa next to Teddy. "You are the most annoying asshole who ever walked the earth. Why are you deliberately turning my words around?"

"Listen, Jamie. I think we should have sex right now. It might calm you down, and I don't mind. We've established that you love fucking and you're not straight, so let's do it. What do you say, hmm?" And that arrogant ass actually stood up and stepped toward me.

My head almost exploded in anger, and I catapulted out of the recliner, intending to take a swing at him. But by the time my body landed on his, apparently I had changed my mind.

My mouth went crashing into his. His arms came around me and my legs circled his waist. He stumbled back onto the sofa, fingers grabbing my ass. Hands were everywhere. He tasted of beer and smelled faintly of cologne and musk. My tongue ate him up while his hands fumbled for the drawstring of my waistband. We attacked each other without reserve. There were grunts and moans.

His lips moved to my earlobe, my neck, my chest. My hands slid down his back under his shirt and into the waistband of his pants, pulling him farther into me. His hard-on pushed against my thigh and I rolled my hips hard into his.

His hands roamed up and down my back, over my shoulders, onto my ass. I felt his thigh muscles moving under my legs and his back muscles moving under his shirt.

Between wet, hungry kisses on my lips, his deep voice rumbled, "So fucking hot." I whimpered like an idiot and kissed him back as though I was starving and his mouth was a pie. My hands found the hem of his shirt and I lifted it over his head. Somehow I was already shirtless and his tongue was sucking one of my nipples into his mouth to grasp it lightly with his teeth. I gasped out his name and my head fell back.

His hands shucked off my sweatpants. Realizing I had nothing on underneath them made him do a comical, lusty double take. I was too horny to make a snarky comment so I spent my energy on relieving the suffering of his trapped erection. When I got his pants down, his cock poked out of the top of his boxers.

I leaned down to taste the drop of wetness at the tip. Teddy sucked in a breath and then let out a deep groan. I shoved his pants and underwear down until I had his entire shaft and sac at my disposal. My tongue started dancing over his hard cock while his breathing sped up and he reached his hands into my hair.

When I came back up to kiss him on the mouth, he slid a hand down my ass to tease my crease. I hummed a little and moved my lips down to his neck. He sucked on two fingers and then moved them to my—*hole-y shit that felt amazing.*

We were frantic with each other, full lust and want and animalistic noises. Before I knew it, Teddy had flipped me around so I was kneeling on a cushion with my forearms resting on the back of the sofa. He was behind me, pulling something out of his wallet on the coffee table, and the next thing I knew, a cold, lubed finger pushed into me. "Oh *fuck*," I cried out.

"So hot, so fucking tight and hot." He growled before latching his mouth on my earlobe and moving the long finger in and out of me.

"Ahh! Right there, Teddy. Don't stop, oh god don't stop," I begged. He pulled his finger out after a few moments of me generally making a blubbery, slutty fool of myself and then sheathed himself in a condom.

He stilled over me for a moment and pressed his lips against my ear. "You sure, Jamie?" he asked in a low voice, making sure I was 100 percent on board. I nodded like a bobblehead. Before I had a chance to beg him further, he breached my hole in one swift, strong motion and slid into me.

"Mmpf!" I mumbled, nearly choking on my tongue from the incredible feeling of him slipping in and filling me.

He used his hips to tease me, alternating between light pulses, lazy circles, and brisk thrusts. I whimpered and begged, clutching his thighs and the sofa cushions. Teddy's body had me wound up so tightly with lust that it only took one stupid word to detonate the bomb inside me.

"That's it, sweetheart," he breathed straight into my ear. My brain short-circuited, stars boomed through my vision, and every cell of my body zinged with pleasure.

He must have come too because I vaguely remember a roar and my name being repeated, but I honestly didn't care. The only thing that mattered to me was the mind-blowing orgasm I'd had and its success at blowing my ex-fiancé off the map of my memory.

My post-orgasmic victory lap came to a screeching halt two seconds later when Theodore Fucking Kodiak opened his shit-for-brains mouth.

"Fuck, Jamie, I didn't really mean it."

Breath still heaving, I gasped, "What?"

"When I said we should have sex. I didn't really mean it." He pulled back and rested his forehead on my shoulder. Panting, he said,

"Jamie. You are incredibly sexy, don't get me wrong, I wanted you more than anything. But I didn't mean for you to have angry revenge sex with me two seconds after saying you don't want serious or casual sex."

Rejection slammed into me like a hammer. I had known he didn't really mean it, but I'd still thought it would be fun. "Anndd, he proves my point exactly. Fucking jackass."

I peeled myself away from him and said, "Good night, Theodore," before walking into my bedroom and closing the door.

# 5

# TEDDY

A*hh, shit. Way to go, Teddy. You have a gorgeous and willing man bathing in the afterglow of mind-altering sex and you pick that moment to open up your fucking mouth?*

I wondered what I should have done in that situation. I shouldn't have egged him on, clearly. But I'd honestly thought I was trying to help him. He seemed to be feeling so sorry for himself, and I wanted him to get angry instead.

And now I'd gone and fucked it up. If he thought he was pissed now, wait until tomorrow when he learned I wasn't planning on leaving. I came here to photograph him and I was damned well not leaving until I did.

After visiting the bathroom, I took my bag and my sorry ass up to the loft. The bed was comfortable but the night was long. Visions of an angry Jamie kept me tossing and turning. At some point I must have drifted into a deeper sleep because I awoke to the sound of gravel crunching under Jamie's tires as he drove off.

I got up and stumbled down to the kitchen. There was coffee in a pot so I found a mug and fixed a cup. Sister wandered over to me and nosed my hip for attention. I stroked her silky ears and enjoyed the warmth of her body leaning against my leg.

When I pulled the Tahoe up to the ranger station, I mentally prepared myself for the standoff. I walked in and found the ranger in charge whose name was Charlie. I had spoken to him at length the day before.

He smiled warmly at me and reached out a hand to shake. "You ready to get started? I think Jamie's out back, so you can head on out and find him."

I thanked him before asking if he'd said anything to Jamie about our conversation from the day before. He replied with a chuckle, "No, I figured I'd let you be the lucky one to tell him."

I headed back outside and around to the grass behind the building. I saw his boots sticking out from behind a big pile of stacked wood. His soft voice spoke to someone with tenderness and concern. While I didn't want to intrude, I was curious to see who he would be having a heart-to-heart with behind a woodpile.

As I slowly approached on the quiet grass, his words became clearer. I heard him sigh and say, "Mmm, Martin, you're so freaking adorable. Do I get one of your massages again today? Come here, baby. Mmm, that feels good. Okay, okay, I promise I won't touch you. You can touch my thigh just there, and I'll keep still."

*What. The. Fuck. So much for giving up on men.*

Before I had another thought, I found myself crashing around the edge of the woodpile to interrupt his make-out session with some asshole. He screamed and I noticed a small brown creature shoot off into the woods behind him. Nobody was with him. Had he been making out with… an animal? That didn't make any sense.

I snapped at him. "Just what does it mean to be an 'animal whisperer'?"

"Teddy? What the hell are you doing here?" he shot blue daggers at me. "You scared off that poor little marten. Do you have any idea how long it will be before he trusts me again? Just as I suspected, you are a bumbling ass."

He got up, brushed off his pants, and started walking back toward the ranger station. Even in his anger, he moved with careful, quiet steps.

I tried to placate him. "Look, I'm sorry. You're right, I made a stupid assumption. I promise to be more careful next time."

He hissed, "Next time? Think again, Teddy Bear. There is no next time. What are you even doing here? You promised me you were leaving."

"No, sweetheart. I didn't say I was leaving. *You* said I was leaving. *I* promised to be on my best behavior last night and refrain from discussing your unmentionables."

He turned around with icy eyes glaring. "Don't call me that. Stay here all you want, but leave me the hell alone. I have work to do."

What I had to say to him next was going to really piss him off. "Jamie, I've already arranged everything with Charlie. I'm shadowing you today whether you like it or not."

If looks could kill, I would be in a thousand bloody pieces right there on the grass. He huffed angrily before rushing through the door and slamming it in my face.

I took a deep breath and entered. He wasn't in the front reception room so I decided to take a seat and give him some time to cool off. I found a magazine on a table and began to idly flip through it.

After a few minutes I heard raised voices coming from somewhere in the back. The volume of the exchange increased as the voices approached the reception area and I saw Jamie and Charlie arguing. *Here we go.*

Jamie came to a stop when he saw me sitting there. Then he snapped two words at me before skirting past me to the door. "Let's go."

I followed him out to his truck, making a quick detour to my rental to grab my backpack before joining him in the truck. He wouldn't look at me as he turned over the ignition and backed out of the lot. Tension was coming off of him in waves, and I started to feel a little bit sorry for manipulating him.

After driving for forty-five minutes, he finally spoke. "How dare you go behind my back to the head ranger? How dare you arrange to shadow me and not even mention it while you took advantage of my hospitality last night? You are such an arrogant prick that I can't even understand how your big fat head fits into this truck. I don't even know what to say to you right now."

I looked over at him. "You don't seem to be having a hard time finding some words."

"Fuck you, Teddy." He stared out of the windshield and fumed some more.

We drove along in silence. After a while he pulled onto a smaller road and switchbacks took us up in altitude. I was grateful I didn't usually get carsick.

When I sensed the homicidal urges had softened to a simmering rage, I tried to apologize. "I'm sorry for blindsiding you. Can we talk about why this upsets you so much?"

Jamie scoffed. "The problem is that what I do is dangerous. So whenever someone publishes a photograph of me interacting with animals, it gives people a false sense of security. They think the animals aren't as dangerous as they thought because there's Dr. Marian touching one.

"A photo came out a couple of years ago showing me cradling a grizzly bear cub. A tourist had lucked into the shot while on vacation in Yellowstone. The guy was able to sell it for big bucks to the media. When it was published, it was insanely popular because it was so rare.

"Only a month after the photo was published and widely distributed, a child tried approaching a bear cub at a campground in Yosemite. The mama bear attacked."

"Oh god," I said. "Did the kid...? Was the kid...?"

Jamie sighed. "The boy survived, but he will always have an enormous scar on his face and shoulder. It should have never happened."

"But surely everyone knows that even when a wildlife vet is interacting with animals, it's because they've had extensive training?" I asked.

"Not if they see photos of it in the mainstream media. Maybe it would be different if this had been published in a scientific magazine. But it was all over the media as a 'cute' moment. Not the medical rescue it actually was," Jamie explained.

"Now I understand, Jamie. I'm sorry. That must have been awful for you." I could see the pain on his face as he remembered it.

"Not as awful as it was for that young boy," he said. "Now do you understand my fear of enabling you to take shots of me with the wildlife?"

"I can definitely understand your fear. But I think there could be a way to honor the job you do while also making sure the public is informed about the risk involved."

We drove along in silence for a while longer listening to a country music station playing softly in the background of Jamie's truck.

When I sensed he might have progressed from rage to acceptance, I asked, "Where are we going?"

"There's a herd of Dall sheep up here. I'm observing a band of rams before and after the rut next month." He slowed down as we reached a closed gate across the gravel road. "Be prepared for major boredom, Teddy. What I do is a waiting game. Lots of sitting around being quiet while the animals get comfortable with me. After today, you're going to be begging for directions back to the airport." He rattled off a four-digit code and told me to open the gate for him.

I almost, *almost*, told him that waiting quietly for animals in the wild was part of my job and I was somewhat good at what I did. I decided not to burst his cocky bubble.

After we drove another twenty minutes he pulled the truck to a stop and turned it off. When I stepped out of the cab I was hit with a profound sense of gratitude for the warmer gear I had grabbed at the airport. It was still cold, but I knew it would have been much worse if I didn't at least have the coat.

I grabbed my camera bag out of my backpack and slung it over my shoulder. He grabbed his own backpack from behind the driver's seat and clipped a can of bear spray on the back of his waistband.

"How effective is that bear spray?" I asked him. "Please tell me you're packing heat or something too."

"I do have a handgun in my backpack, but it's more for putting an injured animal out of its misery. I've never even needed the bear spray, but you never know." He started off toward a thin, barely noticeable trail.

When I followed, I realized we were so high up in the mountains that we were at the edge of the tree line. After we exited the last scraggly trees, I looked out in the distance. The views were amazing and clumps of snow lay on the ground in patches. The trail was hard-packed dirt with loose rock scree and boulders poking up here and there.

He walked along in front of me with his usual quiet grace, and I realized this stealthy way of moving must be part of why animals weren't very afraid of him. Jamie Marian was a study in contrasts. He was snarky and feisty but he also moved with a soft fluidity that begged to be admired. He was probably four or five inches shorter than I was but had a rugged, outdoorsy quality to his looks—sun-golden skin, laugh lines beside his eyes, and hair windblown and messy. The man was fucking stellar to look at.

The air was thin so I was grateful he wasn't hiking fast. He seemed content to wander and take in his surroundings rather than hurry to a destination.

After hiking along a ridgeline for a long time, I saw him slow to a stop and slowly lift an arm to point. There, about a hundred feet away, was a big majestic Dall ram perched on a rock at the edge of a drop-off. His thick horns rounded in exquisite curlicues and his cream-colored coat glowed in the sun. He watched us over his shoulder. I tried to stay as still and quiet as possible, following Jamie's lead.

My fingers itched for my camera, but it was still packed away in my bag. I was trying to go easy with Jamie and not anger him more than I already had. It was unlike me to be outside like this without my finger on the shutter release.

After a moment, the ram went back to eating something off the rock, moss or lichen maybe. Finally, Jamie moved off in his steady quiet way. I followed.

Eventually we came to a grouping of boulders that offered a good place to sit and observe sweeping vistas of the flat rocky areas surrounding us. I noticed he took off his coat and turned it inside out before bundling it in a ball on a rock behind him. I quirked a brow at him and he whispered, "Bright colors scare animals." As a wildlife photographer, I knew that already, which was why I had bought a brown one. I was curious about why he owned a bright red coat in the first place when he worked with animals in the wild.

He sat and removed his binoculars and a notebook as I began preparing my gear. He looked over at me with resignation at the sight of my camera, and I gave him a shrug of apology. Clouds slid across the sun, moving the levels of light around us.

Once I had my rigs set up with the lenses and filters I wanted, I put one around my neck while carrying the other. I climbed over the rocks until I found the spot I wanted. After taking some general test shots, I settled onto my stomach on a rock and focused toward Jamie.

When he turned around to see where I was, I sent up a silent prayer of thanks to the inventor of the silent shutter. I could take snaps without him knowing or without scaring off animals. I took several shots of him sitting in the September sun on the top of that mountain.

He was a natural beauty and the light coming through the clouds loved him. There were moments in my job where I was overcome with grateful disbelief that I was the one getting to witness something amazing. Just watching that man sit on a rock and glare at me was one of those moments. Light blazed golden lines through his hair and created shadows along his cheekbones and jawline. The breeze blew strands of hair across his eyes and he reached up to push them off. I captured it all.

He turned back around to face away from me and sat back with his hands on the rock behind him. I focused on his hands; long, tapered fingers bent on the rough unforgiving rock.

We must have sat like that for over an hour. I wasn't used to prolonged silence when in the company of a gorgeous man, but I found I didn't mind it when I was with Jamie. Even though I knew he was annoyed with me, I felt comfortable in his presence.

My wandering mind snapped back to the present when I saw him straighten up a little. I followed his gaze to the left and saw the group of rams. There were six of them wandering toward us slowly. I froze and tried to remain as still as a corpse.

I noticed Jamie's posture relax as he waited. My fingers went to work, switching dials and selecting settings while I snapped different shots. Group shots, focused shots on some of the males, zoom shots on horns and faces. Mature Dall sheep were intimidating. They strode forward slowly like they owned the place. Which they did.

Jamie's bravery astounded me. He stayed relaxed on the rock as if his doddering old uncles were coming in for a hug and a handshake. Two of the rams moved to within ten feet of him, peering at his face to assess the risks. Did the guy have fucking sheep treats in his pockets? I couldn't understand why these big animals would get so close.

I wanted to move to get a better angle, but I was afraid to scare them off. My toes pushed into the rock to see if I could just shift a bit for the better shot. I lifted my hips and scooted them several inches to the right. Once my hips were back down on the rock I carefully reached out one of the elbows I was leaning on to move several inches to the right too. My movements felt as slow as evolution, but I managed to frame a better shot that had both Jamie and the two sheep in it.

We waited some more while one of the sheep near Jamie leaned down to snack on something and three of the remaining slowpokes came forward. One came up to stand about three feet from Jamie's boots and I felt my heart speed up. It sniffed at his knee. The enormous horns looked as big as hula hoops next to Jamie's smaller form.

He slowly brought his hand up to offer the back of it for a sniff. The ram smelled it and looked back at a noise behind him. Jamie's hand continued up to gently land two fingers on a horn. My camera earned its keep as I held my breath and snapped the shutter release as fast as I could.

The ram didn't mind or didn't notice his touch, and Jamie stretched out the rest of his fingers on the ringed surface. Jamie's head tilted while he stared at the horns, stroking across the bumps of the rings. When the sheep's face turned back toward him, Jamie's hand slid gently off and fell back to his lap.

I heard a hum come from his direction and strained my ears to identify it. The hum changed to murmurs until I could hear soft words of reassurance come out of his mouth. He was talking to the ram.

"Are you the man in charge?" I heard him whisper to huge animal. "Congratulations on avoiding the hunt this year, big guy. You're going to make some lucky ewe a proud mom soon. Don't be too hard on your friends there, because there are plenty of pretty girls to go around. Those horns look dangerous, so be gentle when you decide to start butting heads with your band. No need to be an ass about it. Everyone knows you're a stud."

The sheep looked over his shoulder again, almost as if to say, "See, guys, I told you I'm the man." Jamie put his hand up again, stroking the white fur over the ram's shoulder blade this time. The animal's coat twitched under Jamie's hand. The other rams started wandering away, looking for more plants to scavenge from the spaces between rocks. The main ram turned back toward Jamie, brushing his nose against Jamie's outstretched arm before turning around and following his buddies.

I let out a breath. *That was amazing.*

## 6

# JAMIE

After the Dall band had wandered off, I reached for my notebook and began taking notes. I described each ram in detail. The ring count on the main guy showed him to be over ten years old. Lucky bastard.

I heard Teddy move to sit beside me and rustle through his backpack.

"Jamie," he said in a low voice. "That was surreal."

"It was. Those guys in the band are pretty impressive and mature. You should see the babies in the spring. They're like little white cotton balls with fluffy Afros. And when their horns start to come in they're all tiny like baby devils."

He chuckled softly. "Jamie likes baby Dalls."

I snorted and replied, "Yes, I do."

Teddy laughed and I quirked a brow at him. "You referred to them as 'the guys in the band.' That's just funny."

"You call a group of Dall rams a 'band,'" I replied.

"There are some crazy names for animal groups. It's a little strange there are so many different names when you could just say 'group.'"

I smiled. "Actually, animal group names are kind of a thing with me. I was fascinated with them when I was younger and memorized as many as I could. I get a kick out of them even now."

We stopped halfway back to the truck and I pulled out some water bottles and protein bars from my bag. I handed one of each to Teddy and he thanked me before asking, "Where to next?"

"Well, if we wind up seeing the group of Dall ewes on the way back to the truck, we'll check them out. But I doubt they're around here right now. We'll drive over to a shallow river about thirty minutes away that often has caribou and moose nearby."

"Everything is so spread out. You must do lots of driving."

"Yes, that part is a pain in the ass," I replied. "Denali and the surrounding preserve take up as much land as Switzerland, so it takes a while to drive from one end to another. But I listen to music and audio books, which helps."

We ate and packed back up before continuing on the trail. A fat marmot waddled across the trail, and I stopped to point it out to Teddy. He squatted down to get a photo and was rewarded when the marmot heard the movement and turned back around to look at him.

While Teddy was taking the shots, the marmot's buddy came trundling along from behind a nearby rock and tackled his friend. They ended up in a wrestling match that escalated to a standing version of a comical slap fight. One of them fell back down on all fours and raced toward the tree line. His buddy gave chase behind him, making Teddy laugh.

We got to the truck and stowed our bags. I turned on the CD player and acoustic guitar music started playing softly. "That's nice. What is it?" Teddy asked.

"No idea," I said. "I bought the CD at a furniture store when I heard it over their speakers and asked about it. I love it though. What kind of music do you listen to?"

"I like a little of everything. The playlist on my phone is insane. Because I travel so much, I listen to tons of stuff from all over."

As we turned onto the main road Teddy's phone pinged as a few texts came in all at once. He looked at the screen and then typed on it before turning to me and explaining, "My buddy Mac is having girlfriend problems."

"What do you mean?" I asked.

"Well, he started dating this chick a couple of months ago, but apparently something went wrong after I left for New Orleans. She left him. It's weird because they seemed like the real thing."

"Have you met her?"

He nodded. "Yeah. Gorgeous redhead. I met her just last weekend. I really liked her and he was all moon-eyed over her. He couldn't keep his hands off her the whole time we were at dinner."

I pointed out that sometimes that indicates lust, not love. He agreed but continued, "Something was different with this woman and Mac though. I'd never seen him in love before. They work together, so maybe something happened at the office to fuck it up."

"You should call him."

"I don't know. Maybe. I'll wait a couple of days in case it's just a spat."

After I asked him how he knew Mac, he told me about growing up best friends. Teddy's mother had died when he was young and his father was an alcoholic who didn't have much time for grocery shopping or cooking healthy meals. When he became friends with Mac, Mac's family became like a second family. Being with Mac's family made him feel normal. They were both only children so they became kind of like brothers.

I asked him about his relationship with his dad now. "Are you close to him? Does he live in New York?"

"No, we're not that close, and he still lives in my hometown a few hours away from the city. After I left for art school, I started realizing some of my health issues were created at home. Dad was a heavy smoker. I got away from Dad and felt better. My diet was under my control for once, so I taught myself how to make healthier choices. That's when I learned to cook. My buddies in college thought my healthy cooking was pretty great. I have a group of close friends from

Pratt who credit me for keeping them from the big college weight gain." He chuckled.

"In college, I felt alive and healthy for the first time in years. It made me associate feeling sick with my dad and my childhood. My resentment towards him grew until I just couldn't stand to go home anymore. Now I avoid my hometown like the plague. I feel bad though. He isn't getting any younger, and the drinking and smoking will surely catch up with him soon. He texts me sometimes and I try to make it home for the holidays. It weighs on me more now for some reason."

Teddy looked at me. "What about you? Parents, siblings?"

I saw something ahead through the trees and pulled the car to the side of the road to park. Whispering even though we were closed up in the truck, I said, "Look, grizzly."

His eyes grew wider and he reached into his lap for the camera he had kept out. I pointed and described where to look. About forty feet from the road, a grizzly sow lay in the tall grass snoozing.

Teddy rolled down the window to take several snaps before asking quietly if he could get out to get a better angle. I handed him my bear spray can and told him to hook it to his pants pocket and to stay at least twenty-five feet back from the sow.

Before he reached the door handle, I said, "Make sure you leave the truck door open and stay between the bear and the truck. Don't take your eyes off her. I don't see any cubs, but you never know." His eyes met mine and he nodded. Good, he was taking it seriously.

He got out and moved around, alternatively kneeling and crouching to get some different shots. God, he had a nice ass. He had shucked his coat and fleece when the truck warmed up, so I saw his shoulder and back muscles moving under his T-shirt. I realized I was staring.

Well, he *was* with a bear. Of course I should stare. For safety reasons.

I needed to lust after this cocky photographer like I needed a surfboard here in Alaska. If I didn't get him to catch a plane away from here ASAP, I wasn't sure I could avoid accidentally jumping him again.

*Well then, Jamie. Do what you need to do to get him to complete his assignment quickly and hit the road.*

## 7

## TEDDY

I had taken photos of many animals in my career but never a grizzly bear. I had seen one once, but by the time I had the shot, the grizzly was gone.

There were streams of light filtering down through the trees around the bear. Blades of tall grass were mashed down where she was lying and they shined in different shades of greens and tans. Dark trunks of evergreens split columns of shadows behind the sow and one branch of green needles had fallen on the ground beside her.

The bear rolled onto her back at one point and I thought I might burst. The fur of her belly poked up and a giant paw came down to scratch at it. I was so excited to capture this bear, and if I had been alone, my memory cards would be full of her. Jamie was waiting for me though, so I didn't spend all afternoon there.

I returned to the truck with a huge grin on my face. "That was amazing. Thank you, Jamie. You have eagle eyes."

He laughed. "It's easy to spot them when you're used to seeing them around. I sort of know where to look. I'm glad you got to see her."

My heart began to slow down from the high I felt framing the perfect shot. I couldn't help but laser-focus out the window, looking for other treasures as we drove along.

A light snow flurry brushed flakes across the windshield. I asked Jamie if it was supposed to snow. He said he thought it was just a few flakes, and that he didn't know of any snow in the forecast.

He told me about the snowshoe hare who lived behind his cabin. He had spotted him hopping under some brush a couple of months ago and spent some time sitting with him to see if he'd come out for Jamie to see. He got braver and braver until he began staying out in the open when Jamie was around and hopped across his legs if Jamie was sitting on the grass.

Jamie laughed. "He's actually a good conversationalist. Chatters all the time about nonsense. I told him I can't wait to see how swanky he looks in his fancy white winter coat."

What I wouldn't give to see him chatting with the little rabbit. "Can we see him later? Maybe I can get a shot of him with you."

"Teddy, how long are you here for? I mean, how long do you intend for this whole 'shadowing' thing to go on?" He sighed.

Jamie pulled off to a gravel parking area and turned off the ignition before twisting in his seat to look at me.

I wasn't sure what to tell him. "I don't know. Maybe after I get some shots of you with four or five different animals. I'm not sure how long that would take. But by then I could go home and play with the images for a while to see if I got what I needed."

He set his shoulders back. "Okay, then let's make that happen. Four or five animals. You got the Dall. We'll look for moose or caribou here. Then we'll go into town to get some dinner. I'll let you stay in the loft again because there's no point in looking for a vacancy during the road lottery. Plus, hopefully, you can meet Harry. Then we'll be halfway to your goal. God willing, I'll get you off tomorrow or the next day."

A laugh burst out of me before I replied, "Baby Dall, I would love for you to get me off. But who the hell is Harry?"

He bit back to me, "The snowshoe hare, jackass." Then he opened the truck, grabbed his warm gear, and slammed the door behind him.

I grabbed my camera bag and followed him across a meadow toward a wide shallow river. He got to the edge of the riverbank and looked down to the right and left. Choosing left, he turned and started walking along the river's edge. Even though we were lower in altitude, the temperature had plummeted and my hands were cold. I followed him.

After a few minutes of walking, we picked our way through a clump of brambles. He stopped me before we broke through to the other side and gestured for me to stay quiet for a minute. I looked around him but didn't see anything. We waited. I felt my hands get colder. I had the crazy mental image of snaking my cold fingers up his shirt to warm them on his back, and I almost laughed at the thought of the scream that would come out of him if I did.

Suddenly, a large bird flew into the brush right in front of Jamie and knocked him hard in the shoulder. He stumbled back into me, and my arms went around him to keep him from falling. We stood like that for a beat before he righted himself and brushed off his coat.

He stepped slowly out of the brambles and turned around to me, lifting his finger to his lips. I followed as quietly as I could. At some point I was going to have to tell him I didn't need him to warn me about being quiet while trying to photograph wildlife. It was turning from cutely condescending to annoying as hell.

I lifted an eyebrow at him and pointed to his shoulder. He waved a hand at me like it was fine. I wasn't so sure. That bird was big, and it had hit him at top speed.

He walked slowly along the riverbank to another small group of trees. Through the branches I saw them. A cow moose and her calf stood in the water off to our right.

Jamie really was an animal whisperer. We had already seen more large rare mammals in one day than most tourists do in a week of trying hard. I pulled up my camera and began to sight through the lens. After a few shots, I tapped his shoulder and gestured forward with a questioning look.

He tentatively pushed through the last branch hiding us, and the cow moose's head came up to stare at us. I knew that a mama and her baby together made mama dangerous. That was true across most of the animal kingdom.

Even though I had seen moose before, I was always struck by how tall they were. Jamie moved forward and stepped a boot into the shallow water by the edge. He stopped and waited. The calf moved forward, down the river away from us. It was all long legs and twitchy ears. The cow kept her eyes on us for a few minutes while we stood there. She took a drink of water and started following the calf down the river.

Jamie took a few more steps across the rocky riverbed and stopped again, watching them walk away. He crouched down into a squat and stayed still again. I heard him make a faint clicking sound with his tongue and saw the cow and calf turn back to look for it.

The calf turned all the way around and took a few steps back toward Jamie. The cow looked unsure. I slowly dropped down to a prone position and framed the shot, with Jamie crouching down on the right with a hand extended, the back end of the cow in the center, her giant nose looking over her left shoulder toward Jamie, and the baby taking an eager step toward Jamie on the left of the frame. I couldn't wait to see if one of them turned out.

The calf got about five feet away from Jamie's outstretched hand before the cow decided enough was enough and made a sound that was a cross between a grunt and a honk. The calf quickly turned and blundered back to its mom.

When Jamie put his hands on his knees to push himself back to a standing position, I heard a sharp intake of breath and saw his left arm give a little. I knew that damned bird strike was bad. He pretended it hadn't happened as he made his way back to where I was standing on the shore.

"You look a little pale," I said. "Let's go find you some ice and ibuprofen, okay?"

He rolled his eyes at me and started walking to the truck. By the time we reached it, his shoulder must have been killing him because he handed me the keys and asked if I could drive.

He pointed me in the direction of his cabin and I began to drive. A few minutes later I looked over and noticed he'd fallen asleep. I fumbled with my phone to select the GPS directions from the day before and followed them back to his driveway.

I got out and walked around to the passenger side. Unfastening his seatbelt, I reached to help him out of the truck and up to the front steps when he woke up and slapped my arms away.

"Get off me, you oaf. I can walk for god's sake."

"You were asleep. I was just trying to help you, Jamie," I explained.

"I don't need your damned help. Move." He stumbled down from the truck and reached back in with his injured arm to get his backpack from the backseat. As soon as the stretch of his arm reached his shoulder, his knees buckled and he almost slumped to a heap on the ground. I grabbed him around the stomach and held him up.

"Fuck," he said with a shaky voice. "That hurts like a bitch. You don't think it could be dislocated, do you?"

"Let's get you inside and take a look. It's snowing in case you haven't noticed. We're going to be wet when we get inside." I kept an arm around his waist helping him inside and sat his on the sofa. I helped his take off his boots and handed him the quilt from his chair.

I let Sister out for a bathroom break and started the coffee maker. Jamie pointed me toward painkillers and ice packs. He got up to use the bathroom and when he came back out, he was struggling to get his fleece top off. I stepped over to help him remove it without having to lift up that arm. I put it on the back of the sofa and turned back around to see him trying to get his T-shirt off.

"Can you help me take off this shirt too?" he asked.

"Sweetheart, I've never said no to that question in my life." I reached under the hem and carefully helped him out of it.

When we got it off, he was left in just his pants and colorful nylon webbing belt. His body was sleek and muscled despite his smaller frame. Rounded shoulders and biceps, defined pecs and abs. A tantalizing happy trail leading down into his pants. My mouth watered.

A giant bruise bloomed angrily over the front of his left shoulder. I reached out to gently run my hands from his arms to his shoulders and around the front of his collarbone. He tensed at my touch. Nothing felt broken to me but I wasn't a doctor. I asked if he could slowly move that arm up and around. He did. It went through the motion without any odd jerks even though it was clearly painful.

"I'm not a doctor, but my guess is just a really bad bruise. Let's ice it and use anti-inflammatories to see if it's any better tomorrow."

When I pressed the ice pack to his shoulder, he lay back down and pulled the quilt up to his chest.

"Damned pochard," he mumbled.

"What are you talking about?" I asked.

"The bird. I think it was a pochard. It's like a red-headed duck. What an asshole. I saw him on the surface of the water and then he took off towards us. I tried to duck. I tried to duck the duck. Fuck. He probably thought he was flying into a safe hiding spot. I wonder if he got hurt. We should have looked for him."

I told him to lie down and try to relax. When the coffee was ready I fixed him a cup and brought it over to him. He took a couple of sips before lying back into the blankets and closing his eyes.

When he was asleep, I had an idea. I took some photographs of him lying there, making sure I got his injured shoulder in the shot. The ugly bruise, the ice pack, and his pain-pinched face.

# 8

# JAMIE

I awoke to the sound of typing. Teddy sat at the kitchen table working on a laptop. His camera equipment was spread out all around him.

"Hey," he said. "How's your shoulder?"

"Hurts like a bitch."

"Are you hungry? I can make you some eggs." Teddy sat back and stretched his arms above his head.

I asked him what time it was, and he said five o'clock.

Standing up and heading to the bathroom, I said over my shoulder, "No, let's go into town. I'm in the mood for a burger."

Teddy drove us in his rental and we sat in a booth at the roadhouse about forty-five minutes later. I ordered a burger and fries before handing the menu back.

"I'll have the same. Thanks, darlin'," Teddy said to the attractive young waitress with a wink. I rolled my eyes.

"What?" he asked after the woman gave him a huge smile and walked away.

"Are you always trying to get laid?"

"It doesn't hurt to be friendly, sweetheart. You should try it sometime."

I narrowed my eyes at him. "Who says I'm not friendly?"

He shrugged and smiled. "And what's wrong with trying to get laid? I'm not the one who doesn't want one-night stands, remember?"

"Never mind. Do what you want," I muttered back.

"No, Jamie, talk to me. You did say you aren't interested in hookups like that, right? Because if you are, I'm more than happy to oblige again."

"Okay, well, I changed my mind," I said to him.

His face lit up as he quickly said, "I'll ask for the check."

I rolled my eyes again. "Easy there, cowboy. I didn't mean with you. You're too annoying. Plus, you're not really my type."

He looked at me with a raised eyebrow. "And what type is that?"

"*Not* presumptuous, arrogant, and slutty."

"Ouch," he said, clutching a hand over his heart.

"Maybe more one-night stands would help me move past this shitty feeling I've had since Brian. Maybe my problem was shooting for marriage and monogamy in the first place. I should try sleeping around casually for a while and see if that helps. Sex without the emotional upheaval."

Teddy took a sip of his beer and then asked, "Can we revisit you disparaging me, please? You wounded my pride. I'm quite the catch. Pleasuring people in bed is a special skill I have. Just ask the entire flight crew from Qantas flight 93 from Melbourne to LAX." His grin grew wide, showing off straight white teeth.

I choked on my sip of beer and some shot up my nose. "Are you fucking kidding me? You did not."

He burst out laughing. "No, Baby Dall, I did not. Not the whole crew anyway. But it's awfully fun to make beer come out of your nose."

Our food was delivered and we started eating. I felt a little bad for insulting him earlier so I said, "Well, Teddy, I have to admit that you do take beautiful photos. Working a camera seems to be one special skill you do have."

"You've seen my work?" he asked, surprised.

"I looked it up when you emailed me. The series of the hippos was funny. And there's one of red birds all flying out of a tree that I just couldn't stop staring at. It's mesmerizing."

Teddy was speechless, staring at me. "Really? Thanks, Jamie. That means a lot to me. *Synod*, the red bird photo, is one of my all-time favorites. It's funny, though, because I was in Africa to do a shoot on giraffes. I was setting up to take some test shots of a tree when an assistant I'd hired for the shoot slammed the trunk of the rental vehicle after unloading some equipment. When the loud bang rang out, suddenly hundreds of small red birds came flying out of the leaves. I didn't even know they were there when I was setting up. I found out later they're called bishops."

Teddy was like a different man when he talked about photography. Humble and... maybe a little reverent. "I can tell you really love what you do," I admitted.

"Yes," he said simply. "I'm very lucky."

We ate the rest of our meal as the roadhouse filled up with locals and a few stopped by our booth to say hello. I introduced the people I knew to Teddy and he fell easily back into his usual flirty charm. The music got louder and couples made their way over to the wooden dance floor in the back.

I asked Teddy if he wanted another beer or to call for the check. Before he had a chance to answer, one of the guys I worked with came over and asked me to dance. Josh was the only gay guy in a fifty-mile radius and had been trying to get me to go out with him for months. Teddy's eyes widened.

I opened my mouth to decline when Teddy answered in his deep voice. "Poor Jamie here has a clipped wing so he won't be able to do any dancing tonight. Sorry, buddy."

*That arrogant jackass.* I looked at Josh and said, "I'd love to," before splashing a big smile at him and sliding out of the booth. I didn't look back to see Teddy's reaction.

I did my best to dance without wincing in pain, but I knew I couldn't fake it for more than one song. Josh didn't know about my injury, and I was distracted trying to protect the shoulder without being obvious.

When I realized that Josh was trying to pull me in close to him, I pulled back a little bit. He must have thought I was making some kind of dance move because he grabbed the hand of my hurt shoulder and lifted it above our heads to twirl me. Tears smarted in my eyes and I almost vomited on the floor. I quickly mumbled that I needed to go and would see him later, then I turned and made my way back to the table.

Teddy stood there waiting for me and looked surprised when he saw my face. He gestured to the door with a raised eyebrow and I raced toward it. When I got to the parking lot, I ran over behind a dumpster and leaned over to throw up. Nothing. I took a deep breath to stop the shaking and stayed bent over with my hands on my knees.

I felt a hand on my back. "You okay?"

"No. My pride is crushed. Please don't say you told me so."

"I wouldn't dare, Jamie. Let me drive you home."

I told Teddy to give me another minute, and then I slowly followed him to the vehicle. By the time he started the engine, I reminded him we needed to stop and get some groceries before heading back to the cabin.

When we returned to the cabin, I thanked him for helping me and went straight to bed. I was ready for the day to be over.

# 9

## TEDDY

I went to sleep thinking about Jamie. How stupid could he be dancing with that asshole at the roadhouse? Didn't he see how that would be painful? When I saw him lift his arm up, I stood to go get him. That's when I remembered I wasn't in charge of him. It wasn't like I was his boyfriend or his brother or even really a friend. I wasn't sure he even liked me much. He clearly didn't appreciate me trying to look out for him, or he wouldn't have danced with the guy in the first place.

Forcing myself to stay by the table, I threw down cash to cover the bill with a tip. When Jamie started heading my way, I noticed his expression. His eyes were glassy with pain, and he was pale as shit.

He walked toward me cradling his left elbow with his right hand, and I asked him if he wanted to go. A nod and he was out the door. I grabbed our coats and followed.

After he went to sleep that night, I took care of Sister, put away the food I had purchased, and prepped my gear for the following day. I slept better that night after all the fresh air and exercise.

In the morning I climbed down from the loft and dressed in the bathroom. Jamie was nowhere to be found and Sister scratched at the door. Right before opening it to let her out, I noticed both vehicles still in the driveway. Where was Jamie?

I double-checked his bedroom and noticed movement outside his bedroom window. That was when I remembered his rabbit friend. Grabbing my camera and telling Sister to wait a minute, I raced outside and around to the back.

Sighting through my lens before coming around the final bend, I stopped and saw them. Jamie was sitting on the ground with his back against a rough wooden storage box, his legs stretched out in front of him. There was a light layer of snow on the ground so I knew his pants would be wet when he stood up.

The little snowshoe hare sat next to him, facing away from him toward the woods. Jamie slowly placed his hands down flat onto the ground by his hips and the hare turned back to look at him. They sat like that for a minute.

I slowly eased myself down to the ground on my knees. My movement caught his attention and he looked my way. His face lit up, and I instinctively brought a hand up to rub my chest where it suddenly felt tight.

While Jamie was distracted, the hare tentatively put one paw on the back of his fingers. Jamie turned his face around to see and gently rolled his hand around until the paw rested on his palm. The hare placed a second paw next to the first.

Just like the day before, I was amazed to see Jamie's body language. When he was interacting with an animal, his entire body relaxed. He melted into his surroundings. No wonder the animals weren't afraid.

Jamie tried to curl his hand into a light fist to feel the fur of the paws. That must have been too much because the hare moved sideways and then hopped onto the top of the box behind Jamie's head. Jamie just stayed still again and we waited to see what he would do.

I took minuscule steps forward on my knees and got a little closer before lying on my belly and sighting my lens again.

We waited some more. He winked at me. Fuck that man was sexy.

Only the hare's back end was visible to me beside Jamie's head, so

I was only snapping a few shots while we waited. I hoped to god my shutter caught the wink. I noticed his hair was messy from sleep. He had on a navy blue fleece with the collar popped up under his hair. I saw chest hair peeking out from the open neck of the fleece, and he had green plaid flannel pajama pants on. The skin on his face was flushed with cold and his brown eyes were bright between dark lashes. God, he was beautiful. My heart sped up at the sight of him, and my pants suddenly felt snug. I tried telling my hard-on to take a hike, but it wasn't listening. I shifted my hips to ease the discomfort.

A pinecone or something dropped in the trees off to our right. At the light sound, the rabbit popped its ears up above Jamie's head and they both turned their faces to seek out the source of the noise. I snapped the moment it looked like Jamie had fake bunny ears on and then the moment the rabbit's head popped up fully and both faces pointed sideways, looking in the same direction. It was perfection. I prayed the shots would turn out as good as I thought they might.

After another few minutes the bunny took a big leap over Jamie's shoulder, landed on the snow-dusted grass by his leg, and then turned off into the forest. I tried to get a shot of him in the air but I would have to check the memory card later to see if I got it.

Jamie let out a soft chuckle and got up to brush off his pants.

"Oh my god, I'm frozen." He laughed. "But I'm glad you came out. I forgot to tell you last night that dusk and dawn are the most common times to see him."

"Let's go let Sister out and get you some coffee. She looked like she was going to burst," I said.

"I already let her out earlier. She was probably just anxious to get to me," he replied as we walked back inside.

Jamie showered and dressed while I fixed coffee and breakfast for us. I got a text from my dad asking me how I was doing. I responded with a quick message telling him I was working in Denali. While we ate, Jamie told me about the beaver kits he was observing. He mentioned heading over to their dam to see if we could get them to come out and play. He definitely seemed to be trying to give me what I needed for my photos as quickly as he could so I would leave.

I thought about that for a moment and realized it was probably for the best. I was really starting to like him too much, and if there was one thing I didn't do, it was relationships. Fucking? Sure. Dating, nope. I traveled too much to make a relationship work, and I was used to relying on myself anyway.

It wasn't that I hadn't tried dating people before, I had. It was just that those attempts always left a big mess behind. Guilt trips for being gone all the time. Feelings of betrayal when a someone cheated on me while I was gone. Loneliness when being far away from someone I wanted to be with. I'd rather just fuck. Way easier that way.

I wanted so badly to sleep with Jamie Marian. Run my mouth over all of his delicious skin and feel his body alongside mine in bed. But he deserved better than another guy who fucked him and left.

## 10

# JAMIE

When we parked in the gravel area near the trailhead to see the beavers, I was surprised to see Teddy put on a warm hat and gloves.

"Where did you get those?" I asked.

"They had them at the store last night when I was buying the food. I have to admit this is way colder than I was expecting for September, even in Alaska."

I agreed it was unusual. "Well, not exactly unusual. It happens, but it wasn't really expected this week. This time of the year the weather swings pretty rapidly."

As we started walking down the trail Teddy asked me if I got tired of the extreme cold here.

"The cold definitely wears on me, but I think the short days bother me more. Going without much sunlight is harsh, especially for someone who spends lots of time outside. But I usually book a vacation somewhere warm for the holidays."

Teddy asked if I spent the holidays with family.

"Yes, I have a big family in San Francisco. One sister and seven brothers."

"Seven brothers. Jesus. Your parents must be insane." He laughed.

"They are. Six of us are biological children and then my parents got involved in a LGBTQ youth program. They ended up adopting three of their foster sons through the program. It makes it crazy but good."

"Does growing up with that many siblings make you more or less likely to want kids?" he asked.

"I would be okay either way. Sometimes I want kids because I have a lot to offer them. Adventure, education, love. But then I remember my own parents and think I could never be as good a parent as they were. I don't know. What about you?"

"I think it would be awesome and fun, especially showing them the world one day. But I never want to do something to inadvertently screw them up. I'd rather not have kids if I'm going to fuck them up royally. So, I guess I don't really know."

As we approached the river, I slowed us down, and Teddy pulled the camera around from where it was hanging under his shoulder. I pointed in the direction of the beaver lodge. Then I indicated a log we could sit on while we observed. He sat down next to me. We resumed our familiar waiting silence. I could feel the warmth of Teddy's thigh next to mine, and I had to hold myself back from resting a hand on it.

We could see movement behind the sticks so we knew someone was home. It took about fifteen minutes before anyone poked their head out. It was a mature beaver waddling along the top of a branch and farther down the riverbank away from us. The kits walked out shortly after and climbed up onto the top of their lodge to survey the scene. I saw the moment one of them noticed me because he chattered, twirled around his buddy, and then scampered toward us. His buddy chased after him.

They came with almost no hesitation right up to my boots. They ran around my boots in playful antics and then one of them used the canvas of my pants to run up my lower leg, across the top of my thigh, and onto the log beside my hip. The other jumped from the ground to the log. They played around on the top of the log beside me while Teddy took shots and tried moving backward away from me without disturbing them. He had been too close to get the right perspective.

They weren't skittish at all so he was able to back away without interrupting their play. They tumbled around each other and chased each other everywhere they went. At one point they came back to my lap and climbed my fleece top to the warm black hat covering my head. For just a few seconds, one sat primly on my head while the other draped across my shoulder.

They came down and chased each other around my waist before noticing Teddy and scampering over to him. He remained still, and I didn't know if it was out of fear of them or respect for my wishes.

When they scampered back across to sit on the top of the lodge, Teddy took some shots of the river with the rays of sun lighting up bits of water and the shadows playing along the rocks. I could see speckled fish below the surface in one area and it looked like they had a safe, still spot to hang out away from the water rushing past.

Eventually we headed back to the truck. I saw Teddy pull his phone out of my backpack to check it, and he frowned. As I started the truck, he said he had to call his dad. I turned the music off and began driving while he dialed.

"Dad?" he said. I could hear a muffled male voice on the other end but it wasn't clear enough to know what he was saying. Teddy took a sharp intake of breath before blurting, "What? Tell me that again?" He listened. "Where is he? What hospital? What's his prognosis?"

I looked over at him. His body radiated tension and the hand clutching the phone was white-knuckled.

"I'm in Alaska but I'll be on the next flight out. Tell him I love him and I'm on my way. Thank you so much for calling me. I'll be there as soon as I can."

I wanted to put my hand on his leg to offer him support. I kept my hands on the wheel and drove faster toward the ranger station.

When he hung up, he let out a shaky breath and dialed another number.

"Yes, I need to book travel from Fairbanks, Alaska, to Ithaca, New York, today if possible. It would have to be after one p.m. Fairbanks time."

After arranging a flight leaving at two, he hung up.

"I'm trying to get us back to your vehicle as quickly as I can. Do you want to tell me what happened?" I asked tentatively.

"My dad had a stroke last night. They didn't think it was serious until he had more tests today. He needs surgery, but they're not sure if he's strong enough right now."

"Teddy, I'm so sorry. When are they going to do the surgery? Is it urgent they do it right away?"

He rubbed his hand along his jaw. "I'm not sure."

"I wish I could say or do something to make it better. I feel so helpless."

Teddy looked over at me and I saw a flash of annoyance cross his face. "He's been a smoker and drinker for a thousand years despite my hours of begging him to stop. I had severe childhood asthma. I was sick all the time with various illnesses I caught while my immune system was suppressed. When I left home, it started clearing up, and I finally felt healthy. It wasn't until I was almost done with college that I realized a childhood of health problems could have been prevented if only my dad had gotten his head out of his ass long enough to stop smoking."

"Shit, Teddy."

"Yeah," he said.

I dropped him at the ranger station to pick up the vehicle he'd left there the day before. Back on the road, he followed me home. Eventually we pulled up to my cabin, and he quickly packed his things before putting them in his car. I walked him out.

"Listen, Jamie, I'm sorry about all of this. I was really having a nice time hanging out with you. If everything goes well, I'd love to come back and get more photos. But I understand if you say no. We can wait and see how this first round comes out, okay?"

I didn't want to cause him any additional stress by disagreeing. "Okay. I hope everything goes well with your dad. Shoot me an email and let me know how he's doing?"

He put his hand on my shoulder. "Would it be okay if I texted you? Might be easier."

"Of course. No problem, Teddy. Take care."

He gave me a quick hug before I could protest. I smelled his aftershave and the Teddy smell of him. He pulled back and kissed me on the cheek. "Take good care of yourself out here, Baby Dall."

After he pulled away, I walked back into the cabin and noticed it was more silent than I'd ever heard it before.

## 11

# TEDDY

After close to eighteen hours of travel, I felt hungover. I had managed to buy some new clothes at one of the shops during my layover in Minneapolis. They had lots of good stores in the terminal where I was, and I was happy to change into clothes that hadn't been in rain, snow, or Alaskan dirt.

I rented a car and headed to the hospital. After I parked and went to the reception desk, they gave me directions to his room.

I approached and saw a doctor typing notes on a computer trolley just outside Dad's ICU room. When he saw me, he approached with a handshake. Dr. Whitley told me they had decided to go ahead with the surgery within the next couple of hours. Dad had shown signs of continued bleeding in the brain and they had to go in. The doctor warned me the risks of surgery were high, but it was the only option.

They would begin prepping him in about an hour so I went into the room to see him. He looked significantly older than when I had last seen him. His pallor was gray and his skin looked more wrinkled. Of course, there were tubes and machines everywhere, but I had expected that. He was asleep, or more likely, sedated.

I held his hand gently for a little while until they were ready to take him back. I asked a nurse if there was a place for me to take a shower while we waited. She said I could use the one in the room if I was quick about it. After the surgery, Dad would be back in there so they were going to have it cleaned while he was away.

After showering and putting my clothes back on, I found the small private waiting room for families of surgery patients. I pulled out my phone and a charger from my backpack. After plugging it in, I sat on the floor by the wall and texted Mac.

**Teddy:** *My dad had a stroke. I'm in Ithaca. Surgery this afternoon, not looking good.*

**Mac:** *Oh shit, Teddy. Are you okay? I thought you were in Alaska?*

**Teddy:** *I was. Flew back last night. What's going on there? Things any better with Birdie?*

**Mac:** *Don't worry about me. Do you want me to come out there?*

**Teddy:** *Nah. Thanks tho. I'll let you know if I need you to come. Hopefully we'll know more in a couple of hours, after the surgery.*

**Mac:** *Okay. Just say the word, Teddy, and I'm there. You know that.*

**Teddy:** *I do. Thanks, Mac.*

Then I decided to text Jamie.

**Teddy:** *Hey Jamie. I made it to the hospital about an hour ago. Dad had a stroke and they're doing surgery now. The doctor said it's dicey.*

**Jamie:** *Jesus that was a long trip. Hopefully the surgery will be a good thing and he'll recover. You must be exhausted.*

**Teddy:** *You have no idea.*

**Jamie:** *And you probably smell like ass.*

**Teddy:** *Charmer. Actually I bought new clothes in Minneapolis and just finished taking a shower here at the hospital. Fresh as a daisy.*

**Jamie:** *A tired, wilted daisy.*

**Teddy:** *True.*

**Jamie:** *You okay otherwise?*

**Teddy:** *Not sure.*

**Jamie:** *Fair enough. Have you eaten?*

**Teddy:** *Yes, a little. What about you? Are you cooking the healthy food I bought you?*

**Jamie:** *I'm eating the good stuff, but I put the veggies out back for Harry.*

**Teddy:** *What?!*

**Jamie:** *Kidding. Never give a wild animal people food. You should already know that.*

**Teddy:** *I do. That's why I was surprised, smartass.*

**Jamie:** *Do you have someone with you?*

**Teddy:** *No. I'm waiting to see how the surgery goes. Let's talk about other things to distract me. How is your shoulder?*

**Jamie:** *Ugly as hell. But it's not as painful as it was. I had my friend Daniel at the ranger station take a look at it this morning because he used to be an army medic. He says it's not broken or anything.*

**Teddy**: *Why is the image of some guy looking at your bare shoulder pissing me off?*

**Jamie**: *Because you're a horndog who hasn't gotten properly laid since Qantas Flight 93 a week ago?*

**Teddy**: *Who says I didn't get laid by Alaska Air Flight 124 yesterday?*

**Jamie**: *Fuck.*

**Teddy**: *I didn't. What kind of person do you think I am? Jesus, Jamie.*

**Jamie**: *You're the one who said it, not me!*

**Teddy**: *Plus, you forget that I got laid in Denali. Or was it that forgettable?*

**Jamie**: *Not for me, but I assumed it was for you.*

**Teddy**: *Then you're shockingly unobservant. I remember every single moment of it and will replay it in my mind later when I'm alone and horny. Let's go back to the part about your soldier friend. Danielle, was it?*

**Jamie**: *Daniel. What about him?*

**Teddy**: *I'm picturing a big beefy soldier just back from war. In reality he's probably a skinny nerdy guy who picked medic because it took more brains than brawn?*

**Jamie**: *No. More the first one.*

**Teddy**: *Fuck.*

**Jamie:** *He asked me to take my pants off too so he could check all of me. It was kind of awkward. I decided he was almost like a doctor so it was ok.*

**Teddy:** *Are you fucking kidding me right now?*

**Jamie:** *That depends, are you distracted?*

**Teddy:** *Affirmative.*

**Jamie:** *Then my job here is done.*

**Teddy:** *You are a cold-hearted motherfucker.*

**Jamie:** *Well, I was considering making up a story about going for a ride on the back of a grizzly bear, but I didn't think you'd buy it.*

**Teddy:** *You would have been safer with the grizzly. Just to clarify, you didn't let some army asshole see you naked this morning, correct?*

**Jamie:** *Oh no. I totally did. But it was after a one-night stand, not a medical exam.*

**Teddy:** *You're fucking killing me.*

When the nurse came in to tell me it would be at least another hour, I went out to the car to get my laptop and camera memory cards. I worked on uploading and editing a bit while waiting.

Seeing the shots of Jamie made my chest feel tight and I even felt the backs of my eyes prickle a little bit. I realized just how exhausted I must have been. I closed up my laptop and slid everything back into my bag. Leaning my head back against the wall, I closed my eyes until I heard someone call my name.

The nurse said the doctor wanted to speak to me in a private consultation room. Once I was seated in the little room, the doctor came in and I knew from the look on his face that my father was gone.

"What happened?" I asked in a broken voice. It was as stupid question. I knew what happened. He smoked and drank himself to death, and no doctor on the planet could prevent massive stroke damage.

"Mr. Kodiak, I'm so sorry. Your father's blood pressure dropped during the surgery and we were unable to revive him. If he'd been healthier when it happened, we might have had a better chance at saving him. This was his fourth stroke in the past eighteen months, and his body was just worn out. I'm so sorry for your loss. Is there someone I can call to be with you?"

"Fourth stroke?" I blurted. "I had no idea. He never told me."

"Oftentimes parents are afraid of being a burden to their adult children. Or he could have been ashamed of his inability to stop drinking and smoking. I didn't really know him well, but I'd treated him after one of his strokes here. Honestly, Mr. Kodiak, he wasn't very interested in changing his habits. We went over and over it before he was discharged, but he seemed set in his ways."

"I know." I sighed, feeling numbness take over. What the hell was I supposed to do now?

A hospital bereavement consultant or something like that took charge of me then. She walked me through everything I needed to do to arrange for a funeral home and cremation. I barely registered what was happening and, before I knew it, I was standing in front of my dad's house with a plastic bag of his items from the hospital including his house keys.

Mac and Jamie had both texted several times to ask how the surgery went. When I didn't answer, they each started calling. Finally, I returned Mac's call.

"Teddy, where the hell are you?" he asked.

"My dad's house. He's dead, Mac."

"I'll be there in ten minutes. I went to the hospital when I didn't hear from you, but they wouldn't tell me anything."

I left the door unlocked for Mac and wandered through my childhood home like a ghost looking for something left behind. There was nothing there for me anymore and hadn't been for a long time. Old furniture, broken kitchen items, dirt and dust in every corner.

The fridge was empty with the exception of an opened case of beer. It didn't matter. I wasn't hungry anyway.

I sat in my father's recliner and dialed Jamie. For some reason my tears didn't come until I heard Jamie Marian's voice on the other end of the phone.

"He didn't make it," I said in a whisper, feeling hot tears slide over my cheeks.

"Oh shit, Teddy. Oh god, I'm so sorry. Do you want me to call someone? What about Mac or your friends from school?"

"Mac's on his way. I just called so you wouldn't worry when I wasn't answering the phone." I sniffed.

"I'm still worried. What can I do to help? I'm sorry I'm so fucking far away. I make a pretty shitty friend."

"You're not a shitty friend, Jamie. When I was talking to all of the people at the hospital and kept seeing yours and Mac's names pop up on my phone, I didn't feel so alone. Thank you for that."

"Will you promise to call me when you need a friend to talk to?" he asked.

"I promise," I whispered, trying desperately to keep from sobbing. I heard the front door open. "Mac's here. I have to go."

"Go easy on yourself, Teddy. Take care," Jamie said before disconnecting.

I closed my eyes and felt more tears escape. After talking to Mac for a half hour, I told him how exhausted I was from the crazy trip and the stress of everything. I knew he'd understand, and he knew where to find the guest room. After closing up the house, I finally entered my childhood bedroom and fell into bed.

The next several days went by in a hazy fog of organized chaos. Funeral arrangements, death certificates, accessing bank accounts, and utility accounts. Wills, lawyers, probate, realtors. It was just too much. Mac helped me with everything. He'd been through the loss of his parents a few years before and hooked me up with a law firm to handle most of the legal and financial issues. That was an enormous burden lifted, but it left me too much time to focus on the guilt.

I knew in my brain I couldn't have prevented my father's death, but I couldn't help thinking about how I could have done more, been better, loved harder. At least he wouldn't have been so alone. Mac talked me down from the guilt cliff as much as he could and his words finally began to sink in.

Every day Jamie would text or call in an effort to distract me or make me laugh. I was grateful for his unexpected friendship and appreciated him being there for me even though we hadn't known each other for long.

My Pratt friends came out for the funeral and helped me go through Dad's things. Finally, after ten days at my father's house, I was able to return to my shitty apartment in the city. There were hours upon hours of work waiting for me, and my computer equipment was collecting dust.

# 12

# JAMIE

After Teddy left Alaska, I got back to my usual routine with one exception. I couldn't stop thinking about him.

Whenever I saw an animal in the wild, I imagined the photos he could snap. Whenever I was home alone with Sister, I remembered Teddy sitting on the sofa stroking her as she slept. I thought about how his arm muscles moved when he cooked and the way he smelled and tasted.

All this obsessing about Teddy needed to stop. Surely, it wasn't about Teddy specifically. It was unlikely, considering he had only been there a few days. After the death of his father, we had done a good job at establishing a casual friendship. I enjoyed making him laugh and hearing funny stories about his friends and their artistic craziness.

I realized I was probably just lonely. Or horny. Either way, I needed to start thinking about getting out there again. Despite what I had told Teddy, I didn't want to be alone. But I wasn't interested in trying to trust someone with a serious relationship either. Maybe I should try casual hookups. I thought about how serious I felt recently and I realized maybe I needed to loosen up and have some fun. Maybe I needed to get laid without complications or expectations.

But I was entirely unsure of how people did that. I had never once had a one-night stand. How did it work? Did I get one of those apps like Grindr? I needed a friend I could ask. Surely I knew someone who could give me pointers.

Well, hell. I sure did. Teddy knew all about casual sex. But it would be too weird to ask him. Wouldn't it? Why would it? It wasn't like we were dating. Or having sex. Hadn't he been the one to imply we were friends?

What the hell. When I sat down at a cafe for lunch, I decided to text him.

**Jamie:** *Hey you. Still trying to catch up on work?*

**Teddy:** *I'm almost caught up. It's been four weeks since I left Alaska and I finally feel like I can take the time to check out the photos I took of you.*

**Jamie:** *Hey listen, I wanted to ask you something kind of awkward.*

**Teddy:** *That sounds interesting.*

**Jamie:** *You said we were friends, right?*

**Teddy:** *Yes... What's going on, Baby Dall?*

**Jamie:** *I decided to take your advice and get laid.*

**Teddy:** *Is this about the army medic?*

**Jamie:** *No. The thing about the medic was a joke. Now I'm being serious.*

**Teddy:** *What's this really about, Jamie?*

**Jamie:** *I think I need to get on with my life. After the whole Brian thing I swore off dating because I don't want to have a serious relationship. I don't want to deal with cheating and trusting and expectations. But I don't want* *to be a nun either. I think maybe I should just learn how to hook up instead of date. I've never really done that.*

**Teddy:** *And why are you telling me this? Are you asking me to come to Alaska for casual sex? Let me check the flight schedules.*

**Jamie:** *You wish. No. You're the only friend I have who knows how this crap works.*

**Teddy:** *Who knows how a dick works?*

**Jamie:** *Shut up and be serious. I'm talking about hookups. How do you do this where you just go home with someone, get off, and then not care? Grindr?*

**Teddy:** *I'm not sure that's going to work for you. You'll care too much.*

**Jamie:** *Dude, that's why I'm asking for help.*

**Teddy:** *It's not that easy. You can't always walk away from people you're attracted to without pain or frustration.*

**Jamie:** *What about you? You seem to do it just fine.*

**Teddy:** *I don't always leave without caring, Jamie. Sometimes I leave* because *I care.*

**Jamie:** *What does that mean?*

**Teddy:** *Well, I know that I can't handle a serious relationship because of the unpredictability and travel my job entails. So when I start falling for someone, I try to walk away before hurting them.*

**Jamie:** *Wow, Teddy. That's pretty damned harsh.*

**Teddy:** *Well, I try to do it before their feelings are involved so it's not too harsh.*

**Jamie:** *I mean it's harsh on you.*

**Teddy:** *Oh.*

**Jamie:** *Don't you think?*

**Teddy:** *Yes, Jamie. It is.*

**Jamie:** *So, what's your advice for me then?*

**Teddy:** *You could always try it. Let someone you're attracted to pick you up in a bar or let a friend set you up on a blind date. I would consider Grindr as a last resort. But, Jamie?*

**Jamie:** *Yeah?*

**Teddy:** *That's pretty dangerous too. What if it's a bad guy?*

**Jamie:** *You mean like a bank robber in an old movie? ;-)*

**Teddy:** *No, I mean like a bad dude. Like the kind of guy who puts GHB in your drink or hurts you. I don't like the idea of you going home with some random guy who might do something.*

**Jamie:** *Do the people you hook up with seem scared?*

**Teddy:** *No, not really.*

**Jamie:** *Should they be?*

**Teddy:** *Of course not.*

**Jamie:** *Well, Teddy, sometimes you have to try. And this is a pretty small town where everyone knows everyone.*

**Teddy:** *And you have a gun.*

**Jamie:** *True. But then again, most people here do.*

**Teddy:** *Way to reassure me.*

**Jamie:** *I'll think about it.*

**Teddy:** *Good idea. Maybe it's not worth it.*

**Jamie:** *I need to head back to work. Thanks, Teddy.*

**Teddy:** *Ok, have a good afternoon. Tell Sister I miss her.*

**Jamie:** *I will.*

When I got back to the ranger station, my first opportunity walked in on a silver platter. I didn't realize it first because it was just Josh. But then his face lit up when he saw me at the reception counter working on the computer, and he started chatting me up. He asked me if I was going back to the roadhouse anytime soon because he'd love to dance with me again. I shrugged and he rephrased.

"Would you like to meet there for drinks after work tonight?" he asked with his big, charming smile.

When he mentioned drinking and dancing, I remembered my new plan. Josh looked pretty good in his boots and tight jeans. I tried looking at him as a sexual conquest instead of a guy I knew from work.

"Sure," I said, returning his smile. "Sounds good."

The rest of the day went by fast. I answered questions on my wildlife website and helped Charlie finalize some animal migration reports.

I didn't have time to drive all the way home before meeting Josh, so I did my best prepping in the ranger station bathroom. I brushed my hair and washed all the relevant parts with paper towels and soap and reapplied deodorant I kept in the truck's glove box. I finger-brushed my teeth as best I could and then popped some mint gum.

Pulling in to the roadhouse lot just after six o'clock, I saw we weren't the only people in the mood for dancing that night. Before I turned off the ignition, I heard my phone ding.

**Teddy:** *I have an idea.*

**Jamie:** *Shoot.*

**Teddy:** *If you ever decide to go home with someone, text me and let me know. Then I can text you to make sure you're ok if I don't hear from you.*

**Jamie:** *I think that would be too weird.*

**Teddy:** *Ok, then text someone else.*

**Jamie:** *What, like one of my brothers? No thanks.*

**Teddy:** *Please, Jamie. Or just let me know if there is a possibility, and then I can text you the next morning to make sure you're ok.*

**Jamie:** *I'll think about it.*

**Teddy:** *Ok, sweet dreams.*

**Jamie:** *It's dinner time here. I'm at the roadhouse, meeting someone for drinks.*

**Teddy:** *Drinks? With whom?*

**Jamie:** *Josh. Remember that guy I danced with?*

**Teddy:** *The insensitive asshole?*

**Jamie:** *I'm not getting into it with you. I have to go. I'm already late.*

**Teddy:** *Wait. Just wait a second.*

**Jamie:** *What?*

**Teddy:** *Dammit, Jamie. Please be careful ok?*

**Jamie:** *With Josh? He's like a fucking boy scout.*

**Teddy:** *Not all boy scouts live by the pledge, Ranger.*

**Jamie:** *Let's hope not. I need to get laid.*

**Teddy:** *Goddammit. At least take your phone with you. And condoms.*

**Jamie:** *Sweet dreams, Teddy Bear.*

# 13

# TEDDY

*Fuck.*

I wish I didn't know he was at the fucking roadhouse with that bastard. Why did I text him tonight? If I hadn't, I could have gone to sleep without being pissed off. If I hadn't, maybe I could have gone to sleep *at all.*

*Let it go, dumbass.*

I hated the thought of his sleeping with someone else, but I wasn't there. And I wasn't going to be there. I kept trying to remind myself I'd rather be his friend than nothing at all.

Cat had asked me to meet her at Club Kex, but I'd said no. I wasn't sure I was up to a loud crowded scene yet. After I got the texts from Jamie, I changed my mind and texted Cat I was on my way.

I needed to get my mind off Jamie and blow off some steam. If I didn't, I would stay home and stare at my phone all night.

I made my way to the packed bar and ordered a shot of tequila and a beer. I slammed back the shot and took the beer to a spot at a high table by the dance floor. I drank my beer and watched the dancers for a while before I realized a blond guy was making eyes at me from the table next to me.

I thought about whether or not I wanted to approach him. *What the fuck, Teddy? Just talk to the man. It's better than sitting alone until you find Cat.*

Just as I was about to stand up and introduce myself I heard someone call my name from the direction of the door.

"Teddy! Over here!"

Cat had two friends with her. When they came over I offered them my stool. I gave Cat a huge hug and inhaled her familiar smell of pottery clay and strawberry shampoo. She introduced me to her friends Mei and Len. I assumed Mei and Len were dating because they had their hands all over each other. They offered to get Cat a beer and left to get in line at the bar.

"How are you doing, Teddy? I've been thinking about you so much. I know you and your dad weren't close, but that doesn't make it easy," she said.

She smiled and reached a hand out to squeeze my arm. I noticed the blond at the other table get up and walk away. I'd way rather sit and chat with Cat right now than hit on some stranger anyway.

"Much better now that it's set in a bit more. I don't feel as guilty as I did at first, and part of me thinks that maybe he dodged a bullet by dying quickly and kind of unexpectedly. No months-long cancer battle or painful slow death of lung disease, you know? It helps that much of the probate stuff and listing the house for sale is being handled by professionals. I don't have to come across a new power bill and get surprised all over again with the grief."

"I'm glad it's getting better, sweetie. He was a lonely old guy but don't ever forget how much you tried to be there for him. He always pushed you away."

"I know, but it's good to be reminded. How about you? How are you doing?" I asked, changing the subject.

"I'm good. Lonely as fuck since Adam went back with his ex-girlfriend, but I've been checking out a dating app on my phone. I can't decide if it's good or cheesy. The jury is still out." She laughed.

When her friends brought her beer, we all tried talking over the music but gave up and decided to dance. Cat and I danced like we had in college. It was pretty much a combo of her dancing crazy and me dancing stupidly while laughing. She was hilarious on the dance floor. I had a moment's thought that her ex-boyfriend Adam was an idiot for going back to his ex-girlfriend. Cat was a great catch for anyone. I was grateful to have her in my life. We had tried dating in college, but we quickly realized we made better friends than lovers.

I leaned into her ear and told her Mac had broken up with his girlfriend. If he stayed broken up, maybe I could fix them up on a date. They had always flirted a little but Mac was never interested enough to ask her out. He was always busy with work. If Birdie didn't take him back, maybe he'd consider a setup to help him get over her.

Cat's eyes lit up and she grinned. "Hell yeah. Maybe it's finally my moment with the Mac Attack."

We danced for a little while longer. By the time I was too tired to keep going, I was drenched in sweat and thirsty. I told Cat and her friends I was going to head home. Cat said she'd text me later in the week in case we wanted to get Brody and Jenna and all meet for lunch. That sounded perfect.

When I got back to my apartment, I drank a large glass of ice water and then a Gatorade. I hopped out of a quick shower, wrapping a towel around my waist. One missed text from Jamie was on my phone.

It was 4 a.m. in the city so it was midnight his time.

> **Jamie:** *Ok. I'll agree to your plan. So this is my text to tell you I'm going home with him. Don't bother texting me back to tell me not to because I'm turning my phone on silent.*

And now I might as well have not gone out at all. I couldn't sleep, and I would have to wait until at least noon before there was a chance he would text me to tell me he was okay.

At some point I woke up and went to work at my computer. I put music on my headphones and tried to escape into the music and the images. I finished submitting the Australia job and I followed up on some issues from the meeting in New Orleans. That left Alaska.

I already knew there were absolute breathtaking shots from

Alaska. For the Gramling submission, I had narrowed down my preliminary list to five shots even though I knew which one was the right choice.

The first was one with Jamie stroking the horn of the Dall sheep. The horns were glowing in the sun and the distant snowy peaks were dotted with sun patches and shadow. Jamie's head in profile was tilted, and he was obviously asking the ram something. Thick waves from his hair blew in the wind and one of the other Dall rams watched Jamie with his head tilted too. It was dramatic and breathtaking. The location at the top of the mountain was very clear from the background and you could tell it was a place far off the beaten path. Like another world.

The second shot was the one with the cow moose, the baby and Jamie. Jamie was crouching with his arm outstretched and the calf was obviously curious and naive while the mama was hesitant. The light was sparkling off the water and in the corner of the frame the light caught some of the speckles on a fish through the water. I was sure this one wouldn't make the final cut for the submission but I loved it. It was so symbolic of the different ways animals react to humans and the human trying hard to reach out to the animals.

The third shot made me laugh every time I looked at it. It was Jamie's face opening up in surprise as brown bunny ears stuck up over his head. In the shot, he was looking right at me and his eyes sparkled in the early morning sun. I loved it so much but without another shot showing it was a real bunny, it didn't make enough sense to stand alone.

The fourth was the shot where the bunny sat up behind Jamie's head and they both looked to the side at the same time. Like human and bunny twins. It was a really good shot. The forest had good light and contrast; the colors of Jamie's cheeks and eyes and hair jumped off the shot. The snowshoe hare's coat was rich and full of luster in the morning sun, and there was enough snow on the ground to make you feel the cool bite of the scene.

The fifth shot was undoubtedly the one I wanted to submit. Jamie was sitting on a log. One beaver kit sat up tall on top of his head like he was lecturing from a podium, a great orator with his arm raised in serious explanation. The other was draped upside down over Jamie's shoulder like he was drunk and looking up at Jamie's face with cartoon hearts floating out of his eyes. Jamie's eyes were pointing skyward and he had a quirky smile on his face as though he was getting ready to burst out laughing. His eyes were bright with humor and little lines crinkled on his nose. So much personality. The juxtaposition of the serious kit and the cartoonish kit. The surrounding area with its shadows and textures. The fresh greens and browns of the cluttered forest. The dry bumpy texture of the log he was sitting on. The stunning, beautiful man.

I could photograph Jamie Marian all day every day and continue to see something new. He was breathtaking. And maybe that was partly because he was such a natural in his environment. Clearly at peace in his surroundings, it seemed a Jamie with animals was a Jamie at home in his own skin.

I looked up to realize it was after one o'clock with no text. A sandwich from the deli down the street was calling my name. My intention was to leave my phone behind, but I wasn't quite that mature

# 14

# JAMIE

Waking up in your coworker-slash-date's bed was awkward. Doing it when you had not put out the night before was ten times more awkward. I groaned inwardly at the thought of walking out into the living room and finding him asleep on the sofa. After a nice, heavy session of kissy-face, he had stopped and offered for me to sleep over since it was so late. I agreed and the next thing I knew, he had given me his bed while he slept on the sofa.

*Wait, what?*

Apparently our pal Josh was some kind of gentleman. Selfish bastard.

I was pretty sure it wasn't because he didn't find me attractive. When we were making out on the sofa, I felt his interest against my thigh. The fact he didn't expect more than that made me wonder if he thought I was interested in a relationship rather than a hookup. While that was sweet and all, it wasn't acceptable. I wasn't doing the relationship thing.

I got up and found my boots before heading out of the bedroom and into the bathroom. I made my way out to the living room and found Josh standing in the kitchen drinking coffee. He gave me a sleepy smile. "Hey, Jamie. How'd you sleep?"

"Good, thanks. Probably from the drinks and all that dancing. That was fun."

He offered me a cup of coffee and I declined as politely as I could. I told him I had to run home to let my dog out after leaving her so long. The family that lived closest to me had let her out for me the night before, but I'd be damned if I would inform them she needed to be let out this morning. Plus, I was pretty sure sticking around for the little domestic coffee moment was a no-go on the one-night-stand plan.

Not that we had completed a successful stand. More like a stumble.

I told him I'd see him at work later even though I knew I'd avoid the ranger station today like the plague.

When I got home I let Sister out and fixed my own coffee. I had breakfast and caught up on email and my website posts. I showered and dressed and was loading the truck for a trip to check on a boreal owl nest box when I remembered to check my phone and text Teddy.

**Jamie:** *I'm fine. Just got home.*

Then I chucked it in my backpack, whistled Sister into the truck, and started driving the half hour toward the nesting boxes. When I parked the truck and grabbed my backpack, I remembered the phone was still on silent. I flicked it back off of mute and noticed three missed texts from Teddy.

**Teddy:** *I guess someone got some action last night. It's about time.*

**Teddy:** *That didn't come out right, sorry. I mean, it's about time you texted me. I was getting worried.*

**Teddy:** *Hello? Where did you go?*

I rolled my eyes and texted him back.

**Jamie:** *I was driving.*

**Teddy:** *Oh. Aren't you going to tell me how it went?*

**Jamie:** *That's not part of our deal, is it?*

**Teddy:** *Well, no. But we're friends. You can talk to me if you want.*

I was way too embarrassed to have to admit the guy didn't even want me to go down on him last night. Teddy would get that smug tone, and I couldn't handle any opinions right now. I decided to be vague.

**Jamie:** *No thanks. I need to get back to work anyway. Checking on some boreal owls today. Wish you could see them. Cute little squatty things.*

**Teddy:** *Ok. Have fun.*

**Jamie:** *I will. Thx. BTW, Sister says hi.*

I told Sister to wait in the car while I checked on the owls. I didn't want her to scare them away. The owls were doing fine and the nesting boxes were in good shape. I recorded notes in my journal when I got back to the truck.

The next stop was one where Sister could get out and go with me. We were going to check on some mosses and lichens growing in an area where they had never grown before. Charlie had noticed it on a hike, and I was going to observe and create a record for future comparison.

I bundled up for what would be a six-mile hike round-trip. With my backpack on my shoulders and Sister running up ahead, I was happy to enjoy the midday solitude.

The next few days were busy with fieldwork. I took Sister as often as I could so she could get plenty of exercise before the winter hit. Josh called a couple of times to ask me out again and I politely told him I was catching up on some reports that were overdue and redesigning my website. Lame and obvious stalling tactics. I decided to ask Teddy for help learning how to saying no.

**Jamie:** *So, how do you tell someone no when they ask you for more dates?*

**Teddy:** *Josh wants back in your pants?*

**Jamie:** *No, he's asking me out for a date. I've already stalled several times. I need to give him a hard no, but I don't want to hurt his feelings.*

**Teddy:** *Does he know about the Brian thing?*

**Jamie:** *Everybody knows about the Brian thing.*

**Teddy:** *Perfect. Say, "I've been thinking about it and I'm just not ready for a relationship yet."*

**Jamie:** *Good idea. Will you tell him for me?*

**Teddy:** *I tried that one time already. Remember?*

**Jamie:** *Just kidding. Kind of.*

**Teddy:** *Put your big boy pants on.*

**Jamie:** *Sometimes I feel like I don't own any of those.*

**Teddy:** *Whatever. Just put some pants on. Wait, I don't think I've ever said that before.*

**Jamie:** *No shit.*

**Teddy:** *Never mind. Don't put pants on.*

**Jamie:** *You wish.*

**Teddy:** *I think we should keep talking about your pants.*

**Jamie:** *No. Do you know anyone who does website redesigns?*

**Teddy:** *Yes. My good friend Brody does. Do you want me to connect you two?*

**Jamie:** *That would be great. I am thinking about redesigning my wildlife Q&A site before the new year.*

**Teddy:** *You run a website? Tell me about it.*

**Jamie:** *I get so many of the same questions from tourists that I decided a few years ago to write the questions and answers on a blog so I could refer people to them for more information. It's grown into a large, useful collection but doesn't look very good. I'd love to talk to your friend if you think he won't mind.*

**Teddy:** *He won't mind at all. We've been really close friends for years. He lives in the city and I'm supposed to be going to dinner with him tomorrow anyway.*

**Jamie:** *Great. Thanks, Teddy.*

**Teddy:** *Forward me the website link so I can give it to him.*

**Jamie:** *Will do.*

**Teddy:** *And kick Josh to the curb.*

**Jamie:** *Easier said than done.*

**Teddy:** *Remember the pants.*

**Jamie:** *Don't put pants on before talking to Josh. Got it.*

**Teddy:** *Motherfucker.*

## 15

# TEDDY

I picked up Thai food and we all met at Jenna's studio for dinner. Before meeting up with everyone, I was able to go to the gym, do some laundry, pitch a new magazine spread idea, and send out some proofs to a client.

I loved Jenna's studio because it was one of the places where we had the most room to hang out. It was a warehouse conversion, and she had built in a high loft for sleeping, leaving most of the living space for a couple of old comfortable sofas facing each other across a wooden coffee table and two huge easels with a worktable by the warehouse windows. It was light and vaulted and open. Her paintings were big and they were stacked along the walls, adding splashes of color everywhere.

We ate at the coffee table, sharing food from cartons and pouring wine from the fridge. There had been so many meals like this with the four of us, and it was a comfortable ritual to slide back into every time we got together.

While we were eating, I asked Brody about connecting him with Jamie to talk about his website. He agreed and asked me how I knew him if he lived in Alaska. While I explained about the shoot, everyone listened in and ended up asking me a million questions. I told them how amazing some of the shots came out, but that I really wished I could go back and take more.

They asked me why I couldn't go back. I explained several reasons. One, I had an assignment in Zion National Park coming up soon, and two, Jamie wasn't crazy about the idea of my photos. I explained his thinking and my idea for creating a type of disclaimer on the images. They helped me brainstorm ideas, and I was left wondering if I should try to get Jamie to let me come back. I really wanted more photos. Oh, who was I kidding? I really wanted to see him.

I had brought proof prints of the five photos I'd selected so I could get their opinions about the Gramling submission. They loved them all but selected the beaver shot (I needed to stop calling it that). I was happy they agreed with me, but something about the idea of actually submitting it by the December 31 deadline made my stomach uneasy.

Cat smirked at me. "Dude, this guy likes you." She had the shot of Jamie with the bunny ears in her hand.

"What makes you think that?" I asked.

She pointed to the photo she held before using it to fan herself. "The way he's looking at you in this photo is *hot*."

"Give me that." Brody snorted, grabbing for the proof. He took a look at it and blushed. "Teddy, this guy is adorable. This is who you want me to do the work for? Hell-fucking-yes."

Jenna took her turn with the photo and got a sly smile on her face before looking up at me with a knowing smile. "You fucked him."

Everyone gasped and turned to stare me down, silently demanding the truth.

"None of your business. Give me back the photo," I said, willing the blush to stay the hell away from my face.

"None of our business?" Brody chuckled. "Since when is who you sleep with none of our business? You've always kissed and told. Spill it."

"I have not. That's mean. And this guy isn't like that, so drop it," I said, packing the proofs back up into the envelope.

"Oh my god," Cat cried. "You *like* him."

I looked up at the ceiling, trying to keep my cool and laugh it off. "It doesn't matter. He lives in Alaska. And I don't do relationships, remember?"

At this point, Cat and Jenna were pretty buzzed so they stood up and joined hands, dancing around in a circle singing, "Teddy and Jamie, sittin' in a tree, K-I-S-S-I-N-G!" I quickly escaped to the bathroom to let their teasing die down.

When I returned, we moved on to discussing Cat's breakup and dating adventures, Jenna's attempts to pitch a new art gallery, and Brody's new coworker, who made him crazy. We switched from beer to vodka, which was probably a bad idea.

We ate and drank and laughed. Jenna showed us a new piece she was working on and Brody mentioned his parents had invited us all for Thanksgiving the following month.

We all agreed to Thanksgiving at Brody's parents' house. Since they lived in Greenwich, it was the easiest place to go if we couldn't be away from work for too long. Both Cat and Jenna had part-time jobs to supplement their art, so they wouldn't be able to fly to see their own families. They all knew I sure as hell needed somewhere to be for the holiday.

By the time I left Jenna's, I was happily drunk. I somehow made it to the train and selected the appropriate line to get home. When I got off at my stop, I texted Jamie.

**Teddy:** *S'up dawg.*

**Jamie:** *WTF*

**Teddy:** *I meant, Hi Dall.*

**Jamie:** *Ooookay. Did you by any chance go out tonight?*

**Teddy:** *Who wants to know?*

**Jamie:** *Uh, me?*

**Teddy:** *State the relevance.*

**Jamie:** *Did. You. Go. Out. Tonight.*

**Teddy:** *Asked and answered.*

**Jamie:** *Are you like lawyer-drunk? I didn't know there was such a thing.*

**Teddy:** *I'm not drunk, I'm happy.*

**Jamie:** *Well, good. Where are you?*

**Teddy:** *On a street corner.*

**Jamie:** *Teddy, should I be worried about you right now? Are you with someone?*

**Teddy:** *Some guy offered me some money for a blow pop. I told him I didn't have any.*

**Jamie:** *Good boy.*

**Teddy:** *I mean, who sells blow pops on a Manhattan street corner after midnight?*

**Jamie:** *I don't think he said blow pop, Teddy Bear. You should go home.*

**Teddy:** *I am. Almost there.*

**Jamie:** *Good.*

**Teddy:** *My friends think I should come with you.*

**Jamie:** *Come with me where?*

**Teddy:** *To your place. Alaska.*

**Jamie:** *Did you tell them that you already did?*

**Teddy:** *They know that. I told them all about you.*

**Jamie:** *Then what did they mean?*

**Teddy:** *They know I want to come back. To see you. I mean take you.*

**Jamie:** *What, Teddy?*

**Teddy:** *I mean take pictures of you.*

**Jamie:** *Oh.*

**Teddy:** *Why did that sound creepy? I don't mean take pictures of you like a weirdo.*

**Jamie:** *I know. But there isn't anything fun to take pictures of in winter. It's all boring indoor stuff like grant writing, research, and giving lectures. Not much to take photos of until spring.*

**Teddy:** *Damn. Maybe spring then. Where are you?*

**Jamie:** *Ranger station.*

**Teddy:** *Still? It's late.*

**Jamie:** *I'm finishing a proposal. My printer isn't working at home.*

**Teddy:** *You by yourself?*

**Jamie:** *No. Josh offered to stay with me.*

**Teddy:** *Of course he did.*

**Jamie:** *Don't worry, I already let him down easy.*

**Teddy:** *He obviously didn't take your words seriously.*

**Jamie:** *Why do you say that?*

**Teddy:** *Because it's after nine at night and he's sticking to you like glue instead of looking for someone else.*

**Jamie:** *Hm. I don't know. Let me tell him to go home and see what he says.*

**Teddy:** *Ok.*

**Jamie:** *He said he didn't want to leave me here alone. Then he offered to follow me home to make sure I got home ok. I said that wasn't necessary. I mean, WTF? Now he's acting like my boyfriend.*

**Teddy:** *Grrr*

**Jamie:** *Let me finish up then I'll text you. When you get the text, call me so I can be on the phone when I leave. Sound good?*

**Teddy:** *It's a plan.*

Fifteen minutes later I got the text and dialed his number.

"Jamie Marian," he answered professionally.

"Hey, Baby Dall, how's about that phone sex you promised me?" I rumbled.

"Sorry, that's not possible. Maybe we could arrange another

person to help you with that?" he replied coolly. I heard him put his hand over the mouthpiece and mumble something. I guessed it was a good night to Josh.

I continued, "But sweetheart, I need it so bad. I'm lying here thinking about you and those cargo pants with muddy boots and just, ahhhh, mmmm... Ranger me... Ranger me good, Dall."

He sputtered a little bit before saying, "That is not something I'm able to arrange right now. Perhaps I can send Josh or Charlie to help you."

I purred, "No, sweet cheeks, it has to be you. Only you know how to point my compass north."

I heard his truck door slam and his engine start. I decided to keep going.

"I hear your motor running, baby, and I think I might like to fuck in a truck with the man I saw duck a duck."

He finally spoke with a chuckle, "You ass. I am going to piss myself. Stop talking."

"Let Uncle Teddy deliver you some *wood*. When I get there, my *snake* and your *cock* could just *weasel*—"

"Stop, oh my god, stop." I heard him laughing loudly. "You are so drunk right now."

"It's nice to hear your voice, Jamie."

"You too, Teddy Bear. Are you seriously thinking about coming back here to take more photos sometime?"

I asked him seriously, "Would you let me?"

"Yes."

*Well, hot damn.*

## 16

# JAMIE

Talking to Teddy may have gotten me more hot and bothered than I cared to admit. That deep voice talking about his snake and my cock. *Jesus.* I was rock hard just thinking about it. When I got home I reintroduced myself to my right hand. While it was always good for an O, I was left wanting more.

I decided to get serious about Operation Get Fucked and made arrangements to drive into Fairbanks to visit my friend Gary, who taught at University of Alaska Fairbanks. He was always up for barhopping and dancing. I called him and set it up. He said I could spend the weekend at his place if I didn't have a place to stay.

The rest of the week passed quickly. I had received a few invitations to speak at universities and I decided to tackle them and sort out my schedule. Normally, I declined anything too far away, but there were a few that interested me this time. One was at University of California, Davis near Sacramento. Visiting my family would be hard to pass up, especially if I could request a date close to the holidays.

Another was for a conference in Mexico. The weather in Denali was already cold enough to remind me that the February conference in paradise would probably be a good idea. I could have another winter break paid for by someone else. I replied a definite yes for that one.

The other one was an invitation to speak at Columbia University's zoology and wildlife school in New York. Where Teddy lived. Normally the idea of flying from Alaska to New York would not appeal to me, but if I went and made plans to see Teddy... That could be kind of fun. I could meet his friends and see the city through a resident's eyes. Ah, who was I kidding? He would probably be traveling then anyway. Maybe I would mention it casually to him and see what he thought.

**Jamie:** *I just got an invitation to speak at Columbia University this winter.*

**Teddy:** *Hang on. I'm running. Give me 20 mins.*

**Jamie:** *Why are you running?*

**Teddy:** *Exercise.*

**Jamie:** *Oh, I was picturing you running for your life.*

After half an hour I got another text.

**Teddy:** *Columbia, huh? Are you going to say yes?*

**Jamie:** *I don't know. The flight is a long pain in the ass.*

**Teddy:** *Tell me about it.*

**Jamie:** *Right. But then again, I would love to visit the city. It's been a while. And I have some friends from college who live there. Plus, everyone tells me I need to see the show Hamilton.*

**Teddy:** *I could get you tickets. When would you be here?*

**Jamie:** *They gave me a list of dates. I was thinking about the one in March. I'm going to see my family in California in December and I'm speaking at a conference in Mexico in February.*

**Teddy:** *I think you should come. I'd love to show you around.*

**Jamie:** *But what if I book it and then when March rolls around, you're off in Siberia somewhere on a job?*

**Teddy:** *I won't be.*

**Jamie:** *How do you know?*

**Teddy:** *Jamie, I work for myself. I'll make sure I'm here. I promise. It'll be fun. Email me the dates when you book it so I can mark it on my calendar.*

**Jamie:** *Will do. Gotta run check on the beaver kits before it gets too late in the day.*

**Teddy:** *Happy trails. Be safe.*

When Friday afternoon rolled around I ran by my place to pick up Sister and my overnight bag. There was a package on my front porch from Amazon. It was a brand-new printer with a gift note attached.

*SO YOU DON'T HAVE TO STAY LATE AT WORK. FOR SISTER'S SAKE. - TEDDY*

THAT THOUGHTFUL ASSHOLE. I tried calling him but it went straight to voicemail. I left him a message.

"The printer just arrived. I don't know what to say Teddy. Thank you. That was very thoughtful. Have a good weekend, hotshot."

I dropped Sister at my neighbors' house and thanked them

profusely for watching her for me. I watched their husky when they were gone, so it wasn't an imposition for them.

They had a preteen daughter who adored Sister and took special care of her when Sister visited. I remembered how important my pets were to me at that age. Unconditional love and acceptance. Every kid needed that.

My mom was a veterinarian and I had grown up around her clinic. A life without animals in it was something I couldn't even fathom.

I arrived at my friend Gary's apartment in Fairbanks after six. I changed from my work clothes into formfitting jeans and a black V-neck T-shirt.

We arrived at Bear's around eight. While Fairbanks wasn't known for a gay scene by any means, Bear's was an unofficial hangout for the local guys who were looking. We ate some appetizers at a high-topped table near the bar. After my second beer I started to relax. The music was energizing, but it wasn't blasting my eardrums yet.

Gary had told me on the way there that he had hooked up with a guy at Bear's the weekend before and was kind of hoping to run into him again. He handed me an extra set of apartment keys, so I could go back to his place without him. Then he winked and looked a little embarrassed.

I told him the truth about Operation Get Fucked and he burst out laughing. We agreed we wouldn't worry about each other if someone wanted to exercise their inner slut that night. Once the drinking started, the giggling started. Man, I'd needed this.

After a while a couple of guys came over to chat us up. They asked us to dance and we did. The air heated up and the music pumped louder. My shoulder was healed and I laughed when the guy I was dancing with twirled me around with my arm above my head.

After another drink at the table, Gary introduced me to a guy he worked with named Miles. He was good looking with shoulder-length honey-colored hair. His smile was contagious, and he looked at me like he wanted to lick me in all the right places. We talked and laughed while I drank my beer. When I finished, he asked me to dance.

We danced together the rest of the night. He pulled me in close when the music slowed down, and I liked the feeling of being held. I had missed being touched. After a while the dancing turned to grinding and I was horny as hell. Miles's hands lowered to my ass and he turned his face to brush his lips across my temple. He smelled like woodsmoke and bourbon. He asked if I wanted to come home with him, and I said yes. My stomach flipped with nervous excitement.

I caught Gary's eye and gestured that I was leaving with Miles. He winked and nodded. I grabbed my jacket and followed Miles outside. Before he opened the passenger door to his SUV for me, he grabbed my hand and turned me toward him. His green eyes closed as he leaned in and kissed me. It was a nice kiss, all boozy and warm. His hand glided up my side while the other stayed on my hip. He pulled back and smiled before opening the door for me.

When he pulled into his apartment complex, I realized with relief that it was the same place Gary lived. It was about six buildings behind his, but it made me feel less isolated in case I changed my mind or something. *Why would I change my mind?*

He opened the door to his apartment and led me inside. It was a typical guy's apartment. Mostly empty of all but the basics, with one exception: the giant flat-screen TV. He asked if I wanted a drink, but I declined. He got himself a beer while I went to the bathroom. Inside the bathroom I texted Teddy. I knew I didn't need to because Gary knew this guy, and he also knew where I was. But the stupid part of my brain whined something about having promised Teddy I would text him if I did this. Was there a part of me that wanted to make him jealous? Maybe regret not wanting me? Hell yes.

**Jamie:** *I met a guy in a bar in Fairbanks tonight. I'm at his place. My friend Gary knows, but I promised you I'd text so...*

**Teddy:** *Sweetheart, it's four in the morning. I think you should go home.*

**Jamie:** *Teddy, it's four for you. Midnight for me.*

**Teddy:** *Sorry, I'm half asleep.*

**Jamie:** *It's ok. Sorry, thought your phone would be on mute if you were in bed. Go back to sleep. I'll text you later.*

**Teddy:** *Jamie.*

**Jamie:** *Yeah?*

**Teddy:** *Please don't do this.*

My stomach lurched and the nerves turned to serious nausea.

**Jamie:** *Why not?*

**Teddy:** *This isn't you. I don't think this is what you want.*

**Jamie:** *How could you possibly know what I want?*

**Teddy:** *I just do.*

**Jamie:** *Go back to sleep, Teddy.*

**Teddy:** *Fine. Text me tomorrow.*

I joined Miles on the sofa and leaned against him. He tilted my chin up and kissed me again. His stubble scratched against my face and his hands threaded into my hair. I felt his tongue slide into my mouth, searching for mine.

His hands roamed over my abdomen and reached down to cup my hard-on through my jeans. I remembered when Teddy had his hands all over me during our amazing encounter weeks before. God, that was hot. The sex with Teddy had been so steamy that my heart started racing just thinking about it. I must have let out a moan.

Miles said, "Mmm, you like that, Jamie?"

My eyes flashed open at the sound of not-Teddy's voice. This wasn't right. I didn't want this. It wasn't steamy or exciting or hot. It was... fine.

"Dammit," I muttered.

Miles tilted his head at me. "Are you okay?"

I gave him an apologetic look. "Miles, I am so sorry. I thought I was ready for this, but I'm not. I think I'm still recovering from a bad breakup," I lied.

He looked disappointed for sure, but he said, "It's all right. I understand. There is no need for you to feel uncomfortable. Do you want to just hang out and watch a movie for a little while and see how you feel?"

"Thanks, but I think I should just head back over to Gary's."

He sighed. "Sure thing. I'll walk you to his place."

"Thanks," I said, trying to show him with my eyes how sorry and thankful I was.

I let myself into Gary's apartment and went to sleep. Gary must have gotten lucky because he never made it home. The next morning I left him a note of apology and headed home. Before dropping the keys under the mat, I texted Teddy.

**Jamie:** *I didn't get drugged or murdered. I didn't get fucked either. Thanks for that, asshole.*

I got into the truck and hit the road, ignoring the pinging and ringing of my phone. What the hell did I want? I didn't want sex with cute Miles. I didn't want to date Josh. How could I possibly want to pursue something with Teddy when he lived 4,000 miles away and didn't do relationships?

Teddy needed to be erased from my mind so I could move on. As hard as it would be, I needed to stop talking to him and go cold turkey.

## 17

# TEDDY

To say I was relieved Jamie hadn't had sex with a stranger the night before was an understatement. I felt way too invested in the outcome of his plan to get laid. It had started to feel very personal for some reason.

I was so hot for him and generally desperate for sex that I had even asked out a guy I had hooked up with in the past. After the date, I couldn't bring myself to ask him to my place. I didn't want him like that anymore. I couldn't stop thinking about the damned wildlife veterinarian bundled up in winter layers freezing his ass off in the wilds of Denali.

So after Jamie's failed attempt at casual sex this time, I thought about what the hell was wrong with me. I wanted him. I wanted Jamie so badly it was all I could think about. When I stroked myself at night I imagined his naked body under me. What his tight ass felt like when I pressed myself deep inside him. *Goddammit.* I needed to get him out of my system.

I began to rationalize my crazy thinking. He wanted casual sex; I wanted casual sex with him. Why couldn't that work?

Over the next twenty-four hours I realized he had gone radio silent on me. He blamed me for his lack of getting laid, and I understood.

My fingers almost dialed my travel coordinator about a hundred times to book a flight to Fairbanks, but I resisted. Jamie was not talking to me, so I knew it would be a disaster.

A couple of nights later I met Mac for dinner. He looked like shit. When I asked him about Birdie, I thought he might lose it. I felt terrible for the guy. He was my best friend and he was obviously in pain. I asked him if he wanted me to try to talk to her, but he said no. He had agreed to give her space.

My best advice to him was to not give up on her. I could tell the two of them were meant for each other and suggested maybe it was just taking her a little while to realize it.

We agreed to meet for a run in the park the next day. Mac ran like a bat out of hell and it was hard to keep up. Afterward we grabbed hot dogs and sat eating them on a bench. I told him about Jamie.

Mac looked at me with a smirk before saying, "Holy shit, Teddy. You have a crush on the guy."

"Wanting to fuck him isn't the same as having a crush on him."

"Hmm, well, you say you just want to fuck him, but you've told me about his education, how good he is at his job, his gentle demeanor with animals. Not one word about his nice package or smoking hot ass." He laughed.

"He does have a nice package *and* a smoking hot ass."

Mac looked at me closer, and I felt exposed. "What are you afraid of? That you might actually want to be with a man for more than sex? What's wrong with that?"

"What's wrong with that is I travel too much. You know my track record with trying to have relationships. They just don't work for me."

"I think that's awfully convenient for you. Have you ever thought that maybe after everything that happened with your dad, you're afraid to hand over control of your life to anyone else?" Mac asked.

"Don't psychoanalyze me, Mac. You're a fucking computer geek, not a shrink. Plus, Jamie lives four thousand miles away."

"Imagine for a minute that you and Jamie were good together and wanted a future together. Can you think of a scenario where a *wildlife* photographer and a *wildlife* consultant might be able to bring their careers together in the same patch of *wildlife*?"

I rolled my eyes, but he might have had a point.

After going home and getting myself really worked up, I said *fuck it* and booked flights to Fairbanks for the following week. I knew Jamie would be pissed at me but it was worth a shot.

I developed a big stack of his photos to bring as a peace offering. I arranged to travel from Alaska to my job in Zion a couple of weeks later. It would be easier than coming all the way back east first. If Jamie gave me the cold shoulder, I would find somewhere else to go between jobs.

Because Jamie wasn't communicating, I decided it would be best to just ask forgiveness rather than permission. My plan was to surprise him and use my charm to defend against his anger.

The day of the trip came and I finished packing all the cold weather gear I had gathered. I knew the average high was right around freezing, and I'd be damned if I wasn't prepared enough to follow Jamie when he went on a trek.

By the time I landed in Fairbanks, I was both excited and nervous. I made sure my rental would be able to handle snow, and I got on the road to Denali. There was a layer of snow everywhere and it was gorgeous, especially in the watery setting sun.

I pulled up to his cabin around dinner time. I had stopped and picked up a few groceries on my way, in case he didn't have any food around. If he wasn't home, I didn't know what I'd do.

His truck was there and Sister ran out from around the back of the house, sinking big, heavy paws into the snow on the ground with each step. I parked and got out to greet her with some ear rubs.

Jamie must have heard me pull in because the front door opened and he stood in the doorframe with his mouth open.

"Hey, Dall," I said.

His eyes widened and his mouth moved without making sound. I could tell he was deciding in that moment how he felt about my sudden appearance. He slammed the door closed again.

I looked down at Sister with a shrug. "Well, that didn't go as well as I'd hoped."

## 18

# JAMIE

*What. The. Fuck.*

Was I imagining things or was Theodore Kodiak standing in my front yard? I heard him knock on the door and yell to me.

"Jamie, please let me in. Don't worry, I got a hotel room this time. I just want to talk to you and apologize."

I let out a big breath and leaned my back against the front door. Was it weird that part of me was disappointed he got a hotel room?

Exhaling again, I turned and opened the door. Sister bounded inside and Teddy followed. He shucked his winter gear and kicked off his boots. I wore long underwear with a matching set of dark green fleece pants and a fleece top over them. I had already removed the waterproof outer layer I'd been wearing for the visit to the Dall sheep earlier in the day.

I'd just started a fire and made some decaf coffee. I asked him if he wanted some and he accepted. He followed me into the kitchen.

He said in a soft voice, "I'm sorry for upsetting you and for springing myself on you like this. You wouldn't take my calls, and I couldn't stand you being mad at me."

"So you flew all the way across the country to make it right?" I said incredulously.

"Something like that. You knew I was planning on coming back anyway."

"Yes, Teddy. In the spring. Not in late October when it's fucking frozen and dead here."

He put his hand on my shoulder and pointed blue lasers at me. He started to say something but stopped himself. Then he brushed some hair off my forehead, cupped the side of my face, and ran a thumb across my eyebrow.

He sighed. "I brought some dinner. Let me grab it out of the car." And he turned around to head toward the front door.

My face tingled from where his big warm hand had been. My heart was racing and blood was shooting southward at an alarming rate. That hot motherfucker had turned me on with nothing more than the deep blue pools he pointed my way. I wanted him so badly my mouth watered.

*Get control of yourself, Jamie Marian.*

Why? Why couldn't he be my first meaningless sexcapade? He was hot, he was here, and god knew he was always willing.

Teddy came back in with a couple of grocery bags and unpacked salad fixings and a rotisserie chicken. He'd brought wine too, so I offered to open it. He chopped red and green peppers, purple onions, and tomatoes. He found a large bowl and threw in lettuce and spinach before adding the veggies and some of the chicken.

He held up two bottles of dressing. "I didn't know what you liked so I got balsamic vinaigrette and ranch. Which one do you prefer?"

"Balsamic. That looks great, Teddy. Thanks."

We sat down and ate at the kitchen table. I caught him looking at me a few times as if he was trying to figure out what I was thinking. It was unusually awkward between us, and I hated that feeling.

Part of me wanted to blurt out, "Look, I'm horny, you're always horny, let's just do this." But I couldn't.

Instead, I kicked his leg with my foot under the table. "Teddy, can we go back to being normal, please? I feel like things are weird."

A smile lit up his face and he let out a breath. "Yeah. I'd like that."

After we ate, we sat on the sofa, facing the fire and drinking more wine. I asked him about work and he told me about the Zion job he had coming up.

"They want me to capture some images around the park that they can use on items in the gift shop next summer. Postcards and art prints, things like that. November is a good time for it because the air is crisper and clearer."

I told him that UC Davis had confirmed my request to schedule my lecture in mid-December before classes stopped for the holiday break. "I'll probably stay with Mom and Dad through Christmas."

He looked over at me and smiled. "That'll be good. I'm glad you won't be here alone for Christmas. What do you do with Sister when you go?"

"My neighbors keep her for me. Their daughter dotes on her while I'm away. If I ever turn up dead, check her out as a suspect." I winked at him with a smirk.

"Tell me about your animals. How are they all doing with the incoming winter weather?"

"Well, I checked on the Dall rams today and they are in rut. I stayed well away because they're mean when they're horny," I explained.

"Aren't we all?" He laughed back.

"Tell me about it," I muttered.

"You never did tell me about the guy in Fairbanks. Are you going to get pissed at me for asking again?"

"No. It's fine. He was really nice and cute, but... I just wasn't into it. He was really sweet about it when I put a stop to the make-out session. That's my second failed attempt since trying to become promiscuous. I don't think I'm very good at it."

He turned to face me, resting his back against the arm of the couch and putting one knee up on the cushion between us.

"Two failed attempts. Who was the other one?"

"Josh. You knew that."

His eyes widened. "You went out with him again after all?"

"No, jackass, it was that night I texted you. After the roadhouse."

Teddy looked shocked. "But you slept with him."

Now I looked shocked. "No, I didn't. Why do you think I did? I told you I didn't want to talk about it, remember?"

He thought for a minute. "But when you texted me to tell me you were home, it was the next day."

"I stayed over at his place, but we didn't sleep together. He's the one who stopped it from going that far actually."

"What? Are you sure he's gay?" Teddy blurted.

"Why would you say that? He's been trying to get me to go out with him ever since. Plus, we had a pretty heavy make-out session before he stopped himself."

Teddy's eyes bored into mine. "Sweetheart, if I had you hot and willing in my apartment, there's no way in hell I'd be able to stop myself."

Before I gave myself a chance to think, I launched myself at him. Again.

# 19

# TEDDY

This time when I felt his body land against mine, I knew I wouldn't stop him. I didn't *want* to stop him. If he was willing, then I was going for it. I wanted him with all the molecules in my fucking body. And they had all convened into a tight group below my belt.

The most I could do is mumble against his mouth, "Are you sure?" to which he replied, "Shut up, Teddy."

*If you insist.*

I crushed my lips against his and slid my tongue inside. My hands roved hungrily under his fleece top and I lifted it off him. Returning my hands to his back, I slid my fingers under his shirt to find and savor his warm, smooth skin. Jamie's hands were on either side of my face and his mouth moved from my lips, to my jaw, to my neck. I moaned when he sucked some of my skin against his teeth.

I pushed my fingers down beneath his waistband over his ass and muttered, "Just how many layers do you have on?"

Jamie laughed and stood, shucking fleece pants and silky long underwear, leaving only a pair of boxer briefs. My erection jumped against my fly and I pushed a palm down on it hard. He crawled back on my lap to straddle me. Jamie pulled my top over my head and then my T-shirt followed. His hands roamed along my chest and shoulders, down my arms to lace fingers with mine.

All the while I kissed him for all I was worth. His mouth tasted like wine and I loved it. I used my tongue to search out every hidden delicacy of his mouth. I pulled his hands behind my head and returned my own hands to Jamie's ass, pulling his pelvis against my own. He made a sound of approval as I felt his hands in my hair. His hard cock pushed against mine, ripping a groan out of my throat.

I moved down and kissed his neck, moving to the tender spot behind his ear. My fingers snuck under the band of his boxer briefs and I felt the skin of his bare ass below. "*Fuck.*" I moaned.

"Bedroom," he said, breathing heavy. "Now."

I grabbed him by the ass and stood up, bringing him with me. His legs wrapped around my waist and he kept kissing me as I stumbled toward his bedroom. I turned and sat down on the edge of the bed, moving my hands up to his hair.

He moved his mouth down over the hair on my chest, stopping to suck lightly here and there before trailing kisses down to my navel. I ran my hands through his hair and leaned over to kiss the top of his head.

When he started unbuckling my belt, I almost lost it. He stepped back onto the floor and stood me up long enough to undo my fly and push jeans and boxer briefs down to my ankles. He put his hand around me and stroked. When he started to kneel down, I stopped him, pulling him up gently.

"Not that I wouldn't love that more than anything in the world right now, but I want to taste you first. Please." I lay him down in the middle of the bed. I slowly slid his underwear down his legs and marveled at the beautiful body beneath me.

I climbed over him and looked at his gorgeous muscles. I leaned down to nip his firm, rounded shoulder and nuzzle under his arm, smelling the musky scent of clean sweat and the outdoors on him. My tongue traced his collarbone and kissed its way across to the other shoulder.

He tasted amazing. I pulled a nipple between my teeth and heard him gasp. He ran his hands through my hair and I began to move down, trailing my tongue in a long line from his neck to the top of his pubic hair. I felt my chin brush the curls below and I continued downward, letting my scruffy cheek rub down his hard cock. The swollen length twitched in response.

When my tongue found the base of his cock among those curls, I felt his hands dig into my hair and heard him cry out my name. Pressing in and up with my tongue, I licked his hard cock from root to tip before taking it all in my mouth with a deep suck. He hissed and moaned above me.

I swirled my tongue around his tip and crown before moving down to nuzzle his balls. His words were garbled and his breathing rapid. I tongued the line from sac to hole and saw him clench in anticipation. My finger snuck into the wetness of my mouth before tracing teasing circles around his hole.

I ran my hands under his thighs and grasped them, pushing his knees to his chest. He writhed and moaned as I reached down and slid the wet finger into his tight heat. He arched up and gasped, "Please… please, Teddy… *oh god…*" He tried pulling me up toward his mouth again but I refused to stop tormenting him. My mouth took his cock back in and sucked up and down mercilessly while my finger fucked his tight ass. I wanted him to lose his mind and come down my throat.

I twisted the finger inside him and then pulled it almost all the way out before sliding it back in again with a second one, stretching him while pressing the tight bundle of nerves hidden there. His orgasm hit him in a giant clenching wave. I felt his body move against my finger and his hands pull on my hair. He cried out and shot on my tongue. I took one more stroke with my finger and felt him shudder violently again.

I lightly kissed my way back up to his face and then lay down on the bed next to him, facing him. I watched his breathing slowly calm back down and I palmed my hard dick. Jamie turned to face me. His skin was flushed and his hair stuck up everywhere. A big smile widened across his face. God, he was gorgeous.

We lay there in bed, Jamie's breathing regulating. I held his hand, and our fingers lightly played together. After a while, I leaned over and kissed him, then pulled back a little to gauge his reaction, knowing I had the taste of him on my tongue. He smiled and kissed me back. We kissed and caressed, letting our hands and mouths explore and learn the curves of each other's bodies. He had a freckle or mole in the shape of a heart above his right ass cheek. I nipped it and continued exploring up his spine to the back of his neck.

My heart sped up as he ran a hand behind him to touch my cock and then clasped his fingers around the base of the shaft before pulling up. I almost choked with desire. I turned him back around to face me. He rubbed and stroked me, his fingers glancing across the tip of my erection and nearly making me black out.

Jamie leaned against my ear and whispered, "Fuck me." I was surprised by his confidence, and I liked it.

I mumbled a "yes, sir" before asking if he had a condom and lube. He reached across to open his nightstand and pull them out. I motioned for the condom, but he pulled it back and opened it himself. He gave me a cocky grin and grabbed me before sliding the condom on. Fuck, that was hot.

I leaned back over him, gave him a deep, plunging kiss and then pulled back to watch his face as I slowly pushed into him. My eyes rolled back at the warm tight pressure around me. He hummed and lifted his hips up to take more in. I sank in as deeply as I could and then stopped, trying to not blow it all on the first stroke.

Slowly I began moving in and out, nuzzling into his neck and running my tongue over his skin. I sucked on his earlobe and felt him shiver. I pressed kisses along his cheek to his nose and then took his lips with mine again in a searing wet kiss. Whispering low into his ear I told him he was so sexy and hot and tight. I told him he was beautiful and I couldn't wait to come inside him. He whimpered at my words and clutched my ass, pulling me tighter into him.

"More, harder, *please,* Teddy," he begged. I sped up and thrust harder, feeling my release tingling at the base of my spine. His cock was purple and straining again, pressed between our stomachs.

He cried out, "Yes! *Oh fuck…*" I felt him start to tremble underneath me. I took his nipple in my mouth and gently clamped my teeth around the hardened nub. He screamed as his climax hit and shuddered, squeezing his muscles around my cock inside him.

My own release slammed up my spine and out through every nerve in my body. I growled out his name as I came and it felt like it lasted forever. I collapsed down beside him, holding the base of the condom as I pulled out. After a few moments of trying to catch my breath, I stood up to find a trash can and towel before returning to his side.

After wiping us both down with the towel, I brushed the hair out of his face and looked at him. His hooded eyes, shining face, and slight smile told me he was okay. I smiled back at him and kissed him on the temple, pulling him against my side with an arm under his shoulders.

"Can we go again?" He smirked.

I burst out laughing and grabbed Jamie's hand to kiss it. "Gimme a minute to catch my breath, sweetheart."

After a minute of catching our breath, I asked quietly, "Do you want me to head out to the hotel?"

"No," Jamie said. "Will you stay here instead? With me?"

I quirked a brow at him. His face showed a vulnerability I hadn't seen before but should have. "Are you sure?"

He looked at me and said, with a completely straight face, "I might need your snake to weasel somewhere again before morning."

"Good, because I didn't really make a hotel reservation." I admitted.

"I figured. Almost called your bluff too," he smirked.

He turned to face away from me, scooted back to press me into spooning him, and then fell asleep. My jaw hung open before I thought to shut it and snuggle in behind him.

Because of the time difference between New York and Denali, I woke up a few hours before he did. I gently extracted his arms and legs from where they were wrapped warmly around me. Sliding out of the bed, I found my jeans and closed the bedroom door behind me. After visiting the bathroom, I greeted Sister and her tail started going nuts.

I shouldered on my coat and found the keys to the rental. I let Sister out and got my bag out of the car. Because of the equipment I had, I should have never left my bag in a freezing car overnight. That was really unlike me, but I hadn't spared one thought for my gear after Jamie started touching me.

The early morning was pitch dark and cold as shit. I hurried back inside and kicked my untied boots off again next to the door. I let Sister stay outside to explore for a little while.

Before starting some coffee, I changed into some sweats and thick socks. After booting up my laptop on the kitchen table, I fixed a cup of coffee and savored its warmth. Sister scratched to come back in so I let her in and fed her. I was sure it was earlier than she was used to, but I didn't want her staring at me with those eyes.

My computer automatically pulled up the Wi-Fi in the cabin from the last trip. I had an email from Brody about Jamie's website work. He wanted to double-check with me about whether or not to charge him. I told him to charge me for it and I would sort it out with Jamie later. I wasn't sure about Jamie's money situation, but I had plenty.

The only reason I was able to be a professional photographer in the first place is because I had invested in Mac's tech company before it hit big. Luckily, I had gone to college on a scholarship. All the money I saved from photography jobs during that time went into that company when he started it. Mac's family had plenty of money to help him start, but he didn't want any of it. We both knew without needing to say it out loud that he felt the need to prove to everyone that just because he had a wealthy family, didn't mean he wasn't capable of succeeding on his own.

No one really knew I had money. I tried to keep it quiet because I didn't like the way people treated Mac after they discovered he was wealthy. I didn't have the kind of money he did, but the money I did have scared me a little. My other friends from art school struggled to pursue their art professionally, so I tried to focus on how fortunate I was to have the security blanket I had. Mostly I tried to forget about it.

There was an email from Jenna to all of us telling us that she got the show at the gallery she was trying to get into. I responded it was great news and to let me know when to block my calendar for opening night.

Another email requested me for a gig in late March in Costa Rica for a travel spread. I accepted and marked it into my calendar. I had worked for that magazine several times before, so it was a no-brainer.

After finishing responding to several other emails, I got up to fix some breakfast.

## 20

# JAMIE

My alarm went off at seven and I pressed snooze. I reached over to find Sister missing from beside me in bed. I opened my eyes and saw the empty spot. It looked slept in, and not by a dog. I remembered the night before with a grin. *Teddy*.

Sex with Teddy was pretty damned fun. He was attentive and responsive, gentle and firm. *Mmm*... I stretched, closed my eyes, and went through the highlight reel in my head for a minute.

I heard his deep voice above me. "Now that's a satisfied smirk if I've ever seen one." I opened my eyes and saw him smiling above me, holding out a mug to me. I lifted my eyebrow.

"I heard your alarm. Coffee?" Teddy said.

"Yes, thank you." I accepted the mug and took a sip. "How long have you been up?"

"Since four."

"Yikes."

"No kidding. By the time the sun comes up, half my day will be over." He sat down next to me on the bed and put his hand on my leg over the covers.

"What's on your agenda today?" he asked tentatively. It wasn't like him to be so meek.

"Well, I need to prep for a lecture webinar that I'm doing with SUNY Cobleskill in a couple of days. Also, I told your friend Brody I'd give him some feedback on some of his ideas for the website. Before I do any of that though, I want to check on some pikas I found the other day. Do you know the pika?"

"They're like little rodents. I snapped some on a shoot in Montana a few years ago. Funny little characters."

"Yes. They sun themselves on the rocks during the day. They have these piles of brush and stored food called 'haystacks.' I found a pika haystack the other day that was in a precarious spot where melting snow would pour down a rock and wash the stored food away. They should've figured it out and moved the haystack. I want to go see if they have yet. There's supposed to be a big snow coming in the next day or so. The best time for me to check it is today."

Teddy looked at me with a serious expression on his face. "May I come with you?"

I laughed. "Teddy, I assumed you were coming with me. Don't be weird."

"Jamie, I just don't want you to be uncomfortable with me or with... this. Whatever this is between us."

I looked at him. "How about 'this' is friends with benefits? Does that work for you? We've both already established we don't want something serious. After last night, I'm pretty clear on the fact that I'd like to enjoy your exquisite body some more for major lusty sexual reasons. I like being friends too. You make me laugh. So let's just have fun while you're here. It's not like we can worry about anything more when you live so far away, so that takes the pressure off, you know?"

He let out a deep breath and smiled. "That sounds fucking perfect."

Finally, we could both enjoy what we wanted. Casual sex with no strings.

Teddy's amount of cold-weather gear was impressive. It didn't all look new either. “How do you know how to dress for this weather?” I asked.

He looked at me and snorted. “You really think I just got off the turnip truck yesterday, don’t you? Don’t forget I spend almost as many hours sitting quietly outside as you do. I have waited on my stomach in the snow for hours to catch some images of Siberian tigers. I’ve done shoots in Greenland, China, the Andes, and even on a crab boat out of Prudhoe Bay. It’s a miracle I still have fingers. The only way to succeed in my business is to prepare for a long, cold or hot wait. If anything, I’m often oversupplied.”

“Okay, hotshot, point taken. You da man. I stand corrected. At least I won’t have to teach you how to use the snowshoes.”

“Snowshoes?” Teddy asked a little unsure.

“Yeah, sport. It’ll come right back to you. Kind of like riding a bike.”

As I walked out the front door I heard him mutter, “Fuck.”

We had to drive by a park storage facility to find him some snowshoes. He asked why we needed them if the snow wasn’t that deep yet. I reminded him that the snow is deeper at the higher altitudes where the pikas live.

After finding what we needed, we continued on to the trailhead. It took a while since the unpaved side roads weren’t plowed or treated. The gravel and the truck tires were fine with it, but I went slow to make sure.

Finally we were ready to put on the shoes and start our hike. Teddy took some time to prep his equipment, choosing to fill up pockets rather than bring a backpack.

We started off. He had to admit he’d never used snowshoes. I gave him a tutorial and he was fine. Clearly he was in fantastic physical shape. I remembered his muscled thighs from the night before and assumed he would be just fine with the workout from the hike. I looked ahead to where he took some practice steps. I pictured those naked legs again and thought about what I would find at their junction.

"Dr. Marian, is there something I can help you with? Eyes up here, sweetheart."

I looked up in a flash, blood rushing to my face. He winked. Cocky bastard.

"I was just watching your form in the shoes," I blurted.

"Then why is my dick hard?" He stared back at me with a raised brow. "I think it knew you were undressing it with your brown eyes."

"Shut the fuck up and let's go." I started walking. "Horny bastard," I mumbled. Trying very hard not to think of his erection. *Fuck.*

We walked along in the silence that only comes from a snow-covered stretch of forest.

The air was crisp and cold but not unbearable. Sun filtered through the trees and before long we were exiting the edge of the forest into the area above the tree line. Rocks jutted out from the snowy ground and I gestured for Teddy to go in front of me so he could see the undisturbed animal tracks in the snow around us. Not because he had a sweet ass. He slowed and took photos periodically, pointing out interesting ones to me.

When we came to a large area where the snow was disturbed, he stopped and waited for me to come up beside him. He asked me in a whisper what I thought had happened there.

I turned to answer in his ear, "This is just a guess, mind you, but it looks like a wildlife consultant tripped over his feet and busted his ass. I'm guessing from the impressions in the snow that it happened three days ago, give or take."

He burst out in a strangled snort-laugh, trying to keep quiet. Leaning toward me, he grabbed the back of my neck, pulled me in, and kissed my forehead with cold lips. I grinned and walked ahead of him to lead the way to the haystack.

When we came around the grouping of large boulders, I looked to the spot where I had seen the haystack. It was gone. I let out a relieved breath and pointed it out to him. We sat on the rocks and I brought out the thermos of hot tea I had packed. We shared it for a few minutes while taking in the views.

After a few minutes of sitting quietly, we saw pikas come out to play on the rocks near us. I was happy to see they were still in the area, and I wondered where they had moved their stash. The harder it was for me to find, the better, so I decided not to look for it. They looked happy and healthy, so they probably had it under control.

They tittered and raced around, venturing closer to me without much hesitation. At this altitude, they didn't see many humans and didn't have a built-in fear of us. Teddy moved around slowly, getting shots from different angles. I lay back on my elbows on the rock and let the pikas climb on my coat and snow pants like a jungle gym. I told them how proud I was of them for figuring out the haystack problem and warned them to make sure their foraging game was strong this month before the really harsh conditions arrived.

At one point I looked over at Teddy and saw him staring at me, not through his lens. His dark blue gaze was intense, and for a split second I worried there was a bear behind me. I turned to look but saw nothing. I looked back at him and raised my brow. By the time I did, his face was back behind the camera.

Sometimes I felt as though there was more there than he let on. That the cocky, jet-setting flirt was a front for someone buried inside. I stopped myself right there and reminded myself thoughts like that would get me into trouble. Thoughts like that could keep me up at night, trying to turn a boy toy into a soul mate. *No, thanks.*

## 21

# TEDDY

As usual, Jamie was radiant out there in the snow talking to the pikas who scampered around him. They were not afraid of him at all. They played with him like he was a giant pika or a boulder, and my camera ate it up.

His nose was red from cold and his eyes were bright. I wanted to stay out there forever, but maybe as one of those pikas sitting on his thighs.

Pretty soon, the wind picked up with some flurries, and we decided to head back. The shirring and crunching sounds of our snowshoes seemed to be coming more from me than him. I attributed it to his lighter weight and vast experience.

He stopped a few minutes after we had entered the trees again and pointed up a little ways. It took me a minute, but then I saw him. A sleeping brown bear up in a tree. He was pretty small and his arms and legs hung down around the branch he was sleeping on. It was almost impossible to see him against the brown of the tree and the darkness of the forest shadows. I was amazed Jamie had, yet again, known where to look.

We snuck a little closer so I could try to get some shots. We stopped well before getting too close. He seemed to open one eye at one point but then closed it again. Sneaking back to the trail, we kept an eye on him to make sure he was staying put.

The truck was in front of us before we knew it and we hopped in to get it started. Shucking off some layers, we drank again from Jamie's thermos.

"That was cool. Thanks," I told him.

"I'm glad the haystack was moved. Those guys were awfully sweet even if they are noisy as hell."

Jamie turned the truck around and headed out slowly to the road. I asked him more about pikas. Apparently they didn't hibernate, and they actually laid wildflowers out to dry in the sun so their food storage didn't mold during the winter. He was like a walking book of strange animal facts.

We talked more about animals and Denali on the drive back to his cabin.

When we got back, I showed him the photos I had brought from my previous trip. I thought he liked them, but he blushed looking at images of himself. Spreading them out on the coffee table, I asked him which he would submit if he had to choose one.

He said if he was teaching kids, he would use the moose photo to illustrate the pros and cons of interacting with wild animals. I agreed with him. He said he would definitely love to use the rabbit-ear picture as comedic relief in some of his presentations. Ultimately he chose the one everyone did.

I turned to him. "Good. I'm calling it *Jamie's Beaver Shot*." Then I piled up the shots and put them back in my bag.

"Like hell you are," he cried and slapped my arm. I laughed and poked a finger in his ribs.

"It's pretty easy to push your buttons, sweetheart."

I tickled Jamie some more and he tried to tickle me back. He ended up on my lap and the tickling turned to wrestling, which turned into passionate kissing. I had him pinned beneath me on the sofa and we panted between kisses. We had shucked off our shirts and I felt his chest heaving below mine. I pulled him closer, wrapping my arms as tightly around Jamie as I could without hurting him.

"You feel so good, Jamie. I want you so much," I said in a low grumble into his ear.

I felt his head nod against the side of mine and I picked him up, walking into the bedroom. I laid him down in the center of the bed and unfastened his snow pants. After stripping three layers of pants off him, I started to laugh.

"Winter sex in Alaska is no joke," I told him. Jamie agreed while grabbing my waist.

When we were both happily naked, I lay over him, skin connected from forehead to toes. I ran my thumbs across his cheeks and kissed his eyes, his nose, his ears. My mouth landed back on his and he tilted his chin up to drink me in.

I skimmed a hand down his front and between Jamie's legs. My fingers brushed the insides of his thighs and played around teasingly until he begged for me to get on with it. I chuckled and complied, sliding my fist around his cock and moaning. Good god, he was hard for me.

I pressed my hard-on against his hip before reaching across his to the bedside table and getting a condom from the drawer. Moving back over him, I slid down to replace my hand with my mouth. I blindly fiddled with the lube, squeezing some onto my fingers and then playing with his tight hole. Jamie grabbed the sheet beside him with clenched fists and sucked in a breath.

"Teddy, god. *Teddy...ggnhhh.*"

I pulled my tongue off his cock and circled it lazily around the crown. I repeated the circles and then sucked him into my mouth. His ab muscles danced in reaction to my touch and his legs fell wider open as he lost himself to pleasure. Moans became whimpers and the sounds went straight to my dick. I released his cock with a wet popping sound.

"That's it, sweetheart. I want to see you let go, Jamie."

Returning my mouth to his cock, I sucked up and down and around until he gasped and begged, my fingers stretching him and teasing his prostate to drive him insane. Just when he was close to coming, I pulled back, moving back up to him. He was glassy-eyed and drunk with pleasure.

I tore open the condom, put it on, and drizzled it with lube before sinking deep inside his body with one drive of my hips. He came in a rush on the very first stroke into him, and I thrust as quickly as I could to catch up with him before his orgasm stopped slamming into him. I was already so close just from tasting him and watching him react to my touch. I stroked again. Two, three, and then I felt it. White hot energy buzzed in my head and sang through my body.

Enjoying the aftershocks, I thrust gently once more before starting to withdraw. He clamped his hands on my shoulder and gave me a pleading look. "Not yet. Just wait a second."

I kissed him softly then. Waiting for him to calm down and catch his breath. Kissing his forehead, I said, "Jamie, baby, I have to pull out because of the condom. I'll be right back."

I disposed of the condom and brought a warm wet washcloth back in case Jamie wanted it. I got back in bed beside him and laid my head down next to his shoulder, my nose and lips brushing his skin.

I looked over at him and noticed a tear spill out from the side of his eye.

"Are you okay?" I whispered.

"I'm okay," he lied. "That just felt really good."

I didn't know whether or not I should push him for the truth. Honestly, I didn't know if I was ready to hear it.

Instead of saying anything, I leaned up and kissed the tear away with gentle lips. He squeezed his eyes closed at the gesture and a few more leaked out. I drank them up, wishing I could take whatever bad feeling he was having into my body instead of it staying in his. That might have been when I started to realize I was fooling myself if I thought I could keep Jamie Marian at a distance.

## 22

# JAMIE

I woke up in a puddle of my own drool on top of Teddy's chest. Like a boss.

Quickly sitting up, I tried wiping the drool off him before he woke up. Too late. His rumble came out in a chuckle. "Don't worry, Jamie, I like your wet mouth on me, remember?"

I glared at him. "Ha ha, funny man. It's embarrassing. What time is it? I didn't mean to fall asleep."

He leaned over to check his phone. "It's after two. We should get some lunch."

We got up and put on some comfortable clothes. Teddy offered to make lunch so I said I'd start the fire. I opened the door to let Sister out and saw it had started snowing like crazy while we were sleeping. There must have been a foot of new snow on the ground already.

I started the fire and joined Teddy at the table for sandwiches and soup. My phone pinged with an alert from the head ranger station to shelter in place for the upcoming snowstorm. No problem. I was glad we were safe and sound at home.

After Sister came in, she curled up and went back to sleep by the fireplace. I grabbed my laptop out of my bedroom and settled down on the sofa to work. Teddy joined me and sat in his usual position with his back against the arm of one end of the couch, but this time he stretched his legs across the other cushions toward me. He tucked his toes under my thigh, and I ran a hand up inside his pant leg to stroke the hair on his calf.

"That feels good," he said. I kept stroking his legs with one hand while browsing the Internet with my other. The fire crackled and Sister began to snore. Eventually, I stopped stroking his legs and started typing up my lecture notes.

Teddy worked on his own laptop for a while until I noticed I didn't hear typing anymore. I looked up and saw him studying me.

"What?" I asked.

"Jamie, I didn't hurt you earlier? In bed, I mean. Did I do something that upset you?"

"No, Teddy. What you did to me definitely did not hurt," I said, giving him a smile of reassurance.

He continued to look into me with his intense blue gaze. "Would you please talk to me about what's bothering you? I know you're upset about something."

"I'm okay, Teddy. We're not going to do this, remember? The feelings thing? My body enjoyed your body. End of story. It's good. I look forward to doing it again before I go to sleep tonight," I said with a wink, wishing like hell I hadn't let my emotions leak out after sex earlier.

Why the hell did I need to care so much all the damned time? There was something about Teddy that I just couldn't fucking hold at arm's length no matter how hard I tried.

"Okay. But if you change your mind, it's okay. About the bodies thing or the feelings thing. You can talk to me about either."

I nodded and went back to what I was doing. I tried hard to focus on my job. After several minutes, I heard him start typing again too.

Half an hour later I had an emergency consultation call from the San Diego Zoo wanting to ask my advice about imping an injured peacock they had. It had suffered an attack and lost some of its big feathers. They wanted to try implanting substitute feathers and needed my recommendation about which donor feathers to use.

Teddy watched with fascination as I consulted via webcam while the veterinarians walked through the imping process in their lab. When the call was finished, Teddy asked some questions about it before we both went back to our work.

A couple of hours later I had finished my prep for the SUNY webinar and wandered into the kitchen to see what I could cook later for dinner. I poured a glass of wine and stood in front of the fridge thinking. Strong arms snaked around me and I felt the scratch of Teddy's cheek against mine. I told him I was trying to be clever and come up with a dinner idea from the stuff I had on hand.

"That's my job, sweetheart. Move your ass and let me take over here." He moved me a couple of feet away before leaning his head into the fridge.

"Do you have rice?" he asked. I confirmed I did. "I can make something with that." He got to work.

He pulled out the leftover chicken and vegetables from the night before and created this amazing Basque chicken and vegetable rice with zucchini, tomatoes, onions, bell peppers, and garlic. It was so good. I wished he had made a whole vat of it for me to freeze and eat all winter, and I told him so.

He laughed and said he could make a big batch like that before he left.

"How long are you staying?" I asked.

"That depends on you, really. I have to be in Zion Park in Utah in two weeks. I don't really want to go home and then back west again, but if you don't want me hanging around that long, I could find somewhere else to be." He looked at me with questions in his eyes.

I was quiet for a beat. He broke the silence with, "Jamie, it's okay. If you want me out of your hair, just say so. I'll understand."

"No, that's not what I was going to say. Can we just take it one day at a time?"

"That sounds like a good plan," he said with a smile.

"Just so you know, you cooking meals like this for me greatly supports the case for allowing you to stay the whole two weeks."

"Duly noted." Teddy smiled before taking dishes to the sink.

While I was washing the last of the dishes, my mom called.

"Hey, Mom," I said.

"Hey, Jay, I saw on the weather channel you're getting some snow up there tonight and I just wanted to make sure you and Sister are safe."

I smiled. "We're safe at the cabin. I have a friend here too. Teddy, the photographer I told you about."

"Oh good, honey. Well, then I won't keep you. I was just calling to make sure you weren't trapped on a mountain somewhere."

"Nope. Snug as a bug. Thanks, Mom."

"Love you, Jamie," she said.

"Love you too," I replied before disconnecting.

Teddy looked over with a smile. "That's so sweet that she called to check on you like that."

"I hit the parental jackpot. They're like the perfect parents. If they turn out to be serial killers, part of me will be relieved they weren't quite as flawless as I always thought," I joked.

The snow kept falling outside and we bundled up to walk out with Sister after dinner. We checked the backyard to see if Harry was around but he wasn't. Probably curled up somewhere, trying to stay warm.

After we returned to sit by the fire, the lights went out. I told Teddy I had a generator, but we decided to leave it off and try to make do with the fire and candles for a while instead. The generator was loud, and I was enjoying the silence outside and the crackle of the fire inside.

We lit candles and sat back on the sofa. Sister chewed on an antler I brought out for her. I told Teddy I had some cards or board games if he wanted to play something. We decided on Scrabble. When Teddy's first two words were *helix* and *biaxial*, I knew I was screwed.

After he kicked my ass twice, I suggested we switch to something else. Teddy said I might like strip poker. I informed him strip poker with the heat out in Alaska probably wasn't a good idea. He reluctantly agreed and suggested we come up with other ideas.

We settled on Truth or Dare. Maybe it was because a bottle of wine had been consumed and a second one opened.

I started and Teddy picked truth.

"What is your weirdest habit or personality quirk?"

Teddy thought for a minute. "I have to wear natural fibers when I fly."

"Why?"

He chuckled a little. "I watched a program once about plane crashes. They talked about fire being the worst part, and if you're wearing synthetic fibers, they'll melt to your skin."

"Jesus, Teddy. That's disgusting. You actually think about that every time you fly?" I asked.

"I don't really think about it anymore; it's just a habit. My turn."

I said, "Truth."

"Okay, same question. Weird Jamie thing."

"Hmmm." I thought. "Probably that I'm terrified of squirrels. Like genuinely horrified. To me, they are like Jack Nicholson from *The Shining*."

"You're kidding. How can you be so afraid of one of the most benign wild animals when you do what you do?" Teddy asked.

"One snuck up on me once when I was a little boy and jumped on my shoulder from behind. It was the first touch I had from a wild animal, but it was completely unexpected. Scared the shit out of me. I had nightmares for months. It happened again on campus when I was in college and I had an insane case of the heebie-jeebies for a while. A shrink would probably think I do what I do *because* of it. Now I avoid them like the plague. My turn."

Teddy put his finger to his bottom lip in thought. "Considering I'm terrified of what your dare would be, I'm going to hold off on that for now. Truth."

"Describe your worst date or hookup," I challenged.

"Too many to choose from. Hang on... hmmm... Well, once I was on an overnight flight somewhere and I woke up from a nap to find an old lady's hand gripping my dick under a blanket."

"No, you did not," I cried.

"Yep. Horny old bitch. Then there was the time I was dancing with a woman at a night club in Miami. When I pulled her closer to me I felt the hard ridge of a firearm strapped between her legs."

"Shut the fuck up. You're a liar."

"Nope. Want more? I can keep them coming."

"Of course I do. This is just getting good," I exclaimed.

"Well, once I was at home and a man I had hooked up with earlier that week showed up at my apartment in the middle of the night for sex. I shrugged and stepped back to let him in before noticing he'd brought a man with him for a threesome. It was his twin brother."

"Fuck, Teddy. You are a master bullshitter." I laughed.

"I promise I'm not lying about any of it. Wait, you and your brothers don't…?"

"Good god! Ugh, vomit. Please take back time and make that suggestion not have happened. Seriously, I might hurl."

Teddy laughed. "Okay, okay. Last one for now then it's your turn. When my very straight friend Mac would get stuck on a date he wanted out of, he'd text me. I'd turn up and make a big scene about being his spurned gay lover to scare the date off. One time a woman didn't believe me so I grabbed Mac's lapels and pulled him in for the hottest kiss you've ever seen. I don't think Mac stopped blushing for a week. We still laugh about it."

I giggled. "Man, I wish I had someone like that show up on my bad dates."

Teddy said, "Okay, sweetheart. Truth or dare?"

"Hm, guess I'll break the seal and choose dare. Go easy on me."

He grinned like a cat. "I dare you to let me use your phone to text Brian one word of my choosing."

I waited for my stomach to flip, but it didn't. "What the hell. Okay." I found my phone, pulled up a blank text addressed to Brian, and handed it to Teddy.

He looked at me in shock. "You're really going to let me do it? Are you sure?"

"Sure. I'll bet he'll ignore it. Just don't use something pathetic like 'please' or 'love.'"

He typed onto the screen and hit send. He handed it back to me.

**Jamie:** *Why?*

I snorted. “Good question. Your turn.”

Teddy told me he’d man up and take a dare too.

“I dare you to do a handstand. You get extra points for walking on your hands.”

He laughed and walked behind the sofa. After two false starts he went up on his hands and took a few steps. His T-shirt fell down around his neck and I could see his happy trail leading across his abs to his waistband. I might have stared and gotten a raging hard-on.

He stood back up, his face flushed. “That’s harder when you’ve been drinking and relaxing for a few hours. Your turn, Baby Dall.”

“Truth,” I chose.

“Where would your dream posting be for your job?”

“Hmmm... good question. My favorite post so far was Yellowstone. I love it there. I’ve actually come close to settling there permanently. But I’ve also been considering accepting a teaching job, which would mean moving to a town with a university. I wouldn’t want a huge city, but SUNY Cobleskill and Colorado State are always begging me to come teach permanently. The offers are getting a little ridiculous. I’ve also been approached by the wildlife health center at UC Davis. My parents would go nuts to have me close to home again. It’s hard to not consider it during long Alaska winters.”

“You’d be willing to move somewhere not in a national park?” he asked, looking surprised.

“Sure. I’m in the parks because that’s where the consulting jobs are. But I’ve been doing it awhile and it’s a pretty lonely existence. Moving every couple of years means making new friends and starting over every time. It’s tiring. I think I’d like living in a bigger town. Especially if I had the freedom and proximity to take students into the field. My biggest fear would be publishing if I wanted to go for tenure. I don’t know. But I do think about it.”

He stayed quiet for a moment. I told him it was his turn.

"Dare."

"I dare you to kiss me without getting a hard-on." I smirked.

"Not possible. Next."

I laughed. "What? Surely you can try. Think of the horny old lady on the airplane or the smelliest person on a train."

"I'll tell you what. Let me try and we'll see what happens." He winked and leaned in.

Teddy took a quick peck and was about to pull back for his best chance at winning, but he came back toward me and went for it. All tongue and hands and teeth. That kiss reached into my gut and grabbed it tight. My fingers floated up to his face and lightly landed on his scruffy jaw. After turning me into a puddle of mush, he pulled back and grabbed my hand.

He pushed it down onto his crotch where his erection tented his sweatpants. He was as hard as a fucking steel rod.

"I lose," Teddy said with a sexy grin. "Is there a punishment?"

*That smug motherfucker. How can I knock that smug look off his face?*

"Yes, the punishment is to fuck me up against a wall right now. Like you mean it."

## 23

# TEDDY

I had Jamie up against the wall before the last word was out of his mouth. I yanked off his clothes and fumbled with my own. We kissed like horny teenagers until I pulled away, panting. I told him to wait right there while I grabbed a condom. Before I reached the bedroom door, I looked back at him and said, "Don't even think about changing your mind."

I grabbed the condom and returned to Jamie. Warning Sister not to look, I slid the condom on, slathered it with lube, and picked up that beautiful boy. Jamie's legs went around my waist and I thrust up into him. We groaned at the same time and his hands tightened on my shoulders. I pulled out almost all the way and slammed back into him, slipping my tongue into his mouth and grabbing his bare ass with my hands.

"*Jesus fuck*," he gasped between breaths, and I moved my face down to the top of his chest. I reached one hand down to fist his cock and he pushed into it when he felt me there. His voice got husky, and he mumbled, "*Teddy*."

I kept pushing in and out of him with my hips. His back arched against the wall before he curled back around me and I felt him draw a finger along the top of my ass crack. *Fuck, this guy is hot.*

My climax built and built with each thrust. My fingers stroked his cock with each thrust of my hips until I suddenly felt him shatter around me. The sound of my name came out of his mouth again with his short breaths, and the sound made my legs wobble. I clutched him tighter to me and thrust again, feeling my balls tighten until I reached the crest and rolled down the other side into the sweet feeling of satisfaction and relief inside of Jamie.

I held him against me for a minute until I heard him say, "Christ, Teddy. That was sexy as fuck."

I pulled away with a grin. "*You're* sexy as fuck. Not only can I not just kiss you without getting a hard-on, but apparently I can't just kiss you without fucking you either."

Eventually we cleaned up, threw our clothes back on, gave Sister a pee break, and settled down on the sofa among the candlelight. I reached my arm out toward Jamie in invitation and he snuggled up against me. Part of me was praying the snow would turn into a full blizzard and lock us in together for a week of this. I wanted all of it. The joking, the flirting, the sitting quietly together in front of the fire, and obviously the incredible sex.

I ran my fingers through Jamie's hair as I asked him to tell me about his worst date or hookup. "Besides the obvious with Brian," I added.

He snorted. "Well, there was one time I was set up on a blind date with my brother Blue."

"What? I knew it, you kinky whore!" I laughed. "What the hell happened?"

"Ugh, it was awful. It was the summer after college and I was doing a project at USF. A friend of mine set me up with a guy he knew from college. His name was Will. When I showed up and asked for Will, it was Blue. We were both horrified before we started laughing. Apparently Will was in school with Blue. He had gotten back together with his boyfriend the day before and asked Blue to go on the date in his place. Obviously I made him pay for my dinner, and I ordered lobster. He's still friends with Will, and it's a big joke whenever we all get together."

I kissed his forehead. "I'd love to meet your brother so I can give him hell about it. He still lives in the Bay Area right? So one of your brothers is gay too?"

"Yes, five of nine of us are gay, but before you drop your jaw, let me explain."

"I'm hoping this story includes a poisoned well and a villain. Or maybe a long line of gay ancestry that somehow defied the rules of human reproduction. Or, wait, were you somehow brainwashed into being gay or pressured into it by society? Hm, hang on. I think that's just for making gay people straight," I said.

"Easy, tiger. There is a simpler explanation in our case. Only two biological Marians are gay: Blue and yours truly, plus the three *adopted* brothers my parents met through a gay youth shelter: Maverick, Griffin, and Dante.

"My sister's asshole ex-boyfriend used to call us the Gaydy Bunch. But it's pretty awesome. Most everyone is cool with it and supportive. We were all together in August for Simone and John's almost-wedding in Napa. Blue ended up hooking up with the groom's straight brother. They're together now, and I swear Tristan's homophobic family thinks he caught the gay from us."

I started laughing. "That sounds like an interesting story. Your brother, what? Turned someone gay?"

"Nah, I'm sure Tristan was bisexual all along but tried to ignore it. He was married to a woman. Apparently Blue is hard to resist. Tristan didn't stand a chance." He chuckled.

"Which sibling are you closest to?" I asked him.

"I was closest to Pete most of our lives. He's the oldest and I'm the second oldest. But then he married Ginger and had twin girls. He doesn't have as much time to stay close anymore. Before Blue met Tristan, he was with a real jackass named Jeremy. Jeremy was possessive of Blue, which meant it was hard to stay close to him too. Then there's Thad. He's thirty. Really nice guy. He works on international aid projects, but the travel makes it hard to stay close. And that leaves Jude."

"Tell me about Jude," I said, playing lightly with the fingers of his hand.

"Jude is a country music singer. When he's not touring, he's holed up recovering from touring. He's always been a quiet guy but—"

"Jude as in Jude and the Saints?" I blurted.

He laughed. "That's the one. You've heard of him?"

"Is there anyone who hasn't?" I asked incredulously.

"I was joking. You had the same reaction everyone has when I tell them who my brother is. And before you ask, no, I won't ask him to sign something for you and yes, he is that sweet in real life."

"I'm not really a country music fan, and I'm definitely not an autograph collector, but thanks. I just know who he is from the media. The only thing I really wondered about him is why his eyes always look so sad," I confessed.

"You're the only one who's described them as sad. The media spins it as 'soulful.' You have it right. He's carrying something around. He's been like that since just before he hit it big. None of us know what it is. Well, maybe Blue does. They're really close. He never seems to date anyone loving. Just women who are arm candy for the red carpet. Maybe he's sad because he's lonely. I just wish whatever it was, I could take the burden off him and put it on me, you know?" Jamie turned to look at me.

"That's how it is with Mac and me. He's my brother even though we didn't have the same parents. His parents died a couple of years ago and my heart broke for him. I wish I could carry the pain for him. He's been struggling so much. His girlfriend broke up with him and he's taking it pretty badly. Actually, I was supposed to be home for a fundraising gala after Thanksgiving, but I don't know if we're still going. His girlfriend runs it."

Jamie asked me what I was going to do about Thanksgiving now that my dad was gone. I told him about Thanksgiving at Brody's parents' in Greenwich.

"We've spent quite a few holidays with them because it's so easy to get out there from the city. Getting home to my dad was a four-hour drive, so there have been several years I went to Brody's instead because I couldn't take enough time off. I like it at Brody's parents'. He has brothers who are really cool. The whole family is like the American dream on steroids."

I combed my fingers through his hair some more and smelled his coconut shampoo floating around us. I leaned my nose into his neck and inhaled.

"Jamie, you smell delicious. I can't keep my hands off you," I grumbled into his neck before sliding my hand down the front of his shirt and running my fingers across a nipple.

"Then don't," he said, before standing up, blowing out the candles, and leading me to bed.

That night I had both the worst dream and the best dream ever. First, I dreamed I was in a dark canyon with Jamie. I was separated from him and it was too dark to see. I heard noises and shuffling, then I heard the sounds of a scuffle and a muffled scream. I fumbled for a flashlight and searched frantically, calling out Jamie's name. I was terrified he'd been hurt. I couldn't find him, and the panic rose with every moment of darkness.

The dream shifted and I was outside in the sun on a blanket in a field. It was summer and the air was hot and still. Warm, soft hands were all over me and a hot, wet mouth was wrapped around my cock. I pushed into it over and over again before waking up to discover it wasn't a dream.

"*Holy fuck.* Jamie... oh god...I thought I was dreaming... oh god, baby..." I threw my head back in disbelief and gratitude. I reached down and put my palm against the side of his face. His tongue swirled up and down my entire length and his hand drew light fingernail scratches up the insides of my thighs. He sucked and licked and took me all the way into his throat. I almost exploded in his mouth.

Gasping, I quickly told him I was going to come and tried pulling him away. He stayed, his mouth clasping around me and sucking again. I came deeply into his throat with a cry and a shudder.

I lay there trying to catch my breath. My brain was having trouble catching up as well. Never in my life had I been awakened like that. My heart tried to slow down but it was still stuttering a little.

"Mornin'." He smiled before crawling up and lying back down beside me.

"Jesus, Jamie. That was the best wake-up call ever. Come here." Instead of reaching out to him like I intended, I leaned over and kissed his shoulder and then gripped his earlobe with my teeth. "Thank you," I rumbled into his ear.

He turned his head and kissed me on the lips. Against my lips he said, "You're welcome. Next time don't put the moves on me in your sleep unless you're ready to wake up and act on them."

I leaned my head back and laughed. "How was I putting the moves on you? I was asleep."

He looked at me with a smirk and a raised brow. "You moaned my name in your sleep."

"I did not," I argued.

"You most certainly did, Teddy Bear."

Suddenly I remembered the dream about Jamie being lost and hurt, and my heart sped up at the memory. The dread coiled in my belly again and I looked over at him. He looked at me and then raised an eyebrow in question.

"What is it?" he asked.

"Nothing," I assured him. "I just remembered a bad dream I had before the really, really good one." I smiled and kissed him again before lying back.

"Want to tell me about it?" Jamie asked.

"Not really. I'd rather focus on the one that came after. When a smoking hot guy went down on me and made me see stars." I grinned over at him.

"You're one lucky bastard if I do say so myself. What time is it?"

I looked for my phone but found his instead. I pressed the button to wake it. "Just after seven. Looks like you missed a text." I handed it to him and got up to go to the bathroom.

## 24

## JAMIE

The text was from Brian. That's when I remembered letting Teddy text him from my phone the night before. Damn.

**Brian:** *It's a long story, but you deserve to hear it. I finalized my divorce last week and want to talk to you. Can I call?*

WHAT THE HELL was I supposed to say to that? Even if he did get divorced, the damage was already done. I put the phone back down on my nightstand and got up. I slipped on flannel pajama bottoms, a Cornell T-shirt and an old, worn hoodie that had "Zoologists Do It In The Wild" on it in faded green print.

I started some coffee and let Sister out. The snow had stopped after about two feet. Drifts were piled everywhere and I thought about checking on Harry. I'd wait until after breakfast.

After Teddy came out, I went to the bathroom and had a quick shower. I put the comfy clothes back on and brushed my hair, deciding to forgo shaving and let the scruff stay.

The power had come back on at some point during the night and I was grateful we hadn't left a light on in the bedroom.

I fixed coffee and started making some oatmeal with brown sugar. Teddy drank his coffee and walked up to where I stood at the stove. He turned me around with his hands on my hips and then leaned his forehead against mine.

"Hi," he said softly.

"Hi," I whispered.

Teddy leaned down and kissed me so tenderly my heart almost broke. My chest got tight and I told my eyeballs to forget about betraying me again. I was in so much trouble. This guy was being way too sweet to me. How in the world was I going to spend two weeks with him and then watch him drive away?

I quickly pulled away and went back to stirring the oatmeal. Out of the corner of my eye I saw his head tilt to look at me before he turned and found bowls in a cabinet.

After breakfast we bundled up and went looking for Harry. No luck. I wasn't worried about him, but I wanted to see if his coat had started changing to winter white.

Back inside, I started working again on my laptop. There were some emails from Brody, so I focused on the redesign. Teddy worked on his at the kitchen table while I sat on the sofa. He must have sensed me pull away earlier and was trying to give me some space.

After working for a while quietly, I remembered the text from Brian. I really didn't know how I felt about it. I decided to ask my "friend" for help.

"Teddy, can I talk to you for a second?" I asked.

"Sure." He got up and stretched before joining me on the sofa. I put my laptop on the coffee table and turned to face him. He put his feet on my lap and I grasped them, massaging them and pushing hard pressure into the bottom of one with my thumb.

"Jamie, your forehead is creased, and you're cogitating pretty hard over there. Spill it."

"Brian texted me back."

Teddy looked up at me in surprise. "Oh shit. What did he say? I should have never sent that text. I'm such an asshole. Jamie, I'm so sorry."

"Calm down, it's fine. I think he was going to reach out to me anyway. Apparently he got divorced and wants to talk."

Teddy's eyes narrowed to angry slits. My hands stilled on his feet.

"Please tell me you aren't going to talk to that motherfucker," Teddy growled.

"I knew that's what you would say. But part of me wants to hear him explain himself," I admitted.

He sat up straighter and reached over to grab one of my hands. "Jamie Marian, you deserve so much better. That asshole should rot in hell for what he did to you. He doesn't deserve one single moment of your thoughts or one shred of your heart."

He sat back against the arm of the sofa and muttered, "I should have *never* sent that text." He ran a hand through his hair and then over his face and jaw. Teddy was pissed.

I narrowed my eyes at him. "Dude, seriously? How about this isn't about *you*? This is about *me* needing advice from my *friend*. That would be you, hotshot, remember?"

He looked at me, surprised at my outburst. "You're right. I'm sorry. What do you want to do?"

"I don't know what I want. That's the problem."

"Jamie, if you talked to him, would you be looking for a new beginning or an end?" His eyes searched me for the answer, but I honestly didn't have it.

"I don't know. An end, I think. I want closure for what went on around the wedding. That's the main reason I'm tempted to let him try to explain. Maybe it's because I want so badly to understand how anyone could do something like that to someone they supposedly loved. How can you betray someone like that?"

Teddy suggested the lame-ass technique of making a pros and cons list about whether or not to let Brian call me. We went through every aspect of the situation we could think of and Teddy scribbled it down on a notepad. The exercise quickly devolved into me arguing the reasons why I should let Brian call and Teddy arguing the reasons why not. By the time we ran out of steam, I was emotionally exhausted.

I told Teddy I was getting back in bed. He asked if he could join me and I gave him a glare.

He held up Boy Scout fingers and promised he wouldn't seduce me. I said, "Fine," and let him follow me into bed. His arms wrapped around me from behind and I let out a big breath. His nose found the back of my neck and I shivered.

A small voice inside me whispered, *This one*, as I fell off to sleep.

I awoke to the sound of someone screaming my name. My heart pounded as I sat up quickly and looked around in a daze.

Teddy was grimacing and sweating in his sleep, and I realized he must have called my name while dreaming. But this didn't look like the good kind of moan. This was a nightmare. His jaw was tight and he grunted almost as if he was in pain. I reached out a hand to his shoulder to shake him gently.

"Teddy? Teddy, wake up. It's just a dream, baby."

He grabbed my wrist and yanked it off him while he sat bolt upright. I jumped back and almost fell off the bed. He saw my movement and realization hit him.

"Oh god, Jamie. What's wrong? Are you okay?" he croaked in a gravelly voice.

"You... you had a nightmare," I said. "You screamed and thrashed, so I tried to wake you up. Are *you* okay?"

He scrambled over toward me and pulled me onto his lap and into his arms as tightly as he could. I felt him shaking against me. He kept asking me over and over if I was sure I was okay.

"I'm fine. I'm right here with you. What's going on? What the hell did you dream about?"

"I don't know. I... it was bad. Like earlier. So weird. Sorry. I'm so sorry." He stroked my back and kissed the side of my head by my temple.

"Do you have nightmares often?" I asked him. "Has something happened to cause them? Or just stress maybe?"

"No, never. I've never had nightmares like this. Maybe it's the jet lag or the altitude or something." He took a deep breath and let it out slowly. "I certainly don't think it's stress. I haven't felt this relaxed in a really long time. When I'm here, it's almost like my stress is a million miles away."

I suggested maybe it was the release of stress that comes with significant relaxation. Like maybe the nightmares were a way for his body to let go of the tension.

I leaned my head against his chest and sat there with him. His heart raced and I could feel it pounding under my ear. Something scared the shit out of him and I wondered what it was.

Intending to distract him, I pulled him up and insisted we watch the funniest movie I could think of, which was *Airplane*. He'd never seen it, which made it even better.

Half an hour later we were laughing so hard my cheeks were sore. The "normal" Teddy was back and I was relieved. Until he started quoting from the movie later that night.

His favorite line? "You ever seen a grown man naked?"

## 25

# TEDDY

We basically spent the next two days laughing and having incredible sex. I was so stupidly thankful for the snowstorm that I began to wish I lived there so I could be trapped in a cabin with Jamie anytime there was severe weather.

But reality returned on the third day, and we headed out to the ranger station. He needed to check in and meet with Charlie before we could head out for some fieldwork. Josh was there too, and I could see him assessing me. I assumed he didn't know whether there was more to my relationship with Jamie than just a professional photographer and his subject.

The caveman part of me wanted to claim Jamie somehow in front of him, but I knew that wasn't fair. If I wasn't in this for the long haul, I had no right to fuck things up for Jamie with other guys.

I waited in the reception area and checked my phone. I texted Mac to see how he was holding up.

**Teddy:** *I took your advice and came to Denali.*

**Mac:** *Good. And? What happened?*

**Teddy:** *Snowstorm. A good one. Stuck in his cabin for three days.*

**Mac:** *Holy shit, Teddy. That's divine intervention. God's trying to tell you something.*

**Teddy:** *Well, I have cried out the lord's name a few times, now that you mention it...*

**Mac:** *Slut.*

**Teddy:** *I really like him, Mac.*

**Mac:** *I know. What are you going to do about it?*

**Teddy:** *Hell if I know.*

**Mac:** *Tell him.*

**Teddy:** *I can't tell him unless I'm prepared to go all in. I won't be another asshole who leaves him. You know me. I'm the king of casual hookups. Not relationships.*

**Mac:** *Yes, you've had the quintessential single-guy sex life for several years, but maybe it's time for you to move on. Take it from me, Teddy - grab him and don't fucking let him go. If you leave him without even trying, you'll regret it.*

**Teddy:** *I guess you haven't heard from Birdie?*

**Mac:** *No, but her birthday is tomorrow and I sent her something. Maybe she'll call and at least acknowledge it.*

**Teddy:** *I hope so. Good luck, Mac.*

**Mac:** *You too. Be safe out there.*

Next I texted Cat and asked if she was taking commissions for Christmas.

**Cat:** *For you? Always. What are you looking for?*

**Teddy:** *A vase for the woman at the hospital who helped me with everything after Dad died.*

**Cat:** *Aww, sure, Teddy. Any suggestions on design or size and shape?*

**Teddy:** *Go with your gut. I'm sure I'll love whatever you make.*

**Cat:** *Okay. I'll see if I can finish it by Thanksgiving and bring it to Greenwich. Dinner at Jenna's this weekend?*

**Teddy:** *Can't. I'm in Alaska.*

**Cat:** *Well, well. Tell Kitty-Cat all about it.*

**Teddy:** *No way. You'll tell the rest of the crew and then I'll never hear the end of it.*

**Cat:** *Crap. At least tell me you're happy you went.*

**Teddy:** *Extremely.*

**Cat:** *Awesome.*

**Teddy:** *Tell everyone I'm sorry to miss dinner.*

**Cat:** *Will do.*

By the time I checked my email, Jamie was ready to get back in the truck and head out. We drove for a while before Jamie pulled over to point out some caribou in the distance.

"There's an access road that will get us closer to where they are. Let's see if we can hike in before they move off."

We parked and bundled up before putting the snowshoes back on. The need for them was much greater now with a couple of feet of snowfall everywhere.

I followed his lead and we traveled quietly through the snow. We were on what I assumed was a large open meadow so what sunlight there was shined directly on us. Not that it made a difference in warming us up. We wore sunglasses to cut the glare from the snow, and I remembered a *National Geographic* historical feature with native Alaskans wearing old-fashioned snow goggles to prevent snow blindness.

The old goggles were called *yukłuktaak* and were made out of wood with narrow slits cut into them. Straps were made from seal skin to hold them on. The article stayed with me because I was shocked at the damage you could do to your vision just from being in the snow. As a photographer, the idea of damaging my vision terrified me.

I saw the caribou in the distance and we slowly made our way closer. I noticed an enormous rack sticking up from a snowdrift and wondered if there was a dead caribou lying there. My hand reached for Jamie's elbow and he turned. I pointed and raised an eyebrow.

He leaned toward me and whispered in my ear, "The males lose their racks this time of year. That's just a rack one of those guys has dropped."

His warm breath and beard scruff against my ear went straight to my groin. I quickly nodded and stepped back away from him.

He continued forward. When we got about fifty feet away from them we stopped. Some of them watched us but some nosed through the snow, looking for food below.

Jamie began slowly making his way around to the side, getting a little closer with each move he made. I stayed where I was and brought my camera up. When he was about twenty feet away from the closest caribou, I saw him reach back to move the can of bear spray clipped to his backpack over to clip on the front of his coat.

He squatted down on his snowshoes and waited. I tried not to stare at his ass. The air was electric around us. I squatted down too, trying to find the angle and perspective I wanted. I stood back up and used my snowshoes to pack down the snow around me. Then I carefully lowered onto my front and propped myself up on my elbows to steady the camera.

We waited. I could hear soft grunts from the herd and saw cloudy puffs coming from their noses. Steam rose faintly from their backs in the cold air. One started wandering toward Jamie and another followed.

One of them had a rack so large it made my heart speed up. Those things were amazing, but dangerous too. The one with the rack walked closer to Jamie. He stayed still and looked down where the animal's hooves sank into the snow. Jamie's elbows rested on his knees. Curled tips of his hair blew out from under the cuff of his warm hat. His pink cheeks appeared out of the top of a light blue fleece neck gaiter. He turned his face to look over at me and smiled. I snapped the shutter release button like I was trying to win a speed award. I wanted to capture every single image of this striking man in his element.

As he turned his head back to watch the animal, the caribou walked up and brushed his big shoulder against Jamie's. Jamie fell back on his ass in the snow and my heart lurched. I started to jump up and yell, but he quickly held up a hand to stop me. He gave me a clumsy "okay" sign with his bulky gloves before pulling himself up and getting his snowshoes under him.

The caribou walked past him and turned his head back around to watch Jamie over his shoulder. He didn't look upset and none of the others seemed bothered. Jamie was covered in snow from his hat to his ass. He made his way back over to where I was and I could tell he was trying not to laugh too loudly. It came out in a series of snorts.

I stood up and brushed myself off. Then I leaned toward him and brushed him off, taking my time around the area of his ass. He gave me a raised eyebrow and smirk. I returned it with a wink.

The caribou had wandered closer to us and stood spread out all around us. It was so peaceful and rare. I wished I could go back to tell myself as a little boy that one day I would stand in the middle of a herd of wild reindeer at the base of Denali in Alaska.

Jamie whispered, “Do you want to leave?”

I shook my head without speaking. Instead, I snuck my arms around him, hearing the shushing sound of our outerwear sliding against each other. My face leaned in toward his and our cold lips came together in stolen kisses hidden by the thick white puffs of our warm breath in the cold air.

*No, sweetheart. I don’t ever want to leave you.*

# 26

## JAMIE

When we got back to the cabin, Sister was restless. Teddy offered to play with her and walk with her down the long driveway and back. I went inside and stripped down to my long underwear before starting coffee and booting up my computer.

I answered questions on my website. One of them asked what a group of parrots was called. My answer was: "A group of parrots is called a pandemonium. Just imagine how noisy that would be and you can remember what it's called in the future."

Another one asked: "How fast can a grizzly bear run?"

I wrote back: "A grizzly bear can run about thirty miles per hour, which is about as fast as a car should drive on a residential street."

The last question I answered was: "Why don't snakes have ears?"

I responded they did have ears but they were internal, not external, meaning we couldn't see them even though they were there. I added that snakes could "smell" with their tongues.

By the time I finished, Teddy and Sister were back. Teddy grabbed his computer and joined me on the sofa. He uploaded his photos from the day and started organizing them.

My phone pinged.

**Brian:** *I never heard back from you the other day. I was trying to give you some space, but I'd really like to talk to you. Can I call you tonight?*

Oh shit. I hadn't thought about Brian once since our pros and cons list from the other night.

I looked up at Teddy and opened my mouth before changing my mind and closing it.

"What?" he said. "Who was that?"

"Brian."

"Shit," Teddy agreed.

"Yep."

He thought for a minute then looked at me with a wolfish grin. "Want me to distract you?"

I narrowed my eyes at him suspiciously. "And how would you propose to do that?"

He put his computer on the coffee table and stood. "You ever seen a grown man naked?"

*That smart-mouthed motherfucker.*

"Not since this morning. Remind me again?"

He led me into the bedroom and sat me on the edge of the bed before stepping back and doing a slow striptease. Every piece of clothing he removed was tossed haphazardly around the room and a part of me wished I had some dollar bills.

When he was naked and my heart pounded in anticipation, he reached over to pull my clothes off and then moved me across the bed, laying me on my back. He hovered over me, reaching his lips down to brush so softly across mine that I stretched up to get more. He ran the tip of his tongue along the swell of my bottom lip and my breath hitched.

He brushed the hair off my forehead and then placed a tender kiss there. I ran my hands over his scratchy cheeks and into his dark curls. He moaned my name as he ground his hips into mine. I felt him hard as a rock against my stomach and a trace of sticky wetness led from the tip of his erection to my skin. I wanted him inside me so badly.

"Teddy, need you inside of me." I arched and used my hands on his ass to pull him in tighter against me.

"Not yet, sweetheart, I want to run my mouth all over you first and taste every bit of you before you can't keep yourself from coming."

True to his word, he drove me crazy with his lips. They trailed wet kisses all over me from my wrist to my neck to the sensitive spot behind my knees. His hands caressed and squeezed as they explored every inch of my skin from my face to my toes. I writhed in desperation, begging him to please get inside me.

He growled, "This little spot on your ass kills me. I want to bite it every time I see it." He nipped and soothed and ran his tongue in lazy circles and swirls all over my body.

He came back to my face with a deep, thorough kiss and plunged his tongue into my mouth at the same time his lubed fingers entered my ass. I cried out against his mouth. He slowed the kissing and stroking until reaching over to grab a condom.

When he slowly slid into my body, I felt my eyes fill again. My motherfucking heart. I couldn't help it. I had never been treated with so much tenderness. I spent every molecule of focus and determination I had left forcing those tears to stand down and go back where they came from.

That emotional upheaval added to the physical pleasure until I couldn't even form a coherent thought.

Teddy thrust into me slowly, again and again, swiveling his hips with each thrust. My eyes rolled back and I felt myself about to pitch over the top. I heard him groan out my name as he came, and his last hard thrust into me sent me scattering into a thousand pieces.

As I lay there recovering, smiling a little at the incredible feeling of bonelessness I felt, I sensed Teddy lean over and kiss my cheek softly. My chest tightened at the gesture.

I realized I was going to have to put a stop to whatever was going on between Teddy and me. I was in too far and my heart was engaged whether I liked it or not. To me, this was no longer just sex. But to Teddy, that's all it would ever be.

At the thought of saying goodbye to him, more tears threatened to spill. I ignored them as Teddy softly ran fingertips along my arm.

After lying there for a while, I had an idea. "Let's drive up to the roadhouse and get drunk."

"Hot damn. Great idea, Baby Dall." He grinned. "I'll drive and you can get drunk."

My insecurities stayed home, and I threw myself into having a good time at the bar. I didn't get drunk, but I drank enough to really relax and dance with him. He held me close, and I could feel the hard muscles of his leg between mine. Dancing with him was both exciting and surreal. He made me feel cherished, like I was the only person in the whole place.

When we made it back to the cabin, we had slow, sweet sex again like we had done earlier in the day. It was too much. My heart was so far in it that I thought it would break. I realized I was incapable of just fucking Theodore Kodiak, and I made love to him with every ounce of my soul.

The next morning I woke up surrounded by his warm, strong arms. He smelled like his usual sleepy self and I nuzzled my nose against his skin, breathing in the scent and tucking it away.

Leaning back from him a little, I sucked in a deep breath.

Teddy nudged me with his knee. "Morning, sweetheart. How did you sleep?"

"Like a brick," I lied.

He looked at me with an expression that called bullshit.

"Maybe you're stressed about the text thing yesterday. What are you going to do about Brian?"

I shrugged. "What do *you* think I should do?"

He looked pointedly at me with those piercing blue eyes for a minute before breaking my heart.

"I guess it's not really any of my business."

*Right.*

"I guess not," I said, pissed.

"What do you mean? Do you want me to make this decision for you?"

"Teddy, never mind. Forget I asked."

"Jamie, talk to me. Are you mad at me about this?"

I glanced over at him and snapped. "No. I'm mad at myself. Because I'm a fucking idiot who is so predictable that it's humiliating."

He looked at me. "I don't understand. Because you want to talk to Brian?"

"No! For god's sake. Because I haven't thought of Brian in days since I've been with you. Because despite trying to be an adult and have some casual sex with my hot friend, I fucking can't help falling for him like a schoolgirl."

His mouth fell open and he stared at me.

I muttered, "Never mind, please forget I said that out loud. I'm apparently trying to see just how embarrassed I can possibly get before breakfast."

Teddy reached out his arm to me. "Come here, sweetheart."

"No, and don't call me that right now."

"Can we talk about this, please?" he asked.

"I'm not sure there's anything to talk about, Teddy. You've been pretty up front with me all along."

"Yes, I have, but can I explain something to you anyway?"

I looked at him with narrowed eyes, not sure I wanted to hear it. I shrugged.

"Jamie, I am falling for you too. More than I ever have with anyone, ever. But I just can't do it. It won't wor—"

"I know that!"

He pulled me in closer. He kissed my cheek and held me against his chest. Both his arms wrapped around me, and we stayed like that for a while.

I felt a deep rumble in his chest as he asked, "Do you want me to leave?"

"I don't know, Teddy. Part of me wants you to stay here forever, but part of me is scared that being together longer might make it harder when you do leave."

I felt him nod his understanding against the top of my head.

After a while we got up to fix breakfast. Things were quiet and weird between us. I thought he was afraid of leading me on, and I was afraid of scaring him off.

I went to take a long, hot shower while he finished something on his computer. When I came out of the bathroom, he was gone.

I found a manila envelope on the kitchen table. Inside was his submission packet for the Gramling Prize for Wildlife Photography. The submission consisted of the print of me with the beaver kits as well as an attached smaller square card in the corner that had a photo of me in pain with an ice pack over an angry bruise on my shoulder.

In italic print beside it the injury photo had a caption: "Even trained professionals often sustain serious injuries while in the proximity of wild animals. Please do not approach or feed animals in the wild under any circumstances. Remember to respect wildlife and leave no trace. For more information, please visit nps.gov or your local park ranger."

Seeing the photo of me healthy and happy next to the one of me in obvious pain and injured brought the wildlife risk home so clearly. It would be a great teaching aid, especially for budding scientists preparing to go into the field.

There was a note in the packet for me along with a flash drive.

"Jamie, I'm not going to submit your photos after all. I don't want to do anything to make you uncomfortable. This flash drive has all the original files on it. You can use them however you wish. They are yours now. I'm so sorry I messed everything up. - Teddy"

And just like that, I realized another man I loved had left me. Except this time it was without a doubt the absolute love of my life. The human being I knew would hold my heart inside of his for as long as I walked the earth.

# 27

# TEDDY

When I got to the airport in Fairbanks I was already exhausted. I decided to fly into Vegas before driving the three hours to Zion. I called my contact on the Zion job, letting them know I would be in the area a few days early in case they wanted me to get started on the job. If they didn't, I could always stay in Vegas for a few days.

By the time I landed, they had responded that coming sooner was fine. I was relieved to hear it. Vegas wasn't really my scene and I was afraid with the mood I was in, I would do something stupid.

I found my way to the Zion Lodge and fell gratefully into bed. My phone was dead and I didn't bother charging it. I was going to leave the damned thing behind the next day anyway. Otherwise I would check it all day wondering if Jamie would call or text me.

The first day of the shoot was gorgeous and dry. We started very early in the morning in order to get sunrise shots. A young ranger accompanied me on the hike up Angel's Landing, and I enjoyed hearing about his college internship in the park. He was fit so he offered to help carry some of my equipment. Between the two of us, we got the gear and plenty of water up to the top of the trail.

I wasn't a big fan of heights, honestly, so I wanted to get these shots out of the way first. Angel's Landing was the most famous vista of the park, so I knew I needed to shoot it at several different times of day.

By sunrise, I was snapping away, capturing the beautiful colors of the rock illuminated by the rising sun. I took a few other shots throughout the day but had plenty of down time to wait for sunset. The kid who hiked up with me left, and an older man named Mike hiked up to take his place after lunch. He'd brought me a better sandwich than the protein bar I had packed. I thanked him profusely.

We started talking and I learned he'd done a stint in Denali a few years before. I laughed and told him I had just come from Denali. He asked me all about my trip and I ended up telling him about Jamie.

Mike was so attentive and friendly that I felt like I was talking to the kind of dad I always wished I'd had. I ended up telling that stranger on the red rock all about the captivating animal whisperer who had taken over all my thoughts and a big piece of my heart.

I asked him if he was married and he said he'd been married for thirty-five years to a wonderful woman named Dolly. He explained that for years she'd traveled with him and got a job in whatever park he chose to move to. They had been settled at Zion for ten years now and were thinking about retirement.

I told him about my job and Jamie's, and how I was sure we could never make it work. He said I would find a way to make it work if it was worth it to me. And sometimes things that were worth it took compromise and sacrifice.

"How the hell do I know if it's worth it?" I exclaimed in exasperation.

"Well, Teddy, only you can determine that, but I can tell you one thing. When you find yourself telling a perfect stranger at the top of a mountain about an incredible person you might consider changing your life for, that's a pretty big hint." He smiled big and clapped me on the back.

He had a point.

After I captured the sunset shots I wanted we made our way down the steep trail. He told me about his kids, grandkids, and the new grandbaby on the way. I asked him if he had plans to visit the family for Thanksgiving. He said they were waiting until Christmas so they could stay for three weeks. The family lived in Nashville, and both of Mike's sons and his daughter would be there together with their spouses. It sounded like fun. I told him about my plans with my close friends.

When I got back to the lodge and showered, I had a quick dinner before falling into bed to do it all again the next day.

The next day there was an unexpected visit to the park by a big film star and movie crew. They had to push up the dates of their Zion shooting schedule to accommodate bad weather forecasts the following week. The area filled with vehicles, fans, and entourage until it was hard to bear.

At my request, the rangers moved me from the lodge into the employee dorm to open up a room at the lodge for the film. I spent the next several days trying to stay out of everyone's way. The park was a disaster with media and security. Making sure to stay away from busy areas, I took the time to shoot images in some of the lesser-known corners of the park.

In Kolob Canyons, I found arches and hidden waterfalls. I captured the deep green trees against the warm red rocks. Hikers pointed me toward special spots and by the time I fell into bed each night, my body was so tired from hiking that I fell into dreamless sleep.

Finally the crowds thinned when the week of Thanksgiving arrived. I'd spent lots of time thinking about Jamie. It seemed like everywhere I turned, people had someone they loved with them. When I went to photograph Emerald Pools Trail, I came across someone proposing to his girlfriend. *Jesus Christ.*

On my last day I was scheduled to shoot one of the slot canyons called Knave Canyon. The slot canyons in Zion were absolutely stunning. Zion was known for narrow corridors that had been carved out of water over the course of years. The colors of the red rocks lit by sunlight from above made for stunning photos.

These areas carried flash flood dangers if rains came through the area. Water levels would increase so quickly that hikers could get caught and drown. They weren't my favorite places to spend time because I had heard these stories before. Today, however, there wasn't a chance of rain in the forecast, so I felt like it was as good a time as any to get the shots I needed.

Mike was my guide again, but when we were a mile in, he got a radio call that his wife needed him to turn back because their daughter was in labor, and there were complications. I told him not to worry, that I would be okay.

He said he would let the head ranger know I was in there, and he reminded me there was a small research group with a ranger ahead of us in the canyon. I could try to catch them in the next ten or fifteen minutes by picking up my pace.

I started walking faster to catch up with them, mostly so I could be near a radio if conditions changed. It was never smart to hike alone in a slot canyon. Before catching up with them, however, I found the perfect spot for the photos. I set up my gear and took plenty of shots.

I considered moving farther along the canyon to see if there was another location I should shoot, but I didn't feel like that was the safest choice. My nightmares had done a number on me. Instead, I turned around and hiked out. After I got back to my bed, I took a nap and then made my way to a nearby restaurant.

I sensed a hushed whispering from some of the employees. I tried to eavesdrop to find out what was going on. When I couldn't hear enough, I asked someone.

"What's going on? Did something happen?"

A young waitress said, "Six people got caught in a flood in Knave Canyon this afternoon, and only two made it out. They're still looking for the other four."

The blood drained from my face and my stomach lurched. Surely that was the group I almost caught up with. I had never in my life been so selfishly grateful to be spared. *Good god, how awful.* I couldn't even wrap my mind around it.

I went back to my room with a sick feeling. Those poor people and their families. It should have been me instead. I wouldn't leave behind a spouse or a child or anyone besides my friends and Mac.

I couldn't get to sleep that night until the early hours of the morning. When I finally did get to sleep I had another nightmare about losing Jamie. I woke up gasping and covered in sweat. It freaked me the hell out, and I decided I'd be avoiding canyons for the foreseeable future.

I got up after the sun rose and packed up the car. As I drove to Vegas to catch a flight home, I thought more about Jamie. I felt like flying home to New York was going in the wrong direction. East instead of west.

Dammit, my heart was in Alaska. I realized in that moment I was in love with Jamie. I wanted him in my life, and I truly didn't care what I had to do to convince him. I wanted to wake up entwined with him every morning and fall asleep with my nose in his neck every night. I wanted to hold him on quiet nights in front of the fire and hike with him on summer afternoons.

I had to go tell him what an idiot I'd been to walk away. To find a way to prove to him this wasn't a lark. How could I show him I was serious about him? I didn't want to scare him off with something as insensitive as a proposal after what he'd been through with Brian, but I wanted to make a grand gesture to convince him I was all in.

I booked a flight to Fairbanks and called Brody to tell him that I'd be spending Thanksgiving out of town. My grand gesture was decided. I would tell Jamie I was moving to Denali to be with him.

It didn't occur to me to check in with the head ranger in Zion to let him know I had come out of Knave Canyon alive. When I got off the plane in Fairbanks, I emailed my Zion contact a quick thanks for the visit, and he called me in a panic, telling me I was on the list of people missing.

I talked while I drove. It took about an hour of talking to different people to clear it up, and by the time I was done, I was almost to Jamie's cabin. It was Thanksgiving Day and I had no idea if he would be at the cabin or at a friend's house. I didn't care, knowing full well I would wait for him as long as I needed to. Coming home to Jamie's cabin felt like coming home in a way I'd never felt before.

## 28

# JAMIE

The week after Teddy left fucking sucked. I was hurt and pissed off, but I swung between blaming him for my feelings and blaming myself. The website redesign took up plenty of my time, so I worked late and tried to minimize the time left for self-pity.

I spent many hours working at the ranger station so I could be surrounded by people. Josh asked me to dinner again, and I went. I warned him it was just dinner as friends. He seemed to be understanding even though I was sure he wanted more.

Brian texted me two more times, and I finally called him in an effort to be done with it all. He told me he had royally fucked up and that his marriage was a stupid relic from his high-school sweetheart days when he was still trying to deny his sexuality. He realized it during the weekend of our wedding and raced home to file for divorce. His plan all along was to be with me.

I wanted to roll my eyes.

He was so sorry and wanted another chance. I was the love of his life and if he could just get a chance to prove it to me, blah, blah, blah. It was so clear to me how completely and utterly done I was with Brian. In fact, I could hardly believe I'd ever been with him in the first place.

I had more feelings in my heart for Theodore Kodiak after a few weeks of knowing him than I ever did for Brian after years of being with him.

Even if I wasn't meant to be with Teddy, I knew I deserved better than Brian. I told Brian I was fine now, and I appreciated that his actions had saved me from making a huge mistake.

He suggested he come for a visit so we could talk in person. I said not only no, but hell no. I told him I had been with other men since then, and I was happily moving on. He didn't like hearing that.

The day before Thanksgiving I was at the ranger station preparing to leave early and get home in time for a late lunch. I had plans to hang out with Sister and pretend like Thanksgiving wasn't happening. Charlie had invited me over to be with his family, but I didn't feel up to it. I zipped my computer bag and stood up to leave.

As I walked across the reception area, Josh hung up from a call he was on and told the rest of us there had been an incident at Zion National Park. A ranger friend of his there told him about people being caught in a flash flood in a narrow canyon. My heart skipped and I stuttered, "When? Were they hurt? What happened?"

"Yesterday, I think. There were two fatalities, a ranger and a college professor. Three are still missing. Two are college students and one is a photographer. That's all I know."

I remember my vision narrowing and my legs going out from underneath me. I don't remember Josh grabbing my elbow and catching me at the last minute or Charlie laying me down on the floor and tilting my chin up to help me get some air.

I woke up and remembered what was happening. When I caught my breath, I sputtered to Josh, "You have to find out more about the photographer. It's Teddy."

His eyes went wide, and he called his buddy right back. They confirmed the missing photographer was Theodore Kodiak, and there was no news. I quickly found my phone and pulled up his number. I called him over and over, but it went straight to voicemail.

I couldn't look at Josh or Charlie. I didn't want to see the concern in their eyes. My entire body felt numb. After an hour of waiting for news, they offered to take me home. Josh drove me in my truck and Charlie followed. Josh offered to stay with me, but I insisted he leave. Charlie took him back to the station, both of them promising to check up on me and let me know if they heard anything.

Sister and I walked around outside in a daze and then settled onto the sofa. I sat with my phone in my hand for hours. I called the Zion park HQ late that night to check the status again. Nothing. They hadn't found the missing people. They hadn't found the person I loved more than anyone. That jackass who didn't know well enough to stay out of a slot canyon.

I fell into my bed fully clothed, and after three in the morning, I finally passed out from grief.

Late the next morning I awoke to loud knocking on my door accompanied by Sister's frantic barking. I stumbled out to the front door and saw Brian standing there with his brother and an older couple. He had a huge smile on his face.

I opened the door in shock. He leaned over to kiss my cheek and for a minute, I thought I was having a bad dream. He pushed past me to walk into the cabin and his crew followed him in, carrying trays and bags.

"We've come to surprise you with family Thanksgiving," he said with a grin. "You know my brother and these are my parents, Bob and Gina."

My jaw must have been hanging open, not to mention I was in yesterday's clothes with my hair most likely bird-nesting on my head. "Uh... uhmm... Hi?" I stammered.

They all smiled their hellos and bustled to put their packages in the kitchen. They began unpacking food and it smelled amazing, but I was sick to my stomach. Just then I remembered why I was nauseous, and the uncertainty about Teddy came back in a huge, horrible rush. I raced to the bathroom and made it just in time. I retched and dry-heaved and sobbed until there was knocking on the bathroom door.

I sat there miserable with tears streaming down my face. What in the world was I going to do? I couldn't pretend to be friendly to a group of people I didn't want here. I couldn't face this right now on top of everything with Teddy. I washed my face and came out of the bathroom. I mumbled an excuse and escaped into my bedroom. While there, I packed some essentials into a backpack and walked back out into the family room.

"I don't know why you're here, and I'm sorry to be rude, but there is an emergency at the ranger station I have to attend to. I won't be back tonight. Please let yourselves out when you leave."

I called Sister to come with me and we got into my truck. Grief washed over me again.

When I got on the road to the ranger station, I called Josh and asked for news. He said he would call and get an update for me.

A few minutes after I let myself into the ranger station, Josh told me he had gotten word that Teddy was safe. They had heard from him over the phone. Apparently there was a mix-up and he got out before the flood. He left town before realizing he hadn't checked in with the head ranger.

Relief poured through my body in waves. *Oh thank god.* I stumbled back onto a chair and put my head in my hands.

How could I ever live without this man? I thought about what it would take to make a relationship with Teddy work. What would it take to persuade him to try to make a go of it? Quitting my job? Moving to New York? Going on the road with him? I had to remind myself that he wasn't interested in a relationship. But that didn't mean I couldn't start making some changes in my life.

I went over to my desk and started doing some research.

## 29

# TEDDY

When I pulled up to the cabin I didn't see Jamie's truck, but there was an unfamiliar SUV in the drive. I wondered if he'd changed cars or had a loaner for some reason. I hopped out and strode to the front door, nerves jangling in my stomach. I was both terrified and elated at the idea of seeing him on the other side of that door.

I knocked and someone came to the door. My mouth opened to say something to him when I noticed it was a man I'd never seen. *Oh shit.*

What the fuck had I just stumbled into? My brain desperately grasped at the hope that it was his brother visiting for Thanksgiving. Or another ranger who was here with people from work.

"Hi, is Jamie here?"

He looked at me suspiciously and replied with a simple, "No."

I stared at him, waiting for more information. None came. "Do you know where he is?"

"He had a wildlife emergency. One of his animals, I think," he said.

"Do you know when he'll be home?" I asked.

Just then I heard talking behind him and looked past him to see a family sitting around Jamie's table, a big Thanksgiving turkey on a platter in the center. The older woman caught my eye and said, "Brian, who's at the door?"

*Brian? Motherfucking Brian is here playing happy family with Jamie?*

"You're Brian? Jamie's ex?" I asked.

"I'm Brian, his current. And future," he said arrogantly. My gut clenched at the idea it could possibly be true.

Brian looked me over. "And you are?"

"Theodore Kodiak," I replied, not elaborating.

"Well, Mr. Kodiak, we're in the middle of our family Thanksgiving dinner, so if you'll excuse us..."

"Uh... sure... I was just leaving." I got back into the rental vehicle for the drive back to Fairbanks. I had gone numb. A buzzing sound began in my ears and I couldn't think. Brian. Brian and his family having Thanksgiving with my Jamie. It hadn't taken him long to call Brian back and work things out. I was gutted.

My body made its way to Fairbanks, but my heart stayed behind in Denali. I felt empty, exhausted, and lonely. If Jamie wanted to take Brian back, I'd have to let go. It seemed like maybe Brian had made a grand gesture too, bringing his parents to prove to Jamie that he was serious this time.

I didn't remember much of the drive to Fairbanks. A little voice in my head taunted me over and over, *This is why you don't do relationships—too painful.*

When I got to the airport, I learned I wouldn't be able to get flights to New York until the following day. I chose a route that would at least get me to Denver that night and then I could layover there instead of here. I was afraid if I stayed one more hour in Alaska, I'd go running back to Denali on my knees.

When I got to Denver, I rented a hotel room. I ended up sleeping so long I missed my flight home and had to reschedule.

By the time I got home I was completely wiped out. Tired and heartbroken. Mac called and begged me to go with him to the fundraising ball Birdie was in charge of. Maybe that was a sign there was hope for the two of them.

I felt like I had been run over by a truck and then eaten by wolves, but I knew Mac needed me there. I agreed. Friday night I put on my tux and went to his brownstone.

"What's wrong?" he asked me. "You look like shit."

"Smooth talker," I muttered. We walked into the kitchen, and I took over pouring drinks.

I handed one to Mac and he said, "Fess up. Did the man in Alaska kick your ass out?"

"Something like that. I don't really want to talk about it. Between that and the jet lag, I'm barely hanging in there."

"Sorry, Teddy. I appreciate you coming though. It will mean a lot to Birdie."

We both knew I was there for him, not her, but didn't say it. We went to the ball, and I got a drink at the bar by myself. I didn't blame him for ditching me as soon as we got there.

The fundraising gala was a success for the foster home it benefitted. Mac and Birdie reconciled to everyone's relief. The night ended with a celebration of their engagement. Champagne was opened and toasts were given to the happy couple's future.

It took everything I had not to get up and go home right then. I wanted to be by myself to wallow in the fact that my life right now was the opposite of his. But I manned up and played the part. I was truly happy for them; it was just hard helping celebrate in my current mood. Secretly I patted myself on the back for knowing all along they would end up together.

I wanted that special someone. I envied them their relationship. Someone to stand up for you, support you, be waiting at home with loving arms after a bad day. The person who would beam like a proud peacock when you excelled at something, the way Mac had puffed up watching Birdie give her speech at the fundraising gala. A partner who would always call you on your bullshit. I had never wanted it before I met Jamie, but now it seemed like it was all I had ever wanted.

Did Jamie think that was what he'd have with Brian? If so, then it was well and truly hopeless for me. If I couldn't have that connection with Jamie, maybe it was time for me to look for it elsewhere.

I met Cat and her friend Mace at the nightclub one night. I drank way too much and found myself being dry humped on the dance floor by a beautiful woman. For a split second I was tempted. I thought about taking her back to my place and attempting to find the old Teddy again. The Teddy who didn't give a fuck about some guy with an ass freckle in the frozen tundra thousands of miles away. But I couldn't do it. After a minute, I shot her a look of apology and made my way over to Cat to tell her I was leaving.

In the morning I was hungover as hell. I took my sorry ass to my computer to get to work. I planned on pitching a job in Ireland, but instead I found myself typing in Jamie's website address. I posted a question. I had already done it a few times. It was my own little secret act of desperation to connect with him.

Question: *What do you call a group of owls?*

I already knew it was a parliament. But on the off chance he checked his questions that day, I wanted to know a smile was on his face at least for a moment.

Clicking my way onto a travel-booking website, I searched for flights to San Francisco. I should go fight for him. Tell him to ditch Brian and pick me. If I went there though, how would I find him? I opened another tab and searched for Simone Marian, but couldn't find an address or phone number for her. Was I crazy?

I tried to picture what I would say to Jamie's sister or even Jamie himself. What if Brian was there with Jamie? What would happen? Did I really expect to compete with someone he had been involved with on and off for years? Who had proposed and then divorced someone just to be with him? Did I expect Jamie to jump into my arms, send Brian packing, and then... what? We'd shack up happily at Jamie's parents' place for Christmas? I mentally kicked myself for being an idiot.

The following week Mac called to ask what the hell was going on with me.

"Tell me what happened with the animal whisperer."

I told him everything. It had been eating me up, and Mac was my best friend. Waiting for a lecture, I was surprised when he said, "That sucks."

"Tell me about it," I replied.

"Did the ex say where Jamie was?"

"He said he had to go check on an animal."

"Did you believe him?"

"Well, I know Jamie's been working closely integrating a baby beaver into a new family so it made sense.

"Do you love him?"

"*Fuck*, Mac."

"I'm going to go ahead and take that as a yes."

"Mac, I've gotta go. I can't talk about this right now, okay?"

Mac sighed into the phone. "Okay, Teddy. But listen. Birdie and I are planning the wedding. I'll need you to stand up with me. We don't know when or where yet, but it'll be soon. Promise me you'll be there."

"Of course I will, Mac. Let me know when you figure out the dates and I'll block off the time. Tell Birdie that she has giant balls and I'm proud of her."

Mac laughed. "She's right here if you want to tell her yourself."

"Nah, go back to making out. I need to get back to work," I said before hanging up.

I thought about what to get them for a wedding gift. I remembered a photo I had from the shoot with the pikas in Denali. Because it was one of the ones without Jamie in it, I still had it on my computer.

It showed two pikas arm in arm like they were dancing a reel. Their faces were hilarious and they looked like best pals. Because I was taking the shot from the ground below them, they look like they are standing together on a mountaintop with the entire world spread out around them. I thought Mac and Birdie would appreciate it the way I did so I arranged to have a nice original made and framed for them.

## 30

# JAMIE

I spent Thanksgiving night on the sofa in Charlie's office. Sister slept by my side on the floor and I was happy to be able to reach a hand down and nestle it into her fur. In the morning, I headed back to the cabin hoping like hell Brian and his family were gone. They weren't.

They had spent the night there. I assumed his parents slept in my bed since I couldn't picture them climbing the ladder to the loft. The whole thing gave me the creeps. I tried to remember that Alaskans took pride in welcoming strangers in need of shelter, but I couldn't get past the imposition and terrible timing.

I gathered up my courage and opened the front door. They sat around the table having coffee and danish they must have brought.

"Hi, everyone. I'm sorry about yesterday. There was some park business going on, and it was terrible timing. Brian, can I speak with you in private, please?" I looked over at him and then walked back outside.

When he followed me outside, I spoke with a low growl. "You fucking selfish asshole. How dare you show up here unannounced and force your fucking family on me like that."

He tried to interrupt, but I stopped him. "No, shut the fuck up. You are completely insane if you think that bringing family Thanksgiving to my house was a way to prove your loyalty to me. The way you prove your loyalty to someone is to show up on your goddamned wedding day when they are in a fucking tuxedo waiting for you in front of their friends and family. Apparently, I was this close to marrying a bigamist.

"There is not one single reason, justification, or excuse that you could possibly have to make this right, so I don't want you to waste your breath trying. I am so fucking done. Done with you forever, done with wondering 'what if,' done with wishing for a reality that was never truly mine. And you know what? I am one hundred percent happy with my decision.

"There is no fiber of my being that misses you anymore. I am in love with someone else. Loving him makes even considering you a joke. There will be no more talking to me. You will get your family and leave, or I will make a big fucking scene that you will regret."

I was proud my voice had stayed steady the entire time. He opened his mouth to begin, and I pulled out my phone and dialed Josh. When he answered, I looked at Brian as I said, "Hi, Josh, it's Jamie. I have some trespassers here that are causing me some trouble. Can you come help me, please, and bring some other officers with you?"

"For real?" I heard him say.

"No," I said emphatically, then I put my hand over the mouthpiece and said to Brian, "He asked if he needed to bring extra weapons. I said no. Should I change my answer?"

Brian stormed off and told his family it was time to go. I stayed on the phone with Josh, moving farther down my drive to explain the situation.

Josh said he would swing by anyway to make sure they left. I agreed that would be a good idea.

After everyone was gone, I showered and shared Thanksgiving leftovers with Sister. Having the rest of the weekend to myself turned out to be wonderful. I wallowed in self-pity for a while and then came to some decisions. I decided it was time to stop hiding away in Alaska and move somewhere I could meet people and change things up.

Some of my Denali projects could be handled with two or three trips a year. I loved the teaching I did and the work on my website. I thought about taking a college job. Emailing Colorado State and UC Davis, I requested interviews for positions beginning the following fall. That would give me plenty of time to finish my work here and make the big move. I would enjoy being closer to civilization.

After that, I checked the website. Brody had uploaded the new design before Thanksgiving and it was so much more professional. I looked at the questions that had come in. One caught my eye.

*What do you call a group of owls?*

I wrote the answer: "A group of owls is called a parliament. I try to remember how stately and stuffy owls can sometimes appear, and that's how I remember the group name."

That put a smile on my face. How often do you get to refer to a parliament of owls? I moved on to the next question.

*Is it true that a squirrel's front teeth never stop growing? Just the thought gives me the heebie-jeebies.*

My answer: "That is true. Which is one of the reasons why I stay well away from squirrels. And you should too. They might as well be mini vampires."

I shuddered.

I booked my travel to San Francisco before the fares went up and then I emailed the family my itinerary. An hour later, my brother Maverick called.

"Hey, Jamie, how's it going up there?" he said.

"Cold as shit, what else is new?"

"I got your flight info. I can't wait for you to get here. Blue wanted me to tell you Will is already working on setting you up on a date for when you're here." He laughed. The sound was so familiar it brought a wide grin to my face.

"Har, har. No, thanks. I've had enough guy trouble for years, *thankyouverymuch*."

"What's going on?"

"Well, Brian showed up on Thanksgiving Day with his family, a turkey, and the whole fucking thing."

"No shit? Arrogant bastard."

I laughed. "That's what I said. I managed to get him to leave with the help of my park ranger friends."

"Good for you. I'm proud of you. I'm sure it wasn't easy."

"Actually, Mav, it was very easy. I'm over him. Completely."

"That's great. You definitely sound convinced. Why won't you let us set you up then?"

My throat got tight and I lied. "I just want to forget about the whole dating thing for a little while. I've been on some dates recently, and they just haven't panned out. No need to risk a depressingly bad date over the holidays. I don't want to end the year on a suicidal note. I'd much rather end it on a single-guys-rule note."

"If you say so. I'll pick you up at the university after your presentation?"

"Absolutely. I'll text you when I'm done."

"Sounds good, Jamie. Can't wait to see you."

"You too, Mav."

I hung up and took Sister for a long walk. The following week and a half at work was slow. It was always like that when you were anticipating a vacation.

I spent extra time perfecting my lecture and added two of Teddy's photos into the slide deck. I incorporated the snowshoe hare pics. Hopefully that would break the tension in the room if I came off as stuffy.

While I was looking at the photos I thought about how good Teddy was at his job. It made me strangely proud of him. Like I wanted to stand up and show everyone the photos, bragging about him to anyone who would listen. His talent and passion rang out through those images, and I felt frustrated that his desire to protect me had stopped him from pursuing the recognition he deserved for the images. I wondered if he had selected a different photograph to submit to the prestigious competition.

The day finally arrived when I dropped Sister at the neighbors' with a big hug and kiss, and then stopped by FedEx in Fairbanks before parking at the airport.

## 31

# TEDDY

December is a complete bitch when you're over thirty, single, and have just lost your one remaining parent. Being single had never bothered me much because I loved the freedom, but the holidays were the only time when loneliness snuck in and left me feeling unsure. This year it was a hundred times worse. Everywhere I fucking looked, I saw happy couples and happy families enjoying the holiday festivities together.

One morning, after sending a request for the Ireland shoot, I checked email and found a message from Elkhorn Slough National Estuarine Research Reserve in Monterey, California. They requested special images of the baby sea otters they had. I replied I could do it any day except Christmas Eve or Day.

Later that afternoon I got a call from someone at Elkhorn Slough confirming they could do it the day after Christmas. We confirmed the details of my fees and expenses, and then I called the airline to arrange my flights.

I called Mac.

"Maclean," he answered, sounding distracted.

"Hey, Mac, it's me. Are we still planning on volunteering at Sunshine House on Christmas morning? I got a gig in California the day after Christmas and I was toying with the idea of going to San Francisco from there."

I could hear the sound of him closing his office door and I appreciated his willingness to stop what he was doing anytime I needed to talk.

"Yes to volunteering. What's in San Francisco?" he asked.

"I was thinking about trying to find Jamie," I said pathetically. "He's going to be in San Francisco for Christmas with his family."

"Have you talked to him since the Thanksgiving thing?"

"No," I replied dejectedly. "And I'm going out of my fucking mind. I can't stop thinking about him. Don't give me a hard time right now. I'm seriously fucked up about this."

"I'm not going to. I can tell it's eating you up. Do you know for sure he's back with his ex?"

"Mac, c'mon. His whole damned family was sitting around his table for the Thanksgiving meal."

"Right. So what were you hoping will happen in San Francisco exactly? He sees you and realizes he wants you more than his ex? You're the guy who has convinced him that you have neither the time nor inclination for a serious relationship. How will he believe you've changed?"

My chest was so tight with anxiety that I stood up to pace. "I don't know. What the fuck do I do?" I hoped to hell my desperation wasn't quite as pronounced in my voice as I suspected it was.

Mac thought in silence a moment before answering. "Well, if he's back with Brian, you need to get him away from the dude long enough to plead your case. Maybe wait until he's back in Alaska and Brian is back wherever he lives."

"I'll think about it."

"Good idea. If it's meant to be, it will be. Trust me. I had patience with Birdie and now I get to spend the rest of my life with her. Hang in there, okay? You should spend some extra time in California and get away from this shitty New York weather."

"No kidding, I'm already ready for a break from the cold," I admitted.

"I know what you mean. It's fucking freezing here today. I was going to go for a run in the park but am too chickenshit to do it in this crap," Mac said.

"Yep. And I'm headed out later tonight to help Jenna move some big pieces to a gallery. Gonna freeze my balls off."

Mac hissed, "I'd offer to help but..."

"But you'd rather spend your winter night curled up with a fiery redhead?" I teased.

"Yes, please," he begged.

"Give her a kiss for me. A big, hot, juicy one."

"Fuck you. But consider it done."

When confirming what time Jenna wanted me at her place, I offered to bring food. She said yes, and to bring enough for four. Good. Maybe we'd have help.

Brody was there with a guy named Rocco. I couldn't tell if they were dating or just friends. Either way I was secretly glad the fourth person was a guy instead of Cat. Some of Jenna's pieces were huge and this guy Rocco was built like an gym rat.

After we were done, the guys left and I walked Jenna back to her loft. She asked what I was doing for Christmas and I told her I was spending it with Mac and Birdie but that I was flying out Christmas day for a job in California. She handed me a small wrapped gift and told me to open it at Christmas.

We hugged and wished each other happy everything, promising to plan a delayed New Year celebration after I got back. After I got back to my apartment, I sat down at my computer.

There was an email from the Gramling Group confirming receipt of my entry and inviting me to the awards ceremony in Hawaii on December 30. *What?* I hadn't sent in my entry.

I thought about the submission packet I had left on the kitchen table in Jamie's cabin. Could he have sent it? Would he have done that? I thought he didn't want those photos distributed. I had to ask him. I couldn't very well email Gramling back and say I didn't enter the competition when I wasn't really sure if I had or not.

I needed to know, even though I had promised myself not to

contact him. Not sure I could bear to hear the sound of his voice, I chose to text him instead.

**Teddy:** *Hi stranger. I just got an email from the Gramling Group confirming my submission. Was that your doing?*

**Jamie:** *Yes. That photo deserves recognition, Teddy. Plus, the inset disclaimer was perfect. Thank you for doing that.*

**Teddy:** *I don't know what to say. Thank you.*

**Jamie:** *You're welcome.*

**Teddy:** *They want me in Hawaii for the awards ceremony in a week.*

**Jamie:** *Maybe that's a good sign. Fingers crossed.*

**Teddy:** *Are you at your parents' for Christmas?*

**Jamie:** *Yes. It's been great spending time with them. You're never going to believe the name of a woman my brother Mav works with. Lola.*

**Teddy:** *You're kidding?*

**Jamie:** *Not kidding. I laughed so hard and told him about your Lola.*

There was an elephant in the room and I couldn't help but poke it. I had to know.

**Teddy:** *Did Brian come with you?*

**Jamie:** *WTF? Why would Brian be here?*

**Teddy:** *I thought you were back together?*

**Jamie:** *Why would you think that?*

**Teddy:** *He and his parents were at your cabin for Thanksgiving.*

A moment later, the phone rang in my hand, making me jump. It was Jamie. I quickly answered with a shaking hand.

"Hi," I said.

"How the hell do you know about Thanksgiving?" he demanded.

It was so good to hear the sound of his voice that I couldn't say anything for a second.

"Teddy, answer me," he demanded.

"I… I was there. At your cabin. He answered the door," I admitted, closing my eyes in embarrassment.

His voice shouted through the phone, "You were there? In Alaska? At Thanksgiving?"

"Yes," I said.

"Why, dammit? Why were you there? And why didn't you fucking tell me? Why didn't *he* tell me?"

"I think we both know why *he* didn't tell you. I didn't tell you because I was trying to surprise you. Something happened in Zion when I was there, and I just… I just wanted to see you after that."

He blew out a big breath. "I know about the flood in the slot canyon, Teddy. Our office got the news while you were on the missing list. I almost went out of my mind. On the one hand, I was relieved you were all right. On the other, I wanted to shake you for being in a slot canyon in the first place. What were you fucking thinking?

"I was fucking thinking I was terrified," I admitted.

"Well, join the club. I was terrified for you for almost twenty-four hours," he snapped. "Wait, that was Thanksgiving Day. I was at the ranger station. That's when you came?"

"Yes."

"I was at the ranger station thinking you were dead and you were standing at my cabin? God, Teddy. I don't even know what to think right now. This is so fucked up."

Gathering up my courage, I asked the big question, "So, you're not back together with Brian?"

"Hell no. Not that it's any of your business, because, in case you don't recall, *you left*. You don't do relationships, remember? Why the hell do you care? Because you couldn't get your Thanksgiving fuck?"

He was good and mad now. I knew I needed to proceed with caution to avoid fucking it up even further.

"No, that's not it, Jamie. I..." How did I tell him I was there because I wanted more? "I..."

My throat tightened, clogged with all the words I wanted to say but was too terrified to let escape.

"Goddammit, Teddy, say something," Jamie snapped.

"I showed up there to tell you I wanted to be with you," I blurted.

"Well, that's just great. You're really good at showing up, but you know what? You always *leave*," he yelled.

That was it. He'd pushed my button and I was pissed now too. "Yeah? Well, at least I keep showing up. I'm always the one coming to you, because you're scared. You're so fucking scared of something ending you're too afraid to even let it start."

"Go to hell, Theodore Kodiak," Jamie seethed.

I wanted to tell him I was already there, but Jamie had hung up.

## 32

# JAMIE

I hung up and joined Maverick in the living room. He asked if I was ready to go and I told him I was, even though my heart thundered out of my chest.

"Who were you talking to?" he asked.

"A guy named Teddy," I answered, shrugging on my coat. "We met in Denali a couple of months ago."

Mav looked over at me. "Clearly there's more to the story."

I blew out a breath of exasperation. "Not really. I thought there might be, but it turns out he's not a relationship guy. I don't want to talk about it right now." I gave him the look that one sibling gives another to tell them not to push.

"Understood. Then my goal is to get you tipsy tonight so you start blabbing."

I punched him in the shoulder. "Nice, bro. Real nice."

He shoved me lightly in the shoulder to push me out the door and get me back for the punch.

When we got to his friend Kip's apartment, there were already tons of people there. There was music playing and someone had strung little white lights everywhere. A small decorated tree was next to the television in the main living room and there were big sliding glass doors leading onto a terrace.

We headed into the kitchen for a drink when Kip saw us. He shouted, "Hey, if it isn't my favorite brotherly duo!" before indicating a cooler filled with beer and ice. Mav grabbed two and handed me one after twisting the tops off.

I chatted for a little while with Kip's brother Hal, whom I had met the other night at happy hour. He told me about his job as an attorney at a downtown firm, and I was struck by how different his life was from mine. He wore suits every day in the big city and interacted with people for a living. I wore muddy snow pants and interacted with rodents. It was like we were speaking different languages.

A beautiful blond woman walked up to say hello to Hal. She hadn't been at happy hour, so I didn't know who she was. Hal introduced her as Lola, and I chuckled.

"What's so funny?" Lola asked, smiling.

"Nothing, it's nice to meet you. I'm sorry. I just have a friend who dated a woman named Lola and your name reminded me of a funny story."

"Well, now you have to share it." She laughed. "I always enjoy a good Lola story."

"He was dating her for a little while until the woman left him for the lead singer of a Kinks tribute band." I sipped my beer, still smiling.

"You know Teddy?" she asked with a twinkling smile, and my jaw dropped.

My face flushed Christmas red and I looked at her in disbelief.

"You're Teddy's Lola?" I squeaked.

"Not really. We never really started anything serious. I thought maybe he wasn't that into me, so I made up that story to piss him off." She winked at me.

"So the thing about the Kinks is complete bullshit? He's told that story a thousand times."

She snorted. "Good for him. Glad he got something out of it. As bummed as I was that nothing came of it, I still wish him well. He's a nice guy. Hot as hell. How do you know him?"

I hedged, "He came to Denali a few months ago to do a photo shoot in the park where I work."

She nodded. "He takes gorgeous photos. But do you know that he won't hang any of them up in his own apartment? It's like even though he's an arrogant prick on the outside, he's modest on the inside. I don't know. I never really understood him. Do you keep in touch with him since the photo shoot?"

*Well, how the hell do I answer that? He showed up, I jumped his bones, then I accidentally started falling for him, then he apparently showed up again just when I thought he was dead.*

I blew out a breath. "Not really."

"Well, if you talk to him tell him I said hello. Feel free to let him keep believing that story about me and the band," she said with a smile and a wink.

The rest of the party passed in an enjoyable few hours getting to know Mav's friends better and enjoying being among smart, successful people my age. I realized if I moved to a bigger town, I could have more of a social life like this. The idea excited me, and I started to realize how much I'd been missing.

We got home so late that Mav went straight to bed at our parents' house instead of going back to his place.

The next day was Christmas Eve. I woke up to the smell of coffee and the sounds of Christmas music coming from the living room. Walking out in my pajamas, I saw Mom sitting at the kitchen table reading her e-reader while Mav did something with Mom's laptop. Probably fixing something she'd messed up.

After I finished my first cup of coffee, my sister, Simone, wandered in wearing Christmas pajamas covered in dogs and cats dressed like Santa.

"Hey, baby girl, merry Christmas Eve," I said, standing up to pour her some coffee. "Sit."

Once she'd had a few sips, she asked me how my love life was doing. I was never any good at keeping secrets from my family so I spilled everything. Teddy, Josh, Operation Get Fucked failing, and Brian's aborted attempt to reconcile.

She, Maverick, and Mom listened intently and didn't offer their opinions. When they finally asked what I was going to do about Teddy, I said I wasn't going to do anything. He wasn't the settling-down type and he lived thousands of miles away. What was there to do? Nothing.

In an attempt to change the focus off me, I asked Simone if she'd started dating again since her ex-fiancé ditched her four months before.

"Fuck no. I'm done with relationships. Men can take a long walk off a short pier as far as I'm concerned."

My mom gave me a look that silently begged me to talk sense into Simone. I tried my best.

"Baby girl, don't let one cheating jackass steal a happy future from you. You are going to find an amazing man who will make you laugh and make you feel like a million bucks. Someone who will cross an ocean just to be with you and who will stand in a crowded room and only see you. You have to put yourself back out there though. They're not all manwhores terrified of commitment," I urged.

Simone looked at me with a smirk. "Oh, kind of like a man who would fly across a continent for you three times?"

Well, fuck.

"That's different," I began, trying desperately to figure out how it was different.

"How?" She smirked. Maverick snorted into his coffee mug.

"Never mind how. Now, what's for breakfast?"

Simone rolled her eyes.

While we chatted over coffee and some scones Mom had set out, Dad wandered into the kitchen fully dressed.

"I just finished putting all the presents into the car. I figured we'd leave in a couple of hours for Napa," Dad said. "Rebecca, will you please come help me figure out what I'm missing?"

"Sure, hon," Mom said, standing. She ruffled Mav's hair on her way out of the kitchen.

"I'll go wake up Dante," Mav said. "Otherwise we might forget his quiet ass and leave him behind by accident."

When Simone and I were alone in the kitchen she gave me that look. The sister look that says, *Cut the crap*.

"Fuck, Simone. I'm in love with Teddy."

"No shit."

"What do I do?" I asked.

"Fight for him."

"I'm too scared of being hurt again. I just can't do it."

"You will when you're ready, Jamie."

I finished getting ready and rode to Napa with Simone and Maverick. We met the enormous Marian crew at Tristan's vineyard lodge where we were all staying for Christmas. The lodge was closed to the public for the two days we were all going to be together. A huge Christmas tree sat decorated in the lobby of the lodge with comfortable sofas repositioned all around the tree and the big lobby fireplace. Pete and Ginger's girls had taken charge of gathering everyone's gifts to place under the fat tree. When we all left the lodge that evening to walk to the estate house for dinner, the anticipation for Christmas morning was palpable.

Tristan and Blue had planned a big Christmas Eve feast and it didn't disappoint. Delicious food and wine together with the raucous company of the large Marian clan made the night fantastic. At the end of the night, Tristan proposed to Blue.

It was such a sweet, romantic moment. Blue and Tristan were clearly meant for each other, and I found myself envious of their connection. How had I spent the past eight months denying my desire for a life partner? I had always wanted intimacy and companionship. Commitment and love with someone who adored me and whom I adored more than anyone else.

Was I ever going to be ready to risk my heart for that again? What would it take? Meeting someone who I thought was the love of my life? Done. Being with someone who took my breath away and made me feel cherished? Done. If I couldn't risk a broken heart to go after Theodore Kodiak, then I might as well plan on living a lonely life from here on out.

## 33

# TEDDY

Early Christmas morning alone in my apartment was pretty shitty. I had several presents from friends and had even ordered myself some new camera equipment I'd had my eye on so I would have something to play with after I got home from volunteering.

I opened the gift Jenna had sent with me; it was a lens hood she had hand-painted with a snake slithering around in a bed of flowers. Along the body of the snake it said, "Never be afraid." My friends knew me better than anyone in the world, and Jenna had knocked it out of the park with that one. I knew it wasn't just about my fear of snakes. It was about not letting fear keep me from what I wanted. A message in which the timing couldn't have been better.

By the time I returned home from a full morning at the foster home, handing out gifts, putting together toys, and generally making myself useful, I was in a much better frame of mind. I was feeling grateful for my life and the fact I'd had my dad for as long as I had. No matter what mistakes he'd made, he'd loved me and stayed with me.

I gathered my bags for California and headed to the airport to catch my flight for my next job. After getting through security and finding my gate, I found myself navigating to Jamie's website on my phone. I couldn't help but post more questions. It was like a stupid desperation to connect with him somehow.

Question: *My buddy said that a group of cats is called a clowder, but I told him that's clams he's thinking about. Which one of us is right?*

Question: *What is the name of a group of hamsters?*

The next morning I arrived at Elkhorn Slough early and got to work. The sea otters weren't very interested in being photographed at first, so it was a long day. Baby sea otters are the cutest fucking things you've ever seen, so it wasn't a trial to capture them once they were visible and energized. They rode on their mothers' bellies and snuggled them. Luckily this wasn't a job that was serious enough to require a wetsuit and submersion in the water. I got the shots I needed from land and from a kayak and a small dinghy they had available.

I made my way back to the hotel before flying to Maui the following day.

# 34

# JAMIE

It was Christmas night and I'd gone back to my room in the lodge to grab a sweater before joining the family for dessert.

I couldn't get Teddy's words out of my head.

*You're so fucking scared of something ending you're too afraid to even let it start.*

I remembered Teddy's harassing emails and texts before we ever met. Teddy wasn't the kind of guy who gave up when he wanted something. He had pushed and pushed to get me to agree to let him come to Alaska. Even when I refused, he showed up anyway.

Then he showed up again. Then he showed up a third time. That wasn't the behavior of someone looking for a one-night stand. If he wanted a quick fuck, he could have any number of men in New York or any other bar in any other city. Why me?

Why fly all the way to Denali three times in as many months to see me? The Thanksgiving visit sure as hell wasn't about photography, because he'd already promised not to use the photos he took on his earlier visits. So what was it?

I remembered the morning he left my cabin after the last time we were together. He had said he was falling for me too, more than he ever had with anyone. And then he showed up at my place for Thanksgiving. After he knew he was falling for me.

All these thoughts jammed together in my head as I joined the family in the lobby around the tree.

Pete's girls were busy setting up train tracks all around us with my brother Thad's help. Aunt Tilly, Tristan's granny, and her wife, Irene, played bridge with Maverick at a nearby table. For some reason, Mav always ended up being the dummy and they made him fetch drink refills and seconds on dessert.

Tristan's parents sat quietly together on a sofa taking it all in. They'd been very good sports so far. It wasn't easy for Mrs. Alexander to accept Tristan's relationship with a man, but she seemed to be keeping her mouth closed to the best of her ability. Tristan's dad, on the other hand, had been wonderful, opening up to our family and going out of his way to show his support to his son.

Mom started asking Blue and Tristan about wedding plans. Blue glanced at Simone and me before speaking.

"Mom, we've decided we might just elope to save everyone the hassle and stress," Blue said.

Simone's face darkened. "Absolutely not. Just because Jamie and I had a bad year for weddings doesn't mean you two should miss out on your special day."

"I agree," I added. "We all want to be there. We were here when you got together and when you got engaged. We want to be there when you make it official."

Jude sat on the fireplace hearth strumming his guitar quietly. He looked up with a grin. "Plus, I hear there are some gnarly T-shirts being made, and I can't wait to see what they say."

Tristan choked on his coffee and turned to Blue. "You asshole. You did not tell him about that."

"Hush," Blue said, laughing. "Never you mind about the T-shirts, babe."

Pete snorted. "Now you have to let us all come."

I noticed Jude's bodyguard, Derek Wolfe, chuckling in the background where he sat against the wall. He'd been with my brother for at least eight months and it was always a trip to catch him doing anything other than staring stoically.

Tristan thought for a minute. "Another idea would be to just all go somewhere together, like a vacation, and get married while we're there. That way it's not all about this big wedding plan, but everyone will still be together."

"I like that idea, and the sooner, the better," Blue said. "But where?"

"It would probably work if we did it right away before the holidays were over," Pete said. "Maybe anytime between now and the second week in January."

My heart sped up until I could feel it slamming against my chest. "I'm not available December 30. I'm going to be in Maui," I blurted, surprising myself more than anyone.

Everyone turned to look at me. Blue tilted his head with a smirk. "Is that right?"

I could feel my face flush, only then remembering I'd mentioned the Gramling event in Hawaii to some of my siblings the night before. Instead of walking it back, I sat up straighter. "Yes. I'm going to go to the Gramling Awards whether Teddy wants me there or not."

"Well, good for you, brother," Jude said, grinning. I noticed Maverick wink at me and flash me a thumbs up.

Tristan looked at Blue with a smile. Excitement lit up Blue's face. "What do you say, beautiful? Want to get married in Maui on New Year's Eve?"

"Absolutely. I can't think of a better plan," Blue agreed before looking at everyone else sitting around the room. "What does everyone else think?"

Simone studied me with a silly grin. "Sun, sand, love... celebrating new beginnings. What's not to like?"

Mom caught Dad's eye. "We insist on paying, but it's such short notice. Will everyone be able to make it? Jude, honey, what's your schedule like?"

"I can make it work," Jude said.

Mom frowned. "But weren't you supposed to be in—?"

"I wouldn't miss this for the world," Jude interrupted. He looked straight at me with a grin. In fact, almost everyone seemed to be staring at me instead of the happy couple. I squirmed, cheeks burning. Was I that obvious?

"We'll all be able to make it work," Simone said. "Marians will do anything for love. Plus, third time's a charm, right?"

We all looked around at each other. Those of us in school still had time off until mid-January. Those of us with jobs could work around it if it was for something as important as a Marian wedding.

We spent the rest of the evening making plans. Jude grabbed his laptop from his room and made some calls. His assistant arranged to charter a jet leaving a few days later from SFO to Maui, and he called a musician friend of his who had a house on the island to ask advice on finding last-minute rentals.

The following day, everyone returned to their respective homes to pack for Hawaii. Excitement built, and Mom was in her element, coming up with ideas for little surprises for Blue and Tristan.

Only one family member wouldn't be able to make it to the wedding on such short notice: Tristan's brother, John. The Alexander brothers weren't exactly getting along these days and the decision was best for everyone involved. Especially Simone who was relieved to find out she wasn't going to have to face her ex so soon after breaking up.

Everything seemed to be falling perfectly into place. The only thing left to do was wait for the big day to arrive.

Three days later, I landed at the airport in Maui in a cold sweat of nerves. When the warm sun of the islands hit me it thawed out the winter I didn't realize was still deep in my bones. I felt lighter once the sun soaked into my skin. The clear blue sky was surpassed only by the incredible blue waters of the ocean.

Never having been there, I had no idea Maui was as beautiful as it looked in photographs. Absently, I wondered if Teddy had brought his camera equipment. Then I shook my head with a laugh and realized of course he would have. He probably never went anywhere without it.

There were several town cars waiting for us outside the airport building to take us to the estate. We spent the afternoon settling in and had a casual dinner by the pool that night. My nerves were getting the better of me, so I turned in early. I couldn't stop thinking about Teddy, wondering if he'd already arrived. Wondering where he was staying. Wondering if he was also thinking about me or if he'd moved on.

The next day Simone and I went shopping in Maui.

We wandered into several stores and treated ourselves to new bathing suits and some other goodies. Spending time with Simone after the shitty year we'd had was really special, and I was secretly glad we had that chance to hang out just the two of us. Plus, she did a good job distracting me from the Gramling award ceremony that night.

By the time we got back to the house, everyone was lounging by the pool. We changed clothes and joined them until it was time for me to shower and make my way to the conference hotel where the award ceremony was.

I wore my most formal suit. My brother Griff had managed to get me a press pass for the event. Officially, I was covering the ceremony as a freelance journalist, which meant I couldn't be there for the dining portion of the evening, but I could stand in the back while they gave out the awards at the end.

When I arrived and was allowed into the ballroom, my stomach lurched like a greenhorn on a crab boat in the Bering Sea. I couldn't see Teddy anywhere, and I wasn't sure if I wanted him to see me.

I'd spend so much time focused on actually getting there that I wasn't sure what exactly I was going to do after that. All I knew was I needed to be there for him. Win or lose, he shouldn't have to be alone for this. He was about to be recognized in some manner by the most prestigious panel of wildlife photography judges in the world, and he deserved to have support from someone who loved him, whether he knew it or not.

## 35

# TEDDY

By the time the day of the awards ceremony arrived, I'd spent three days alternately lounging in the sun and exploring local wildlife with my camera. On the spur of the moment, I even did a little shopping.

I'd tried to get Jamie out of my head, but knowing Brian was no longer in the picture made me wonder why the hell I didn't just show up again to convince Jamie to give me a chance. Despite knowing I should let him make the next move, I decided I couldn't wait any longer.

Unsure how long I wanted to stay in Hawaii after the ceremony, I finally decided I would fly straight to Denali from Maui to convince him I was ready to commit. My heart was already his, and living without him was killing me.

The night of the ceremony, I put on the tuxedo I had brought and wished for the hundredth time I had someone to take with me to the ceremony. I knew many people from the industry who would be there, but it was different having someone you cared about there to share it with you. I pictured Jamie all dressed up, arm tucked in mine as we walked into the ballroom and I almost turned around right then to head to the airport.

Screw the award, I wanted Jamie. But I forced myself to take a deep breath and focus. Jamie would be pissed if he found out I'd ditched the ceremony to go after him. Plus, there weren't any flights that would get me to Denali tonight anyway. I'd already checked.

Being invited to the ceremony meant I was at least a runner-up for the prize. There were several levels of awards, so there was no way to know what kind of mention I would receive. If I didn't win the Gramling, then I would try again the following year. I knew it was something I would keep striving for in order to keep getting better at what did.

I walked into the ballroom and greeted several of the magazine photo editors I knew. The top entries for the prizes were framed and hanging around the room for everyone to study. I couldn't help the pride I felt when I saw the image of Jamie smiling with the baby beavers playing on him. My heart raced and my chest tightened. God, he looked so happy and alive in that shot. So at home surrounded by his animals. The disclaimer inset was included just as I had insisted in the paperwork. As more and more people saw the photo, they sought me out to congratulate me on a magical composition and capture.

When we sat for the dinner, I was pleasantly surprised to be sitting near the front next to a photographer I'd worked with before named KJ Harrow. She was bubbly and a little nutty, which was my favorite combination. After giving her a big kiss and hug, we caught up on industry gossip and she told me how her two kids were doing in middle school in Dallas.

When it was time for the prize announcements, the room hushed. As each prize level was announced, my stomach tightened until we were down to the nitty-gritty.

"And finally, the coveted Gramling Prize for Wildlife Photography grand prize winner is... Theodore Kodiak for the photo titled *Trusting Him*."

I sat there, stunned for a moment before KJ nudged my shoulder. Standing up, I smiled appreciatively and made my way to the stage to accept the award. I couldn't believe it had happened. If only my parents had been there to see it, or Jamie or Mac or anyone else I loved.

When I shook the presenter's hand and took the plaque from him, I turned to the room to say a few words of acceptance. It would be a lie if I said I hadn't thought about what I'd say if I won, but I hadn't prepared any kind of formal speech. I glanced up at the winning photo of Jamie projected onto a massive screen behind the podium.

Suddenly, I knew exactly what I wanted to say.

"The Gramling Prize is an honor that truly humbles me. Thank you so much for the recognition of the photograph, but in this case, the credit goes to the subject rather than the photographer. When I took this photo, I knew it was one of the best days of my life, but I didn't realize until later the magic of this particular shot.

"Sometimes photographs tell you the truth. You look at the moment you were lucky enough to capture and see your very heart reflected back in the image. In that way, photography offers permanence. Moments, like relationships, can be fleeting, but a photograph captures the moment and sets it in stone."

I paused and looked back down at the picture framed inside the plaque. Remembering what it had been like that afternoon, the chill in the air and the way Jamie smiled at me, not even needing to tell me to be patient for the kits to come out, that it would be worth it. And it had been.

"The moment I captured in this photo turned out to be a collection of love stories. The love between Dr. Jamie Marian and the animals he looks out for in the wild, the love of a photographer pursuing the elusive magical shot, the love between two beaver kits brought together by chance, and finally, the love that jumps out and grabs me now every time I look at the photo. My love for Jamie."

I paused, letting the statement hand in the air for a moment before continuing. "Jamie was hesitant to let me photograph him, and I didn't understand at first. Then I thought it was because he didn't want people to get the idea that it was okay to approach animals without proper training. Which, by the way, he'd kick my ass if I didn't make sure you knew to always be cautious approaching wild animals. Even the animal whisperer himself carries bear spray."

At that, everyone chuckled, and I smiled.

"But now I think I understand the real reason Jamie was hesitant. Because the real photographs, the ones that suck you in, are the ones where you catch a glimpse of truth in the person being photographed.

"I didn't realize it at the time, but this was the gift that Jamie gave me. The chance to see that in him. I've learned that being in love with your subject changes your definition of beauty in those fleeting moments. The way the sun lights up their best features, the way their body language changes as they interact with their surroundings. The patience you have for dimples you know are just waiting for the right moment to show themselves. And the instinctive knowledge you have of when to hit the shutter release to catch them being their truest self.

"It's a difficult thing to open yourself up to that kind of vulnerability, to allow someone else to not only see the real you, but to capture it and make it permanent for others to see as well."

I felt the back of my throat burn, and I hesitated, taking a sip of water. I needed to do this, to make myself as vulnerable as Jamie had. I owed it to him and to myself to tell the world just how important this man was to me. Because he was the real reason I'd won this prize.

"If Jamie were here tonight, I would want to thank him for giving me the honor of his trust. I would also want to tell him I fell stupidly in love with him, which led me to take the best photograph of my career. Thanks again to all of you for the highest photography honor I've ever dreamed of," I finished, holding up the plaque again.

As I walked off of the stage, several people reached out to shake my hand or slap me on the back. Everyone was clapping and there was motion rippling through the crowd at the back of the room. As the presenter wrapped up the ceremony and folks got up to leave, I saw heads turn my direction and I wondered what was going on.

Then I saw a couple step aside revealing Jamie Marian standing a few tables away. I blinked, not sure I was seeing right.

It was too good to be true.

People always said Hawaii was like paradise, but when I'd landed a few days earlier, it had seemed to be missing something. Not quite paradise. Not until I saw Jamie being nudged through the crowd by people who obviously recognized him from the photograph.

My Jamie.

If it really was him, then my life had just gone from an old sepia print to a high-definition full-color showpiece.

His eyes were wide and he looked terrified, like a wild animal getting ready to bolt.

I smiled the most genuine smile I had ever felt. "Hey there, Baby Dall."

He hesitated for a moment and then crashed into me, causing me to stumble back a step as I laughed and caught him against my chest. I smelled his familiar coconut shampoo and buried my nose in his hair to soak in the scent.

I pulled back from Jamie and saw his gorgeous face, eyes shiny from unshed tears. My hands came up to cup his cheeks and I looked into those eyes, searching, trying to determine what he was thinking.

"*Teddy*," he said.

"Jamie, what are you doing here?" I asked incredulously.

His smile faltered and I quickly backpedaled. "No, no, I mean thank god you're here. I'm so happy you're here. I'm just surprised. I mean, how did you get here? How did you know where to come? Sorry, I'm blabbering now."

Jamie's beautiful lips slid into a smile again. "I wasn't about to miss seeing you win your first Gramling."

## 36

# JAMIE

I couldn't believe Teddy's words during his acceptance speech. My mouth hung open and I stood transfixed, feeling my eyes fill when he got to the part about being in love with me. He'd stood up there and described his passion for photography in a way that made it sound like a love letter to me. The man put his heart on his sleeve in front of a room filled with his peers.

As he spoke, heads turned toward me, recognizing me as the subject of the night's top photo.

Once Teddy's speech came to an end, people began encouraging me forward with smiles and pats on the back. I hadn't really known if I was going to approach him during the event or how I would tell him I was there, but the decision was taken out of my hands as the crowd pushed me toward his table.

When he called me Baby Dall, all bets were off. I was in his arms before my brain even registered the endearment, and holding on to him was the best thing that had happened to me since I'd woken up in his arms the day he left me to go to Zion. The day he walked out to spare my heart. As if sparing my heart had even been possible.

After I told him I'd never miss his big win, he leaned over and whispered in my ear. "Stay with me?"

I nodded and gave him a smile of reassurance. Stay with him. If only he knew.

I wanted to stay with him for the rest of my life.

He put his arm around my waist and held me close while he accepted congratulations from everyone and introduced me. It became clear that, while he was certainly being lauded as the photographer of the year, I was also somewhat of a celebrity in the room. The attention was unnerving and I began to feel uneasy. When Teddy's arm wasn't around my waist, his hand held mine with our fingers laced together. Having him physically connected to me anchored me throughout the rest of the evening.

When it was finally time to say our goodbyes, I trembled with nerves. Teddy handed off the award and a bag of goodies from the event to a bellhop to put in his room. We walked out the conference section of the hotel and along the paths through the palm trees dotted around the pool area.

I led Teddy toward the beach and we stopped to take off our shoes and socks before stepping onto the sand. We hadn't spoken since we left the crowd of people at the ceremony, but we automatically found each other's hands again.

I was nervous, not knowing where to begin when we spoke at the same time.

"Teddy, I—" I said.

"Sweetheart—" he began. We started laughing.

"Me first," I said, wishing like hell my hands would stop shaking. "On the flight here I thought about all the things I wanted to say to you, but really it boils down to one thing. I'm in love with you." I saw Teddy's eyes widen and I thought, not for the first time, about how ruggedly handsome he was. I tried to ignore the thudding in my chest.

Teddy didn't say anything and I started to freak out a little. "I don't want to scare you or pressure you or anything. I know you said what you said on stage, but you didn't know I was there when you said it, and well, lord knows I didn't see this coming when we met, and I know you don't—" His lips crushing mine stopped my stupid babbling.

The kiss was molten passion, all tongue and heat. He devoured my mouth and all I could think of was wanting to feel that mouth devouring me all over. I brought my hands to his hips as he stepped closer to me. His own hands were on either side of my neck, and I felt his thumbs graze my cheeks.

Fire burned deep in my gut and blood rushed in my ears. I heard Teddy groan into my mouth as one of his hands brushed my hair back and then smoothed its way down my back to pull me in closer. I dragged my own hands from his hips up his ribs to his chest, loving the feel of smooth fabric over over curvy muscle. He groaned again and pulled away from me.

"You're killing me, sweetheart," he panted. I leaned in to kiss him again but he held up his hand to stop me. "Hang on, let me catch my breath," he said, smiling.

He paused for a moment before taking my hands in both of his. "My turn to say something, okay?" I nodded.

"Jamie, you asked me why I came to your cabin at Thanksgiving, and I didn't answer you fully. I was scared you wouldn't believe me if I told you. The truth is I'm in love with you. I love you so much I can't think straight without you. There's no place on earth that feels like home to me without you there.

"The idea I could ever be happy alone in the world again after being with you is incomprehensible. And honestly, I never thought in a million years I would find someone who made it all come together for me. But I have.

"I'm not perfect, and I'll probably disappoint you somehow at some point, but I would really love a chance to prove myself wrong. I will do anything to be with you. Move to Denali? Done. Stop traveling? No problem. You name it, I'll do it. Just give me a chance to prove to you that I am all in."

"How do I know you won't leave again?" I asked, looking down at our bare feet in the sand. I wanted to be sure of him.

He leaned toward me again and put his finger under my chin. "Because since I met you three months ago I have flown over fifteen thousand miles and thirty hours just to be in the same room with you. Because even when I left, I came back. And I will keep coming back until you feel secure in the knowledge that I am not leaving you ever again."

His hand came up to caress the side of my face. "Sweetheart, I'm not Brian. Please don't punish me because of his stupid decisions. If it weren't for him, I would propose to you this minute. But I won't. Because I don't ever want you to worry that I would put you in that situation. If you decide one day that you want to get married, say the word and we will go immediately together. No waiting for me in a church. I'm ready to marry you right this minute if you will have me, but if you don't ever want to make it official, I'll be happy just being by your side."

I stood still while I thought about his words and about the last time I had trusted a promise like that. Was I really going to let old fears slip back in? Hell no. This incredible, sweet man was handing me his heart and I was going to hold on to it for the rest of my life.

My arms went around him and I kissed him for all he was worth. Teddy broke the kiss long enough to whisper in my ear, "I love you Jamie. So much. Please say you'll have me."

I pulled back and looked him in the eyes. "Of course I will. I love you so much it makes my eyes leaky."

Dropping his hand and stepping back from him, I noticed Teddy's brows furrow. Then I got down on one knee.

His eyes widened.

*Here goes nothing.*

I held out a little platinum ring on the tip of my index finger. "Did you mean what you said about getting married?"

I'd never seen him cry before that night. His eyes were full, and the tears began to reflect like little crystals hanging from his eyelashes. In that moment, I wished Teddy could have seen himself the way I saw him. I wished his camera could have captured that magical moment where my entire future was written as bright as day in salty tears spilling down his gorgeous face.

# 37

# TEDDY

I was speechless. Jamie Marian had gotten up the nerve to propose to me just months after someone had left him at the altar and shattered his trust. I wasn't sure I'd ever known someone so strong.

"Oh fuck yes," I exhaled in a rush before grabbing him and lifting him off his feet into a huge embrace. My mouth landed on his, taking him by surprise. As I kissed him, I felt the smile on his face and his giant sigh of relief.

We laughed against each other's lips and I spun him around on the beach, leaning my head back and yelling out a *whoop*. Two couples walking down the beach turned their heads to us and I called out, "The love of my life just asked me to marry him!"

Jamie tucked his face into my neck as I continued to hold him. "Damn, you're ballsy," he laughed. The couples cheered and whistled for us before continuing on their way.

"Me? You're the one who flew to fucking Hawaii and proposed. I think you're the ballsy one," I told him. "Now, did someone flash a shiny ring in my face only to pull it away when he got the yes?"

Jamie stood back and held up his index finger with the ring still on the tip. "You mean this little old thing?" He smirked.

"Gimme," I said, holding out my hand for him to slip it on. I assumed it wouldn't fit until we had it sized, but it did. Once it was on my finger, I grinned at him again. I felt like the goofy smile etched itself permanently on my face.

"Baby, I know this is all a dream, but I'm loving every minute of it. Don't pinch me. I've never had a dream of winning the Gramling and a hot guy proposing on the same night. This is epic." I winked.

"Seriously, Teddy. Are you just caught up in the excitement or—?" Jamie began. I shut him up with a kiss and put as much passion and convincing in it as I could.

"Am I caught up in the excitement? Hell yes. Does that mean I have any doubts about spending the rest of my life with you? Hell no. Believe it, James Marian. You're stuck with me now."

He shook his head at me in disbelief. "You're impulsive aren't you? Should I be worried?"

"Sweetheart, I have a little something for you back in my room that will prove to you I'm not making an impulsive decision," I informed him with a grin.

"Showing me your cock isn't going to prove to me that you're serious," he teased.

"Hmm, I beg to differ." I looked at the platinum band to reassure myself it was real. "So now I'm an Alaskan, huh? Never thought I'd move to Alaska, but at least I have someone to warm my bed at night."

"You're not really moving to Denali," Jamie warned.

My heart dropped, and I started to let go of him. "Oh yes, I am," I said firmly.

"That's not what I mean, hotshot," he said, tightening his arms around me. My body stayed stiff in his arms as I prepared to argue with him about it. "I'm applying for teaching jobs in Colorado and California. I don't want to live in the middle of nowhere anymore. We'll live together, but we'll also figure out *where* together. Right now, though, I want you to take me back to your room and do naughty things to me."

I let out a big breath and grinned.

# 38

# JAMIE

An evil grin lit his face and I almost took off running toward the nearest bed. If only I'd known where his hotel room was.

"Your wish is my command, Dall," Teddy teased before lowering his mouth onto mine again.

I wanted to jump his fucking bones right there on the goddamned beach. Instead, I pulled back, gasping, and suggested again we go to his room.

He laughed and ground his hard-on into me before kissing me once more before pushing me away. "You might have to walk in front of me so I don't get arrested for public indecency," he said, smacking my ass as I turned back toward the hotel path.

"As if you're the only one sporting a gigantic boner," I muttered.

When we got into the elevator, Teddy's hands were all over me again and I was a willing participant. He grabbed my suit jacket out of my arms so he was holding both our coats. While he was juggling those, I tried to untuck his shirt to find some bare skin to touch. No dice. Damned cummerbund. Instead, I grabbed his hand again and took out the cufflink at his wrist to ruck up his sleeve and kiss the inside of his wrist.

His skin was warm and delicious. I wanted to rub myself all over it for hours. I ran my other hand over the front of his pants, and he groaned out my name. When the elevator door opened, we raced down the hall trying not to laugh too loudly.

Teddy fumbled the key card and it fell onto the carpet. I grabbed it just before Teddy took it from me and hoisted me over his shoulder. While he tried to get the key in the slot, I smacked his ass and snaked my hands down into his pants, causing him to hiss before entering the room and slinging me down on the bed.

I stood up on my knees on the mattress and took off my tie, locking eyes with him as he did the same from where he stood in front of me. After the ties came the shirts. Teddy's blue eyes were dark pools of lust sparkling more with each button my fingers twisted open on my shirt.

When I was finally bare chested, he grabbed me and tackled me down until he was kissing my chest and fumbling open my fly. His hand grabbed the outline of my cock and stroked through the material. He quickly shucked off my suit pants and dropped them in a puddle on the floor.

As he saw me lying there in just my underwear he got a devious smirk on his face. Teddy took his own clothes off quickly and came back to kneel beside me. Then he looked right at me with a wolfish grin and leaned down to peel my briefs off with his teeth.

He returned up my body just far enough to settle his face between my thighs. I felt a warm wet tongue exploring my cock, teasing and kissing and sucking.

"*...oh god... Teddy... yes...*" I moaned when his mouth started making me lose my focus. His hands grasped the back of my thighs and I could feel his scratchy cheek against the tender skin of my inner thigh. My hands bunched in his hair and I could hear my breathing speed up. He moved his mouth down to my hole and continued sucking and licking.

His tongue pushed inside me and I gasped, almost climaxing on that one strong thrust. I writhed and felt myself reach the edge and almost crest over it. Just as I thought I might come, he stopped and sat up, grinning.

*That cocky motherfucker.*

"Why are you stopping? Come here, you jackass!" I panted.

"Jackass? I thought you loved me?" that sexy asshole said with a smirk.

"I changed my mind. I think I need some convincing. Try harder," I suggested, crooking an index finger for him to *come here*.

"You want me to show you how *hard* I can try when I really want to?" Teddy drawled as he leaned back over me and ground his cock against mine. I stifled a cry.

He leaned down to whisper into my ear in his deep voice. "Jamie, do I need to get a condom?" He rolled his hips again, sliding his cock against mine and sending pulses of sparkles through me.

"Wha..uhn?" I asked, trying to get clarification.

"I'm clean, annual doc appointment a few weeks ago. Can I come inside you without a condom, Jamie? I want you so badly I am going to explode the minute I thrust myself deep inside you," he growled, the vibrations rumbling against my chest.

In one quick whoosh I blurted, "Yes, clean. Tested after Brian's bullshit. Yes... *Please...*"

After a couple more minutes of torturous teasing with lubed fingers, he thrust inside me and my eyes rolled back. The feeling of his hot bare skin inside of me almost put me over the edge.

I heard him say, "God, baby... you are so hot... so tight ..." as he pulsed in and out, going deeper with each thrust. He sucked on my neck and ran his tongue along the curl of my ear. I ran my fingers up his spine and into his hair, down to his shoulders and over his arms.

He thrust harder and faster until I mumbled I was about to come. He stopped, pulling out immediately and leaving me with a horrific feeling of emptiness. I started to cry out in frustration but he reached for me and flipped me over onto my hands and knees, sliding a strong arm around my stomach to pull my ass back against him. He slipped right back into me from behind and took one hard stroke deep into me, jacking me at the same time. Just two more hard slams did the trick, his cock nailing my prostate and causing me to see stars. I shattered. The orgasm shut everything off and left me convulsing with tingles of pleasure so intense I couldn't even scream. My hot come shot onto the bed and his shot deep into my ass.

When I finally caught my breath and started to sense him beside me again, I tried to act nonchalant. It didn't work.

I wanted to express my appreciation. "Mmmmhhhh...fhhhtthhh," I told him.

He chucked and replied, "That good, huh?" before leaning over to press a soft kiss on my temple.

I nodded. "Mmm..." I licked my lips.

He laughed and grabbed my hand, intertwining our fingers. "God, you're so hot right now I could go again."

I smiled and said in a gravely sex-drunk voice, "Prove it."

His eyes lit up and he started to move toward me when I started laughing and held up a hand to stop him. "I'm kidding! Jesus, Teddy, I'm like an empty sock over here. How could you possibly still be hard?"

He smirked and raised a cocky eyebrow. "If you had a mirror right now you'd know." He nipped my jaw and then kissed me on the lips. His kisses turned slow and tender. My tongue tasted his soft familiar mouth.

Teddy pulled back to look at me, his face turned serious.

"I love you, James Marian."

I gazed back at those intense blue pools. "I know you do. I feel it every single time you look at me like that."

I reached up to trace one of his eyebrows with my finger and then drew it down the side of his face to run across his bottom lip.

"My heart is completely yours, Teddy."

His face relaxed into a heartfelt smile, and for a while we just lay there, touching each other and remembering each other until we drifted off to sleep tangled together.

## 39

# TEDDY

The next morning I came awake early to the feeling of soft lips nipping my shoulder. I felt Jamie's warm body tucked against mine and smelled the musky scent of him floating around me. Heaven. But as much as I loved the man, I decided a little teasing was in order.

I pretended to catch a glimpse of my ring and freak out about it. "Holy shit, I didn't actually say yes to you, did I? Fuck, what was I... YEOW," I cried as I felt a chest hair get plucked. I saw Jamie's furrowed eyebrows and burst out laughing.

"Oh, geez, Dall. If it means that much to you, I guess I'll go through with it." I laughed, rubbing the sore spot on my chest.

His hand roamed down to clutch a hair in a way more sensitive spot than my chest, and I winced. "Okay, okay, uncle!" I gasped, pulling him in to rub my nose against his and then kiss him softly on the lips, the eyelids, the cheeks, and forehead.

Jamie's stern face melted under my ministrations, and I let my hands get in on the action of making him forget my tease. After thirty more minutes and a thorough reminder of my incredible sexual prowess, Jamie laid gasping with his head hanging off one side of the bed, there were pillows thrown around the room, and a lamp lay knocked over on the bedside table. I tried to pretend I wasn't mentally singing Queen's "We Are the Champions," but I'm pretty sure Jamie saw right through me.

"Smug bastard," he mumbled.

"I'm hungry. Let's hop in the shower and go get something to eat," I said as I got up and pulled him to his feet.

On the way to the bathroom Jamie stopped mid-stride and looked down at his hand.

"What the fuck?" he asked. "How did your ring end up on my finger?"

I couldn't suppress the wide grin on my face as I held up my hand to show him my own ring on my own finger. "Huh," I said. "That's strange. I still have mine on."

He looked up at me, confusion etched in his forehead until realization dawned.

"*What the fuck?*" he repeated.

"The ring fairy must have visited you in the middle of the night." I shrugged and started to continue toward the bathroom. Jamie followed and grabbed my arm.

"How the hell did you go ring shopping in the middle of the night while I was sleeping?"

I barked out a laugh. "I'm not that sneaky. I bought it two days ago here in town when I decided to fly to Fairbanks after the awards ceremony," I said.

Jamie couldn't seem to process the fact that I'd bought him a ring before he'd shown up in Hawaii.

"But –" he stammered.

"Jamie, I love you. I was coming to Denali to convince you that I was one hundred percent committed to you. To us. I wasn't going to propose to you yet because of the whole Brian thing. But I bought this to have in case you were ever ready. It was kind of a way of holding my promise to you even if you weren't ready to do the same," I admitted with a shrug.

"Jesus, Teddy. Really?"

"Nah. Not really. I carry that ring around in my bag in case I ever need to pretend to be married," I said with a straight face.

Jamie tilted his head and stared at me with a smirk.

"Oh my god, you don't seriously believe that, do you?" I asked. "It's engraved for god's sake."

His eyes sparkled as he pulled the ring off his finger to look inside.

*J & T - Our Adventure Awaits.*

He slipped it back on and held it over his heart, covering it with his opposite hand. "Who the hell are you? This whole thing is too good to be true."

I wrapped my arms around him and kissed him. "Believe it. I was an idiot, Jamie, to think I could ever live without you. It killed me thinking of you dating other people. Of me thinking I could be happy with anyone else after being with you. I was an idiot. Every time I boarded a plane heading anywhere besides Fairbanks, it felt wrong."

"Thank you, Teddy. I didn't realize how much it would mean to me to know for sure that you're ready for this. You know I don't ever want to pressure you into something you're not ready for."

"You weren't the one who kept flying to fucking Alaska, sweetheart. I'm pretty sure that showed you how ready for you I am." I reminded him.

"Good point, hotshot," Jamie said, grabbing my hand and pulling me into the bathroom.

I turned on the shower and we both stepped in, my arms circling around Jamie under the hot spray.

Jamie looked up at me with a mischievous grin. "So, ah, speaking of marriage, how would you feel about being my date for a wedding?"

"Is it our wedding?" I asked.

"It's crazier than that, I'm afraid."

"Who's getting married?"

"It's my brother Blue's wedding to Tristan. My entire family is here. You'll soon learn that the Marians don't do anything by half measures." Jamie said.

"What? Where the hell are they?" I asked, pretending to look behind me.

"They're at an estate around here somewhere. I'm a little embarrassed to tell you the whole story," Jamie said, blushing.

"Spill it, Dall." I said. "Is this the part where you tell me that the Marians do *everything* together?" I started the enjoyable task of washing his hot body.

"I'd like to say no, but… On Christmas day we were talking about planning Blue and Tristan's wedding. They wanted us all to go somewhere fun together so they could get married quickly without too much planning and fuss. I said it couldn't be this week because I was going to be in Maui for the Gramling thing. I guess they thought Maui at New Year's sounded pretty good for a wedding."

My heart squeezed in my chest and I felt a goofy grin spreading on my face. "Really? Your family is all here because you wanted to find me?"

Jamie laughed. "Don't get cocky. I can see your chest puffing up. You're not that special. It didn't take much to convince twenty people to take a private jet to a superstar's Hawaiian estate."

"Is your family expecting us? Should we head over there?" I asked.

Jamie smiled at me. "Yes, but we don't have to rush. The wedding is tonight, and it's pretty casual. More like a quick ceremony to make it official and a big family luau."

"Are you sure they'll be okay with you bringing me?" I asked.

"Of course they will. You're my fiancé," he said.

"I like that word, fiancé. But I'm going to like calling you husband even better," I said, feeling a sweet rush of possessiveness.

We finished showering and I handed Jamie some clothes to wear. I had an extra pair of flip-flops but they were comically big. Then we headed down to the cafe in the hotel for breakfast. After we sat down with our muffins and coffee, I remembered Jamie mentioning changing jobs.

I looked over at him. "Tell me about the jobs you applied for. What brought that on?"

He explained about feeling ready for a change, about wanting to be around more people our age to have more fun and spend less time in studious solitude. Teaching was fun for him, but he told me it had to include some kind of fieldwork. He described the two programs he was looking at and explained why each appealed to him for different reasons. Then he shrugged and admitted his heart wasn't set on any particular course. He was just tired of being isolated.

I turned to face him. "Jamie, I've been thinking about this a lot since I left Alaska. Mac said something to me that really struck me. He asked if I could think of a scenario where a wildlife photographer and a wildlife consultant might be able to bring their careers together in some way."

He looked at me and muttered, "Wow. He makes it sound so obvious. We're idiots."

I laughed. "Yep. That got me thinking of examples of us doing just that. I thought maybe you and I could work together to pitch magazine articles or even a book that uses your animal knowledge and my photography. I have plenty of connections at magazines, and I know people who could hook us up with book publishers. We could travel together to work on it."

Jamie smiled at me. "That's a very tempting idea. But then I'd have to put up with your sorry ass, like, all the time."

"Sweetheart, I'm a catch. You'd be lucky to have this ass all the time," I said, leaning over on one hip so I could pat the ass in question.

"Mm-hm," Jamie said, assessing said ass. "Maybe it would work, but I think we should negotiate the terms and set some office rules if we plan to work together."

"What did you have in mind?"

"Like if we argue about something, I get to have the deciding vote. You know, things like that."

I snorted. "And whenever we get a work email, you have to read it naked?"

"Right. And whenever you say the word 'shoot,' you have to use finger guns," Jamie suggested.

I put my finger to my lips in thought. “And whenever you say the word ‘wild,’ you have to swipe your claws out like a tiger and say ‘rawr.’”

# 40

# JAMIE

"All conversations by the water cooler should be done with one hand on a coworker's junk," Teddy declared.

I thought about that seriously for a moment. "Hmm, okay, but I was thinking mouth on the junk instead of hand. We'll go with your plan." Teddy tried to interrupt, but I kept talking. "No, Teddy, you're right. Hand only. Let's see... another rule should be achieving membership status in the mile-high club every year, don't you think?"

His eyes took on a hungry look before he added, "Indeed, Dr. Marian. Your ideas are compelling, and I'm willing to work *hard* to achieve them."

*Fuck, that man oozes sex.*

"See that you do. What other *penetrating* issues should we *slip in* to the rules?"

His pupils dilated as he formulated his reply.

"Okay, Dr. Marian. During office hours I think it would be best if you call me 'sir' or 'Mr. Kodiak.'"

"I think I'd rather call you Mr. Marian."

Teddy looked me straight in the eyes. "I can't wait. But are you sure, like really sure? I keep waiting for you to stress out."

"Teddy, absolutely nothing about this worries me except for the thought that you might be the one scared off."

"Nope. I kind of like the idea of having a sexy-ass science nerd for a husband." He shot me a quick wink.

*Husband.*

A word that used to make me feel lost now had the power to make me feel found.

*How did I get so fucking lucky?*

As we pulled up to the house where my family was staying, I realized I should probably warn him about the Marian crazy he was now a part of. "Don't freak out. They're mouthy but harmless. Except for the old ladies. Be careful of them," I said with a wink.

He laughed. "Old ladies don't scare me, sweetheart." He opened the car and stepped out, admiring the expansive views of the island and the ocean beyond.

I saw the front door swinging open and my family come pouring out. Poor Teddy had no idea what he'd just gotten himself into.

## 41

# TEDDY

"Now that's a hot piece of ass," said a tiny woman who had to have been a hundred years old. I froze and looked at Jamie, who burst into laughter.

"That's Tristan's granny. Ignore her." Jamie grabbed my hand and led me into the fray.

Suddenly I was jumped by another petite woman. This one was much younger and had a mane of curly brown hair. "Teddy," she cried. I held her in the hug to keep her from sliding onto the pavement.

Jamie mouthed the word "Simone" at me and I smiled.

"Hey, baby girl," I said, remembering the brothers' nickname for Jamie's sister. She pulled back and looked at me with an enormous smile on her face.

"Granny's right. You're hot as shit. How come my brothers find better-looking men than I do?" she complained.

I noticed a tall, Italian-looking guy puff out his chest and wink at a strawberry-blond guy standing next to him. "She's talking about me," he said.

"You won't hear any arguments from me, babe. Why do you think I'm in such a hurry to put a ring on your finger?"

Ah, Tristan and Blue. They were both nice-looking, and I could tell right off how into each other they were.

Jamie made a shooing gesture to Simone and grabbed my hand again. "Everyone, this is Teddy. My fiancé." He held up our hands, flashing our rings.

There was a loud squeal but it was hard to tell which Marian it came from because they were all talking at once as they swarmed with hugs and congratulations. It was a lot to take in, but everyone was very laid back and fun to be around. They made me feel immediately at ease.

By the time Mrs. Marian got to me, she gave me a huge hug. "Teddy, honey," she said. "I'm so sorry about your dad. We know we'll never replace your own family, but we are so looking forward to making you a part of ours."

Her words took me by surprise and made my eyes sting. "Thank you, Mrs. Marian. By sharing Jamie with me, you've already done the very best thing I could ask for."

She wiped her eye and smiled up at me. "Please call me Rebecca until you ever decide you'd like to call me Mom." I caught Jamie's dad's eye as he stood behind her nodding and smiling.

I was floored. This family had known me for all of ten seconds and they'd already welcomed me with open arms. My mouth refused to work and I was worried about losing my composure in front of everyone. Rebecca must have sensed it because she ushered everyone back into the house.

"All right, let's not overwhelm the poor guy. Back to decorating. No one gets out of helping me out back," she said to a chorus of groans.

When everyone but Jamie and I were back in the house, I turned to him.

Jamie's smile faltered at the emotion in my face. "Too much?" he asked.

I shook my head and pulled him to me, leaning my forehead against his. "More than I ever hoped for," I whispered. "They're fucking amazing."

He grinned again. "Yes, they are. They seem to think you're amazing too."

I kissed him and enjoyed the familiar taste of his mouth. "God, I love you." I said against his lips, feeling his turn up in a smile in response to my words.

At that moment when all seemed right in the world and a fresh new year was being born, I felt an incredible sense of peace wash over me. I couldn't think of any place I'd rather be than with this man on this piece of earth and the rest of my life dazzling before me.

LATER THAT NIGHT, after Blue and Tristan's ceremony, Jamie and I walked down to the beach to witness the start of the new year coming in with a bang. Tristan had arranged fireworks for Blue and colored lights reflected off of Jamie's features. We were closing the books on a year full of endings and new beginnings. And we were welcoming a brand-new one full of exciting times ahead.

"Happy New Year, Teddy." Jamie smiled at me before catching my lips in a kiss.

"Happy New Year, baby," I said against his lips. "It's going to be different, isn't it?"

"I have a feeling that life with you is going to be a crazy adventure," he laughed.

There was so much I wanted to say to him. My voice sounded gravely before becoming clearer. "Jamie, I can't believe that I get to be the one standing here with you right now. In all of my life I never imagined feeling this way about another person, but then I met you. You are without a doubt the love of my life, and I plan on spending all of my days proving it to you. You are kind, smart, loving, and so very beautiful. I love the way you laugh with me, and I appreciate the gentle way you approach the world around you. Thank you for loving me back and for agreeing to marry me. I can't wait for the adventures we're going to have together."

Tears brimmed in Jamie's eyes and he tried to dash them away with his fingers. “Teddy, you’re talented, adventurous, and engaged in the world around you in a way that excites and inspires me. You’re kind and loving toward your friends, and more tender and loving with me than anyone has ever been before. I can’t think of anything I want more than to be your partner and explore the world with you. Whether it’s a quiet trek in the snow or a rowdy dance in a bar, being with you is the most fun I’ve ever had. I love you.”

He leaned forward and took my mouth in a deep, sensual kiss full of promise and trust. It was also full of hot fucking lust. “Maybe we should get a room,” I suggested.

“Ah, the future Mr. Marian has the best ideas,” Jamie said, tugging me toward the house.

As we made our way back to our bedroom, I held the hand of my best friend. My finger rubbed over the metal of his ring and I pulled his hand up to kiss it. He squeezed my hand and smiled at me.

“Jamie, I want to come stay with you in Denali until we figure out where you’re going to be. I don’t want to be apart anymore. I just...”

He turned and tilted his head up toward my face. “Thank god.” He laughed, pulling me down for a kiss. “My stomach was already in knots thinking about leaving you again.”

We entered our room and found it full of lit candles and champagne chilled in a bucket next to a couple of glasses. Jamie looked at me with a sweet expression on his face.

“Did you do this?”

“Of course. You only get engaged once or twice, right?” I teased.

“In your case, once. *Once*, hotshot.”

“C’mere, Dall,” I growled, grabbing a belt loop on the back of his linen pants. He squeaked and then laughed as I pulled his back against my chest. I wrapped my arms around him and spread my open hands on his stomach and chest while I nibbled the back of his neck.

Jamie hummed in approval as I slipped one hand under his shirt and began to raise it up. When I got it off him, I turned him around to face me, resting my hands on his hips. I moved my hands to his fly to drop his pants. He wore a sexy-as-shit blue jockstrap.

"What's this?" I asked, running my finger along one of the straps. His skin pebbled with goose bumps, and seeing his reaction to my touch made my blood thicken.

"A little reward for dealing with my crazy family all day," he breathed.

My eyes widened and my heart rate jumped. "Is there more?" I asked, hearing my voice come out huskier than I imagined.

"That's for me to know and you to find out," Jamie smirked.

I fumbled for the button of my own shorts, and my fingers felt like they didn't work right. They were shaking with need. "Please," I muttered. "*Please* let these be magical shorts that automatically come undone when my dick gets this hard."

Jamie laughed and helped me. When we were finally, blessedly naked, I noticed he was still trembling.

His entire body shuddered under my hands and I scooped him up to take him to the bed.

After I laid him down, I began worshipping his body with my lips and fingers, sweet words, and soft touches. His nipples were tight against my lips, and his hips arched up to meet my greedy fingers. He was hot and hard and so willing to let go. Jamie's pleasure was like a gift to me and I unwrapped it as slowly as I dared.

I ran a single finger up his side and he shivered. My finger moved to the inside of his thigh to skim down toward his ankle and he cried out for me to stop teasing him. If he only knew how much teasing him turned me on. But of course he did. The sounds coming out of him went straight to my cock; I rocked my erection against his. Precum leaked along his belly and hip as I was driven even crazier by his kisses and hands on my body.

Jamie finally lost patience with me and pushed my shoulder to roll me over, taking charge by straddling my hips. He teased my hard-on with his ass and his cock stood up temptingly in front of me. His body was like a buffet for me, and I realized it was a feast I would have access to for the entire span of my lifetime. The realization sent my desire into overdrive and I almost came just from the thought.

Jamie must have sensed the electric jolt that went through me because he raised an eyebrow at me.

"*Mine*," I growled. "*Forever*."

His questioning glance turned to a sweet smirk. "*Yes, yours, always*."

After lubing himself in front of me and riding his own fingers with dazed eyes, he settled back on top of me. He teased the head of my cock with his slick entrance until I was begging him and grasping desperately at his hips to hold him steady so I could slam up into him. He held me off, smugly teasing me that what goes around comes around.

"Yes, dammit, I want to *come* around," I grumbled. "Please, Jamie."

He leaned forward to kiss me gently on the lips, touching the tip of his tongue barely against the seam of my lips. Then he came down over me, sliding his body over mine and sheathing me in his tight heat.

"*Oh god, oh god*," I moaned. "*Sooo good*."

Jamie rocked up and down, swirling his hips and driving me mad. I couldn't take it anymore and I flipped him over, cupping his face with my hands as my elbows rested next to his shoulders on the mattress.

"Love you so much, baby," I whispered as I stroked firmly into him over and over. He looked at me with wide eyes, and he sucked in stuttering breaths until I stopped hearing him breathe at all. My lubed hand worked his cock as my balls slammed against him with every thrust of my hips.

I looked into Jamie's face right as I was on the edge of coming and saw the moment his own climax hit him. His eyes rolled back and his entire body contracted, squeezing around me and arching under me. His face was flushed and his lips were dark and swollen. He cried out my name just as I felt the waves wash over me. My vision narrowed and lightning bolts of pleasure surged from my balls to my toes. My brain short-circuited, and I think I made a sound that was a cross between Jamie's name and a sob.

When reality snuck back into my consciousness, I allowed myself to collapse next to Jamie, hearing a whimper of protest as I pulled out of him. I pulled him in to my chest and his head rested over my heart.

My lips found his nose and I dropped a kiss there.

"Baby Dall?" I said after a few minutes.

"Mmm?"

"You're making all of my dreams come true."

He lifted his head up and leaned in for a kiss on the lips. "You're welcome. Still laying on the charm, aren't you?"

I smirked at him. "What, you thought you were getting some new-and-improved Teddy?"

"Nah, I guess you're okay the way you are. Pretty much too late for me to change my mind anyway."

"Hey, I'll have you know I'm a great catch. Just ask the flight crew on United flight 1725 from SFO to Maui."

He smacked me on the chest. "You cocky fucker." He laughed.

"*Your* cocky fucker now. I guess that means I need to cut back on the one-night stands, huh?" I teased.

"Just remember what I said about what comes around goes around. I still have Josh back in Denali. Might need to work late nights sometimes." He smiled.

My smile disappeared. "Not funny," I grumbled, tackling him until I had him begging for mercy. Among other things.

Much later that night while half asleep, Jamie and I made love in a way I'd never done with anyone. That was when I finally realized why Jamie had cried when we'd made love in Alaska. I hadn't allowed myself to feel it fully then, but I did now. I worshipped his body as tenderly and slowly as I could.

Hands ghosted over skin, lips caressed, tongues slid and teased. Tears slid out of Jamie's eyes before I'd even entered his body and by the time we were both close to coming, our eyes locked and we both felt overwhelmed with emotion and connection.

I repeated those three words over and over again while I continued to roll my hips into him. *I love you. I love you.*

The sweetness was almost unbearable. Jamie's thumbs came up and wiped my own tears away as he smiled. In that moment, I knew we would be together forever, no matter what.

# EPILOGUE

## Jamie - Six Months Later

I walked into the grassy backyard with a tray of cheese and crackers. Teddy and Tristan were trying to fix something on our new grill, and Simone, Blue, Griff, and Maverick sat playing cards with the trio of old ladies at the picnic table. Ginger was inside going to the bathroom for the millionth time, and Pete was busy pretending not to notice Teddy and Tristan needing help with the grill. Mom and Dad were out of town, so Teddy and I had offered to have Sunday family dinner at our place.

Our new house was in a tree-lined neighborhood within walking distance to the UC Davis campus. The big yard was perfect for Sister, but she was currently panting in the June heat, taking cover in the shade of a big oak tree.

Motherfucking squirrels lived in that tree, and I had tried to impress upon my husband the need for drastic measures to exterminate them. In return for my pestering, he had a shirt made for me that had a fat squirrel on it and "I'm Nuts" written below it.

*Jackass.*

I set the food down on the picnic table just as I heard Teddy yelp and bring his hand to his mouth. Sister's head popped up to see what happened. I walked over to check it out and reached for the injured hand.

When I brought it up to take a look, what struck me wasn't the sight of the small cut on his knuckle, but the sight of Teddy's wedding band on his large, masculine hand. It never ceased to get me right in the gut. He was mine. Forever.

I looked up at him and kissed him on the lips. "Just a scratch, hotshot. You'll survive." I walked back to sit down and ask Blue some questions about design for the book Teddy and I were working on.

Behind me I heard Teddy mutter, "See? My husband doesn't give a shit. I almost lost a finger and he just blew me off."

*Don't do it, Pete...*

"You only wish he'd blown you off," Pete said with a chuckle.

"Pete Marian, you're a pervert," I heard Ginger say when she walked back out onto the patio.

Pete replied, "You love it when I'm a perv, Ginge."

Ginger rolled her eyes as her auburn hair caught the sun. "Not when your pervy ass knocks me up I don't. This shit sucks. Jamie, don't do it. No matter how much Teddy begs."

"Don't worry." I laughed. "Despite his many attempts, Teddy has failed to impregnate me thus far. Plus, Teddy and I have too many travel plans right now to think about kids for a while."

Maverick reminded me he could Sister-sit the following weekend if we needed him to. I said that would be great. Pete asked where we were going.

"Teddy and I are headed back to Yellowstone to capture bison and mule deer photos for our book project. I can't wait," I said with a big smile of anticipation. We had the whole summer to enjoy each other's company before I started teaching in the fall. Teddy had cleared his schedule by only booking jobs that took us to places we wanted to visit together. After winning the Gramling, Teddy had the pick of the litter when it came to what jobs he wanted to take.

Teddy grinned and winked at me and went back to working on the grill.

After he fixed the grill, Teddy sat back down to play poker with Aunt Tilly, Irene, and Granny. Those ladies were good. He still hadn't learned their secret trick of distracting people. Every time he needed to concentrate, one of them asked him something designed to fluster him.

"So, Teddy, Jamie says you got a big dick," Aunt Tilly said, studying her hand.

"What?" he sputtered, looking around to see if anyone else heard her. No one from the Marian clan batted an eye. "Repeat that, please?" he croaked.

She looked up innocently after Teddy missed the chance to swap a card out. "He said you got a big tick, hiking last weekend. In your hair. A tick. What did you think I said?"

"Cut it out, Aunt Tilly." Blue laughed. "We don't want him to change his mind and decide Jamie's not worth the Marian baggage after all."

Teddy's head shot up. "That will never happen."

I came up behind him and put my arms around his neck with my mouth next to his ear. "Take it easy, hotshot. I implanted a microchip in your ass while you were sleeping so I can track you like an animal in the wild."

Teddy turned, giving me a look.

I rolled my eyes. "We're not working!" I protested.

"Don't think I didn't hear you talking to Pete about the book project. That totally counts," Teddy insisted.

*Fuck.*

"Rawr," I said swiping my fingers through the air.

He laughed and turned to lay some kisses on me until Granny put her foot down.

"Quit that crap or Irene and I are going to go at it in front of all of you. Teddy, focus on your shit. I'm getting ready to take you for all you're worth," Granny said from under her green poker visor. I didn't even know such a thing existed in real life.

Tristan sat on the other side of Blue. "You don't want to see these two making out. Take my word for it. Dentures come out and joints creak. It's not pretty," he muttered while focusing on his cards.

The rest of us chuckled. Tristan looked up at me with a grin after taking his turn. "You laugh, but that's how those little fuckers end up taking your money." And he was right.

I looked around at my family making themselves at home in my new backyard and was struck by how happy I was to have made the decision to take the UC Davis job.

After returning to the kitchen to grab some more ice, I heard noises coming from the laundry room. I peeked in through the doorway and saw my brother Jude pushed up against a wall being absolutely manhandled in a noisy, passionate kiss. His wrists were held above his head with one big strong hand, his long hair was tangled over his flushed face, and his breathing was, ah, labored. To say the least.

I scrambled back before they could mistake me for a voyeur, and I felt the hot rush of embarrassment in my face for having seen such an intimate moment. As I quickly made my way back outside, all I could hope is that the two men hadn't caught me staring.

I walked out in time to see Teddy throw down his cards in disgust while Tilly swiped his remaining cash with a snicker. When he saw me, Teddy's face lit up, and he reached over to pull me onto his lap.

"You okay, sweetheart?" he breathed into my ear as he wrapped strong arms around me.

"Tell you later," I murmured, and he nodded.

Griff scooted closer to where I sat at the picnic table. "Hey, Jamie, I keep forgetting to ask. Mom wants to know if you've heard from the San Diego Zoo lately to see how the peacock is doing with the implanted feathers."

Teddy's face split into a wolfish grin, and he turned to shoot cobalt lasers at me. "Yes, Jamie, how *is* your cock now? Is it in good hands?"

*That smug motherfucker.*

"My cock has never been better, Griff. Thanks for asking."

## LETTER FROM LUCY

Dear Reader,

Thank you so much for reading Taming Teddy! Check out the other Made Marian novels where Jamie's brothers find their Happy Ever Afters.

Be sure to follow me on Amazon to be notified about new novels when they are released.

Please take a moment to write a review of Taming Teddy on Amazon and Goodreads. For a self-published author, reviews can make all the difference in helping a book show up in Amazon searches.

Feel free to sign up for my newsletter, stop by my website or visit me on social media to stay in touch. To see fun inspiration photos for all of my novels, visit my Pinterest boards.

Happy reading!

Lucy

# ABOUT THE AUTHOR

Lucy Lennox is a mother of three sarcastic kids. Born and raised in the southeast, she is finally putting good use to that English Lit degree.

Lucy enjoys naps, pizza, and procrastinating. She is married to someone who is better at math than romance but who makes her laugh every single day and is the best dancer in the history of ever.

She stays up way too late each night reading M/M romance because that shit is hot.

For more information and to stay updated about future releases, please sign up for Lucy's author newsletter on her website.

For other Lucy Lennox books, please turn the page.

~

*Connect with Lucy on social media:*

www.LucyLennox.com
Lucy@LucyLennox.com

## BORROWING BLUE - MADE MARIAN 1

**Blue:** When my ex walks into the resort bar with his new husband on his arm, I want nothing more than to prove to him that I've moved on. Thankfully, the sexy stranger sitting next to me is more than willing to share a few kisses in the name of revenge. It gets even better when those scorching kisses turn into a night of fiery passion.

The only problem? Turns out the stranger's brother is marrying my sister later this week.

**Tristan:** I have one rule: no messing with the guests at my vineyard resort. Of course the one exception I make turns out to be the brother of the woman my brother's about to marry. Now we're stuck together for a week of wedding activities, and there's no avoiding the heat burning between us.

So fine, we make a deal: one week. One week to enjoy each other's bodies and get it out of our system. Once the bride and groom say I do and we become family, it'll all be over between us. Right?

# JUMPING JUDE - MADE MARIAN 3

**Jude:** Reaching the top of the country music charts brings out the crazy, and there's no one crazier than my ex. Unfortunately, his threats to out me are escalating. Enter the bodyguard of my dreams.

I'd probably chafe under his constant presence if his attention to my body wasn't so… ah… thorough. Now I have to worry about outing myself to millions of fans if I can't keep my hands off him in public.

**Derek:** Now I'm an ex-Marine turned babysitter. If I have to hear Jude sing his mega-hit Bluebells one more time, I might murder him myself, and after 6 years in special ops, I know my way around a weapon. Unfortunately, so does he. Except his arsenal includes washboard abs and a killer set of pipes.

I've faced guns, knives, explosives and yet it's Jude Marian who may end up bringing me to my knees.

## GROUNDING GRIFFIN - MADE MARIAN 4

**Griff:** I learned early on that the easiest way to avoid a broken heart is to always be the first out the door. Caring about anyone or anything is asking to be disappointed, which is why I avoid relationships and chase freelance gigs — ghost writing restaurant reviews and penning articles about the efficacy of cheesy pick up lines — instead of chasing my dreams.

Besides, dreams don't come true for people like me. And no one, not even the sexy-as-hell bartender at the club can convince me otherwise. Because I'm never risking my heart again.

**Sam:** As a bartender I've watched a million pick-up artists work their magic, but none as talented as Griffin Marian. He's a flirt, a good time. Hooking up with him was supposed to be just a fling. I wasn't supposed to care abut his fractured past or his buried dreams. I have my own future to worry about, especially after that stupid food critic scuttled my hopes of finally opening my own restaurant.

But, the more time I spend with Griff, the more I'm beginning to realize that my plans mean nothing without him. If only I can convince him to give us a chance to follow our dreams together.

## MOVING MAVERICK - MADE MARIAN 5

**Maverick:** I haven't been back to Rabbit Island, South Carolina, since my parents died and my grandmother, Mimi, rejected me. I'm only returning now to attend her funeral and sell an estate I never wanted. But the moment I step foot on the island and fall into Beau's arms, I realize it might not be so easy to say goodbye after all.

Beau Talmadge was always the boy next door, but now he's no longer a kid. The man is hot as hell and pushes all my buttons in the very best way. I'm supposed to leave in a week. Sell everything, close the door on my past, and walk away forever. So why am I letting myself fall for someone who lives thousands of miles away? And how the hell am I going to break it off when it's time to go?

**Beau:** It took one short summer to fall in love with Maverick Mitchell and fifteen long years to forget him when he left. I'd never expected to see him again, but when he shows up at Mimi's funeral looking lost and lonely I can't resist doing anything I can to comfort him. Falling into bed with Maverick is easy and the nights we spend together are as hot and steamy as a South Carolina thunderstorm.

I know it's not smart. I know it's not what he planned. But dammit,

Mav belongs in my arms, in my bed, and in my life. So how the hell do I get him to stay?

## DELIVERING DANTE - MADE MARIAN 6

**AJ:** I know Dante's story better than anyone. After all, I was the one who rescued him from his homophobic, abusive father eight years ago. Since then, I've kept my distance, but when I run into him at the Marian House gala and he doesn't recognize me, I can't resist the incredible, sensitive man he's become.

I would do anything to protect Dante Marian, but what if his past keeps me from being part of his future?

**Dante:** Every new relationship has obstacles, it just turns out that ours involves my bumbling inexperience (ugh), an octogenarian naughty toy party (don't ask), and being on the run in an RV with Aunt Tilly (it involves the Secret Service— no really, don't ask).

When my biological father takes his homophobic views to a national platform, the only way to stand up for what I believe in is to claim my past and confront him. So now it's time to decide: do I put the past behind me and walk away from AJ for good or face my biggest fear and fight for what's mine?

# FREE MADE MARIAN SHORT STORIES

**Brad: A Companion to Borrowing Blue**

When Brad opens his Vegas hotel room door to find a hot police officer waiting on the other side, he assumes crazy Aunt Tilly has sent him a strip-o-gram. But instead of getting naked, Detective Gorgeous pulls out his cuffs. Turns out, the badge and uniform aren't just props, this cop is the real deal.

~

**Keller: A Companion to Borrowing Blue**

**Keller:** After watching my long-time crush marry the man of his dreams, I realize I'm not so much heartbroken as envious. I want what they have – love, companionship, a hot body to tangle the sheets with. But as long as I'm spending most of my time at the vineyard, I'll never meet someone like that, right?

But then I stumble into Aunt Tilly's art class and catch sight of the nude model in the center of the room. I can't stop thinking about all of the ways I'd want him to pose if I was ever lucky enough for a solo session.

**Eli:** When my brother convinces me to take his place as a nude model for a painting workshop in Napa, I reluctantly agree. What harm could come from dangling my naughty bits in front of a room full of tittering old women? But those little ladies are actually dirty-mouthed matchmakers in disguise and my entire concept of being laid bare is put to the test.

Just when I'm figuring out how to handle the gossiping artists, the handsome host shows up to paint me into a corner.

~

*Both stories are free at www.LucyLennox.com.*

~

## LOST AND FOUND - TWIST OF FATE 1

BY LUCY LENNOX AND SLOANE KENNEDY

**He promised to never leave me. But when I needed him the most, that was exactly what he did...**

From Bestselling Authors Sloane Kennedy & Lucy Lennox comes an exciting new series about how a twist of fate can change everything...

**He promised to never leave me. But when I needed him the most, that was exactly what he did...**

Wilderness guide Xander Reed has spent fifteen years trying to forget the night he turned to his best friend in his darkest hour, only to find the young man who'd sworn to always have his back was turning his on Xander instead. Two thousand miles and fifteen years of building a new life in the quiet backcountry of the Rocky Mountains should have been enough to put the memory of Bennett Crawford out of his mind forever, but old wounds run deep and when Bennett suddenly reappears in his life as part of a wilderness expedition Xander is guiding, the scars he thought long healed break wide open.

**I'd only ever wanted to protect Xander from getting hurt again. I never considered the one he needed protection from was me...**

Bennett Crawford was faced with an impossible choice the night his best friend needed him.

He chose wrong.

As the only son of one of the wealthiest families in New England, he should have had the world at his feet, but losing his best friend at the tender age of fourteen changed everything. And even though Bennett's managed to hide behind a mask of contentment as he takes his place at his father's side in the family business, inside he's searching for the piece of himself that's been missing ever since Xander Reed walked out of his life. Bennett's only saving grace is his work with a group of inner city kids, and when he's given the chance to show the troubled teens that there's a bigger world out there waiting for them if they just have the courage to reach for it, he takes it.

But when he steps off that bus for what was supposed to be a week of fun and adventure, he's instantly returned to the past when he discovers their expedition guide is none other than the boy he let go so long ago. Only, the soft-hearted, insecure little boy Bennett once knew is gone, and in his place is a brooding, bitter man who isn't interested in second chances.

**People leave. I know that now and nothing Bennett has to say to me will change anything...**

All Bennett wants is another chance to show Xander that friendship was only the beginning. But when a stubborn Xander refuses to even hear him out, Bennett realizes he's going to need to fight dirty.

Because now that he's found Xander again, he's not letting him go a second time...

Made in the USA
Columbia, SC
27 November 2018